I0460579

Murder Most Melancholy

Penrose & Pyke Mysteries, Book 2

Rose Pascoe

Published by Flax Bay Books, 2022

Copyright

MURDER MOST MELANCHOLY

ISBN: 978-0473636166 (softcover POD)
978-0473636180 (Kindle)

Publisher: Flax Bay Books, New Zealand

Cover design: Rose Pascoe
Cover images from Adobe Stock Images by Stefan Schierle, dervish15 and Irina Korsakova

Acknowledgements & Notes

Acknowledgements

A huge thank you to my fabulous beta readers – Mary, Jenny, Kathy and Angela – whose enthusiasm is very much appreciated. Thanks also to my son for website development and sundry techie stuff, and to my friends for their encouragement.

Special thanks to the train enthusiasts at Ferrymead Heritage Park for taking the time on a dismal day to show me a beautifully restored rail carriage from the era.

Dedication

This novel is dedicated to all the people who work tirelessly in support of mental health. As many eminent people have noted, including Thomas Jefferson and Mahatma Gandhi, *the true measure of any society can be found in how it treats its most vulnerable members.*

Note

This fictional story uses the vocabulary of the late 1800s to describe mental health and women's health conditions. Words like "lunatic" and "hysteric" are appalling in retrospect, but they were in common usage at the time, as outlined in the Historical Notes at the end of the book.

Acknowledgements & Notes

Acknowledgements

A huge thank you to my adoptive born teachers — Mary Jenny, Ruth and Angela — whose enthusiasm is very much appreciated. Thanks also to my son for the development and steady topic talk, and to my friends for their encouragement.

Special thanks to the man of my mana at the studied Dancing Talk for taking me home on a dismal day to enjoy me a beautiful good time and arrange Ronald's ride.

Dedication

This novel is dedicated to all the people who wrestle tirelessly in support of mental health. As many chronic people have noted, including Thomas Jefferson and the famous Franklin, the true measure of our society can be found in how we treat its most vulnerable members.

Note

This fictional story maps the popularity of the late 1800s to describe mental health and women's health conditions beyond the "feminine" and hysteria law, highlighting a snapshot that they were in common usage at the time, as outlined in the Historical Notes at the end of the book.

4

Table of Contents

Location Map

Early 20th century South Island railways, New Zealand. (In 1891, travel between Wellington and Christchurch was by steamer). Source: LINZ /natlib.govt.nz. Crown Copyright reserved.

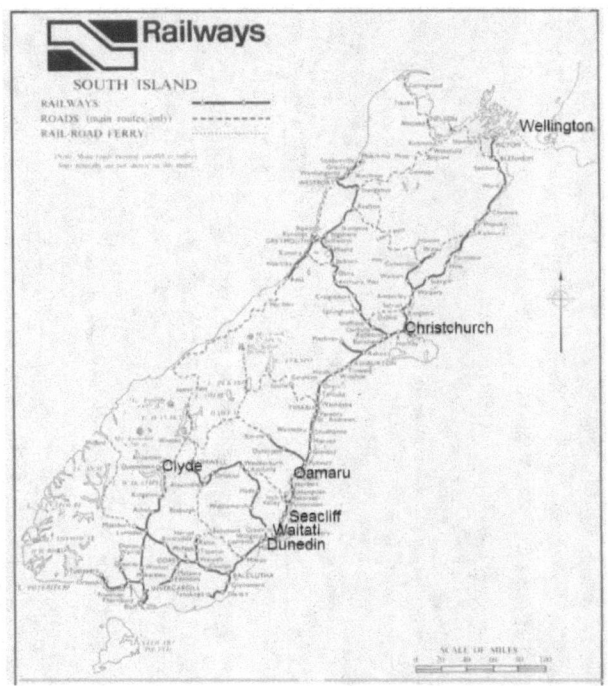

Runaway

Grace Penrose hated sitting still at the best of times, and today was far from the best of times. The part of her anatomy in contact with the hard bench seat managed the medically impossible feat of being both numb and excruciatingly painful at the same time.

It had been her own fault, for allowing herself to become distracted by the railway workers swarming the steam locomotive during their stop in the coastal town of Oamaru. Coal men, water men, oilers and greasers, and goodness knows what other varieties of broad-shouldered, grimy-faced men, all to keep the massive iron beast champing at the bit.

If only she had gone with the other passengers to the tearoom, where refreshments were served in cups so thick that not even the NZR's infamous stewed tea could erode them. Instead, she had failed to see the porter heading her way with a baggage trolley. The sharp edge of a trunk had caught her buttock, causing her to utter an unladylike oath, which fortunately was drowned out by the clatter of smaller items of luggage raining down upon her head.

The young porter tripped over in his eagerness to right the wrong, ending up on his knees in front of her, a supplicant begging forgiveness. He lifted the face of a crestfallen cherub, complete with a lock of blond hair curling over his pale forehead. "I'm sorry, Miss. I couldn't see you over the stack of trunks."

She could well believe it. What on earth had the New Zealand Railways been thinking when they recruited a stripling to do the heavy task of manhandling enormous shipping trunks?

Grace handed him back his cap and forced a smile to her lips. "No harm done. I should have seen you coming."

She resumed her stroll along the platform, trying not to limp too obviously. Far too soon, the guard had blown his whistle and she had

had to scramble to get back into her carriage for the long journey south, stopping at every paltry little station between Christchurch and Dunedin. For the hundredth time, she cursed her foolishness for not taking the express train, especially as endless delays meant that the express was now not too far behind them, despite leaving much later.

The train set off again, winding its way through green hills dotted with gambolling lambs on a perfect summer's day. No doubt the birds were singing rapturously, as nectar-drunk bees zig-zagged through the fields of wildflowers, buzzing with delight. While she sat in a second-class carriage, brushing coal smuts off her white shirtwaist, fuming at the vagaries of fate.

When she next looked up, having awakened with a start, her head was on the shoulder of the woman next to her. The train appeared to be suspended above the sea. A blast of the whistle and a screech of brakes signalled a stop at yet another small-town station.

Grace stammered an apology as she removed her head, hoping that the slight damp patch on the woman's shoulder was not her drool. "I'm so sorry. Must have dozed off."

"Didn't like to wake you, love. You looked as if you could do with a nap." The woman gathered her possessions, which included a startling number of children, and herded them towards the door in an orderly line.

The train pulled up beside a plain weatherboard building, with a sign saying "Waitati". No more than a short platform, a ticket office and a modest shelter for the waiting passengers, within a wider sprawl of ugly storage sheds, stock yards and sidings. Beyond the shroud of coal smoke belching from the locomotive, the scenery was undeniably pretty. A large inlet stretched out beyond the flat coastal strip, framed by green hills and a distant sandbar and island.

Grace distracted herself from her pummelled posterior by studying the few passengers embarking at Waitati. A gentleman dressed in a dark suit got into the first-class carriage. Obviously a professional man, carrying a smart leather case, which made her wonder what he was doing out here in the back of beyond.

Three rumbunctious children scrambled into second class and ran squealing to an empty space under a window, where a squabble broke out as to who would get the best spot, although there was plenty of room for all three on the bench seat that ran lengthways down the carriage. They were followed by an older woman laden with baggage and trepidation. No prizes for guessing this one – grandma must be taking the little terrors for a visit to the big city. A beaming woman with rosy cheeks waved the party off from the platform with ill-disguised glee.

Grace was about to return to her pathology text book, when she noticed a figure running up to the off-side of the train. The young woman had a desperate look about her – not just in her windblown hair and muddy hem, but in the whites of her eyes. She slipped on at the rear of the carriage and took the seat nearest the door, in the expanse of empty space created by the departure of the large family. She wore neither gloves nor hat, and carried no coat. Her only luggage was the reticule dangling from her trembling fingers.

Instinct took over as Grace recognised a woman in need. She strolled down to the end of the carriage, as if stretching her legs, and leaned forward, close to the woman's ear. "Come and sit with me. You will be less noticeable."

The woman's eyes widened at the unexpected words, but she hesitated only long enough to look into Grace's eyes and read her sympathy. When she moved up the bench, Grace realised that the two of them were similar enough to be mistaken for each other by a stranger. Slim, dark-haired, average height, even wearing an unmemorable combination of grey skirt and white shirtwaist, although the woman was probably three or four years younger than Grace's twenty-two, and obviously terrified.

"I'm running away," the woman admitted, unnecessarily. Her hand dropped to her belly as she pleaded with Grace. "Please don't let them take me back to that dreadful place."

Grace had been a student at the Otago Medical School for the past two years and had assisted at her father's medical practice since she was old enough to hold a stethoscope in her chubby toddler hands. The

11

woman's unconscious gesture was unmistakable – she was with child, although it was not yet showing. And there was no ring on her finger.

Out on the platform, the last of the baggage and freight had been loaded and the guard was raising his flag. With a shrill blast on his whistle, the guard stepped aboard the front carriage. After a reluctant shudder, the locomotive lurched away from the platform in a shower of soot and steam.

"Put on my shawl and hat." Grace handed over her plumed hat and, reluctantly, her much-cherished ruby-red silk shawl, edged with a gold band and adorned with flowers. She pressed her train ticket into the woman's hand.

The train rattled over a pair of trestle bridges, frightening flocks of waders into flight out across the water. The air seeping under the sash windows was alive with the smell of salt and mud, as they gathered speed along the curving coastline. Before long, the guard entered the carriage, checking tickets.

The guard dealt with the other new passengers, whom he knew well enough to exchange a few personal remarks with. He wasn't much older than thirty, although the years sat hard in his face, but he went about his job with the practiced ease of one who has done it hundreds of times before. His brow wrinkled uncertainly when he approached Grace and the runaway, but it was Grace he spoke to, ignoring the dozing woman in the distinctive red shawl. "Have I checked your ticket, Miss? I didn't see you get on."

"It was rather chaotic, with so many people getting off." Grace held out the money for the fare. "A single to Dunedin, please."

The guard ran a hand over his bushy moustache, but reached out to take her money and issue a ticket with no further questions asked. "Lovely day, Miss. Off to the big smoke for a spot of Christmas shopping are you? Where did the year go, eh?"

She took the ticket with a smile. "Indeed I am. A Merry Christmas to you." Christmas was still two and a half weeks away, but the excuse was as good as any. It seemed scarcely possible that eighteen ninety-one was nearly over.

The guard moved on down the carriage, taking a seat by the rear door. When he took a sheaf of papers out of his satchel and busied himself with paperwork, the woman beside her let out a long breath.

"Thank you," she whispered. "I'm Isabelle Forsyth. May I know the name of my saviour?"

"Grace Penrose, at your service." She paused. "Miss Forsyth, you may think it presumptuous of me, but if you are in need of help, my great-aunt runs a refuge for women in Dunedin. We provide medical care and compassion, no questions asked."

"Again, I thank you. I have no need of a refuge, but the thought was kind." Isabelle rubbed her fingers together nervously, suggesting that her confidence in her situation was more fragile than she was admitting.

"I have some sandwiches and cake, supplied by the lovely women of the Christchurch Suffrage Committee, if you are hungry."

"Thank you for your kindness, but I feel too ill at ease to eat." Isabelle twisted the end of the shawl into a knot, before clasping her hands together to stop her fretting. "Perhaps you might tell me a little about yourself, Miss Penrose. You are a suffragist?"

"I am. I have been giving a series of lectures in Christchurch on the need for women to take charge of their own medical decisions. We are barely eight years away from the start of a new century, yet men with no understanding of our needs still claim the right to make our decisions for us."

Grace realised she sounded a little strident, as she launched into her favourite grievance, but Isabelle was nodding her agreement, her hands still at last. Even her relentless scanning of the surroundings ceased, as she looked at Grace properly for the first time.

"Life would be so much better if we could make our own choices," Miss Forsyth agreed. "But, surely, doctors would never allow it?"

"I'm training to be a doctor myself. I'm sure there will be many other female doctors soon. Anything will be possible once women get the vote."

"Do you really think it will happen?"

"The women of New Zealand may have missed out again on getting the vote this year, but I am positive it will happen next year, and then politicians will be forced to listen to our concerns." Grace paused before she got carried away. "You must forgive me, Miss Forsyth, I tend to get rather carried away by my enthusiasm."

"Do call me Isabelle. You have no need to apologise. I must admit I am impressed by your accomplishments. Would it be impertinent to ask if your husband approves?"

"I am not married. My future husband, if there is one, will certainly approve of my opinions, or he wouldn't get within a mile of the altar."

"Do you have a young man?"

An image sprung to Grace's mind unbidden. A tall, black-haired man with gold-flecked green eyes and a beguiling grin. "I have – I had – a good friend, but he lives in the North Island now. Sometimes I think it might as well be London. I haven't seen him for a long time."

Grace fell silent as the train passed through fields and patches of bush, gathering speed for the climb into the hills ahead. Charlie Pyke was supposed to have visited her while she was in Christchurch, but his work had taken precedence. After one year and ten months apart and three unsuccessful attempts to cross paths in their busy lives, she had just about given up hope of seeing him again. Given the impersonal tone of his letters and failure to meet her yet again, perhaps it was for the best.

Ironically, he now lived in Wellington, near where she grew up. Charlie saw her family regularly and was often conscripted into escorting one or other of her female cousins to dances or other events. To rub salt into the wound, she received regular letters from those cousins, gushing over his easy-going charm and good looks, and telling her she was a lunatic for ever having let him out of her sight.

Good advice in theory, but he had been offered the opportunity of a lifetime in Wellington, while she had achieved her dream of being accepted to medical school in Dunedin. A staunch belief in a woman's right to sculpt her own destiny came at a cost, as did most other things worth having.

Isabelle startled her by unexpectedly ducking her head below window level as they passed a large building, even though it was some distance off, half hidden by trees. Beyond the building, the sea and a small island appeared in glimpses between the trees, passing by slowly as the train chugged up a steep incline.

She wasn't sure what to make of Isabelle's reaction, other than that she was scared of something. Or, more likely, someone. Grace wondered what the building was, but did not want to ask for fear of damaging the trust between them.

Isabelle straightened up again. "That's the place I escaped from. My father abandoned me in a home for wayward women as soon as he found out I was with child. He refused to allow me to marry my sweetheart. Stillwaters Sanctuary, they call it. Stillwaters Madhouse more like."

"Isabelle, I have a friend who is a policeman. Constable Pyke is a fine man. He can help you if you are in trouble."

Isabelle jerked her head up at his name. "Constable Pyke? What an odd coincidence."

"Have you heard of him?"

"I met a woman called Charlotte at Stillwaters. We had both found a way to sneak out at night to savour a moment of freedom. I admitted to her that I was planning to escape, but hadn't bargained on there being no way over the walls. She said she would help me if I promised to get a message to a Constable Pyke, who lived in Clyde. Or his son – what was his name? Bertie?"

"Charlie?"

"Yes, that's it. It would be such a weight off my conscience if you know him and could pass on her message."

"Yes, of course I will tell him. What was the message?"

"She asked me to tell them that Amelia was still alive. And Josiah too."

"Amelia? Josiah? Do you know to whom she was referring?"

"I have no idea. Charlotte only said that the Pyke family would know whom she meant. I assume Amelia was one of the other women at Stillwaters or perhaps someone from her past. I must admit I was more interested in getting her help to escape than questioning her motives."

"And did she help you?"

"Charlotte was magnificent. She knocked over a brazier that was burning dead leaves, which set off a small fire. When I got to the rear wall, she helped me to get over it. I owe her a great deal. Knowing her message got out would be a relief."

Grace tried not to think about why Charlotte wanted to get a message to Charlie from a home for unwed pregnant girls. Right now, Isabelle was her first priority. Despite the fact that she had got away safely, her agitation was growing with every turn of the wheels, as the train ground slowly up the hill towards the steep cliffs ahead.

She was about to ask Isabelle for more details about Charlotte's message, when a tap on her shoulder startled her.

"A word please, Miss." The train guard gestured for her to follow him to the empty end of the carriage. "I can see you are trying to help that young woman, which speaks well of your charity, but I must ask you – did that girl get on at Waitati?"

Faced with a direct question, and knowing the guard had likely seen Isabelle ducking out of sight when they passed the house in the trees, Grace had no choice but to tell him the truth. "She did. She seemed in distress, so I thought it best to look after her."

"I don't know what story that girl has spun, but I fear she has escaped from the Stillwaters Lunatic Asylum. She may appear harmless, but the women there are a danger to themselves and others."

"A lunatic asylum? Are you certain?" Was this the reason Isabelle seemed so jittery?

"See them come and go all the time, Miss. The patients have a look about them. For everyone's safety, I am obliged to report her to the doctor, who is in first class. Please try to remain calm until I return." The guard strode up the aisle at a sharp pace, casting an anxious glance at Isabelle as he passed.

16

Isabelle jumped up and stared after him. "What did he want? Where is he going?" Her voice rose to a high pitch of hysteria, causing heads to turn their way.

"Sit down, Isabelle. The guard is concerned for your wellbeing, so he has gone to fetch a doctor. Don't worry, I shall remain with you all the way to Dunedin. You will be safe with me."

"No! Grace, you must stop him from getting the doctor. He'll kill me and my baby if they take me back to that place." She clawed at Grace's shoulders, shaking her. "Don't let him near me, please. I'd rather kill myself than let them take me back." She pushed Grace towards the door with unexpected strength. "Stop him!"

Grace fought down the panic that was seeping into her from Isabelle's hysteria. She dared not leave Isabelle alone, yet she feared what the doctor's unwanted presence would do to this troubled woman's mental stability. "Stay here, in your seat. I'll be back as soon as I can."

She hurried up the carriage, dodging the brass spittoons in the middle of the aisle, to the door at the far end. When she pushed it open, she found herself on a narrow wooden platform, joined to the next carriage by an even narrower gangway. The noise of the train was amplified out here, tearing at her eardrums as she gripped the rails and forced herself across to the door opposite.

Midway across the gangway, she made the mistake of looking down.

The wind tore at her skirt, whipping it between the insubstantial safety rails as the train travelled along the edge of a steep hill. Far below, a narrow passage of deep turquoise water cut a path between the base of the slope and a sandy spit on the opposite side. It would have been beautiful, had she not been so thoroughly terrified. Looking down from a height gave Grace the heebie-jeebies, but doing so while travelling at speed was far worse. And she had to do it all again to get through to the next carriage.

When she finally hauled open the door to the first-class carriage, the calm of the interior was like stepping into paradise. Padded seats dulled the roar of the train down to a softer rattle, as she staggered

17

forward to where the guard was talking with the man in the dark suit, who had joined the train at the last station. Presumably this was the doctor from the asylum.

The doctor rose from his seat and hurried towards her, weaving across the aisle with the movement of the train, his relatively youthful face creased with concern. "Excuse me, Miss."

Grace put out her hand to stop him. "Please, stay where you are. Your patient is in a very fragile state of mind and I fear your presence will only alarm her further."

"Please, step out of the way, Miss. You needn't worry. This is what I am trained for."

There was no way to stop him as he pushed past her with a determined shove. He was out of the door and across the gangway before she could steady herself. Medical doctor he may be, but his slurred speech and weaving gait suggested he had let his professional standards slip to the point of being slightly the worse for drink in a public place.

The guard followed a few paces behind. "Best you keep out of the way, Miss. You never can tell what such people will do. I've seen a few in my time on this train turn from calm to hysterical in an instant, for no reason known to man. Some of them would strike terror into the devil himself."

Despite the logic of his words, there was no way Grace would desert Isabelle in her moment of need, even though the thought of crossing the gangways again terrified her.

When she stepped out through the door, she saw that the train was now running hard up against a sheer cliff, right at the very edge of a precipice. Indeed, when she looked down, she caught a flash of the sea through the rails below.

The train shook and twisted, determined to tip her into oblivion, as she stepped from the relative safety of the platform onto the narrow gangway. With grim determination, she clung to the rails and inched her way across with her eyes fixed on the opposite door.

As she reached the halfway point, the train rattled around a curve, throwing her onto the widely-spaced rails of the gangway. She teetered on the edge, hanging over a dizzying drop of over a hundred feet to the waves crashing on the rocks below.

The Express

Detective Constable Charlie Pyke rested his head against the padded cushion of the first-class seat, watching the farmland and seascape pass by at astounding speed. The guard had told him the average speed of the express train was more than twenty miles per hour. A true wonder of the industrial age.

Picturesque as the view was, all he could feel was the deadweight of the flimsy telegram in his pocket. The words on it were direct and to the point: "Depart Chch early GP". Brevity was the norm for a telegram, but he still felt the whiplash of Grace's stark words on his conscience.

His own telegram to her had read: "Sorry leave cancelled CP". For a few more pennies, he might have made it sound more contrite. "Very much regret leave cancelled, hope to see you soon" would have been better, although not nearly good enough to atone for a third offence.

He and Grace Penrose had arranged to meet in Christchurch – their first time together in almost two years. Grace had already returned to Wellington twice to see her family and both times he had been required for duty in the far reaches of the region. Third time lucky had been anything but. Grace had every right to be fuming mad, or worse, to believe him uncaring.

"If you sigh one more time, Pyke, I'll banish you to the second-class carriage."

"Duly noted, sir. Thought you were asleep on account of the snoring."

"Not much chance of that on these cursed long-distance trains." Detective Inspector Stewart pushed himself upright in his seat. "Don't worry, lad. Grace will be so glad to see you when we get to Dunedin that she will forgive you for the change of plan. Whether she will forgive me for cancelling your leave again is another matter."

Stewart squirmed in his seat and let out a long sigh. He caught Charlie's smirk. "Don't even think of saying anything, Pyke. Sitting down for hours on end makes me irritable."

"I'm grateful for the comfortable seat. A whole day on a wooden bench in second class would have been murder." Especially given the black and blue state of his body.

Stewart had paid for first class by way of apology for cancelling Charlie's leave yet again. He was taking the express train from Christchurch to Dunedin for his own week of leave, so Charlie had joined him as soon as he realised that Grace had already departed.

Detective Inspector Stewart had been his commanding officer long enough that Charlie could read his moods, which were almost always on the cheerful side of the ledger, when he wasn't focussed on the serious business of catching criminals. People who met him for the first time took one look at his spare frame and dapper attire and assumed he was a gentleman of leisure. His glossy moustaches, which curled in perfect symmetry above his barbered cheeks and perfectly tied cravat, did nothing to dispel that entirely misleading impression.

Charlie had long believed that Stewart cultivated this look by way of disguise. A long list of criminals had underestimated his brilliant mind and rattlesnake speed. It was always a pleasure to witness their shock when they found their wrists in handcuffs.

People underestimated Charlie for the opposite reason. He fit right in amongst the labouring classes, with his cloth cap and clodhopper boots. The top hat and bowler brigade would nod politely at Stewart and either fail to see Charlie at all or take him for a thick-headed plodder, with nothing but muscle to recommend him. Grace Penrose had been one of the few people who saw through him. Without her, he would no longer be a policeman, let alone a detective working alongside the best in the business.

"You did a fine job bringing down those anti-immigrant agitators, Pyke. I'll never forget the crazed look in their eyes when they attacked those Chinese shopkeepers."

"It was my pleasure, sir."

21

The ringleader's arrest had been one of the most satisfying moments of Charlie's career. The kiss he had received from the age-wizened wife of one of the shopkeepers, as he restrained her after she delivered a well-deserved boot in the kidneys to her attacker, more than made up for the pain he was now trying to ignore.

His shoulder ached where he had brought the vile lout to the ground in a flying tackle, landing in the gutter and jarring the old knife wound on his upper arm. The surrounding thugs had made the most of the chance to imprint their boot-marks on his back, before he had scrambled to his feet again and arrested the lot of them, with the help of a band of uniformed constables, who had emerged a moment too late from an alleyway, with truncheons and handcuffs at the ready.

"Lily will be proud of you. I hate to think what abuse she must suffer for being half-Chinese, although she never says a word about it."

"My aunt is used to dealing with the many bigots in the world." Charlie took after his English father in looks, so he didn't suffer from prejudice as his mother and aunt did. "Does Aunt Lily know we are coming?"

"We wrapped the case up so fast, I didn't have time to send a telegram to say that we could make it after all." Stewart pulled a letter out of his pocket, pausing to sniff the lingering scent from its pages. "She seemed to be looking forward to the visit." He started reading the letter again, not bothering to hide his pleasure at its contents.

Charlie wished he could be more like Stewart, who had no trouble expressing his thoughts in writing, even to the extent of penning poetry. In contrast, Charlie struggled to know what to say in his infrequent letters to Grace, so they were mostly about their shared interest in detection. The gory details of victim autopsies might be fascinating to both of them, but it was not exactly the conventional way to correspond with a young lady.

Not that there was anything conventional about Grace Penrose. They had been thrown together during a murder investigation, which had come close to claiming both their lives, sparking a connection between them. Grace's letters gave him no hint as to any lingering feelings, although they did contain many useful suggestions on his autopsy notes. In contrast, Aunt Lily's letters left him in no doubt as to Grace's busy social life and many admirers, which she fitted in around the long hours required for her medical studies.

He stifled another sigh and caught the eye of the passing guard. "Excuse me, sir. Can you tell me if we are running to time?"

"We are right now, but we've received a telegraph message to say there may be a delay up ahead."

"Nothing serious, I hope?"

"A fatal incident, I'm afraid. I am not at liberty to disclose the details."

Detective Inspector Stewart perked up instantly, as the words "fatal incident" triggered instincts honed by thirty years of policing. He had his badge out before the guard had finished his sentence.

"I don't know much more myself, Inspector. A young woman and a gentleman fell from the previous train and died on the cliffs beyond Waitati. We have been ordered to proceed with caution."

A chill finger of misgiving crawled up Charlie's spine. He told himself he was being foolish. Just because Grace Penrose was on that train, and had a magnetic attraction for trouble, did not mean that anything had happened to her.

On A Precipice

Grace thought she heard a scream, as she focussed on pulling herself along the railing to the door.

Although it had felt like a lifetime, not more than a minute or two could have passed since the doctor and guard had entered the last of the second-class carriages, yet she saw no sign of them or Isabelle when she finally made it inside.

Every face on the train followed her as she stumbled down the aisle. Isabelle was not there. Her reticule lay discarded under the empty seat.

"What happened?" Grace asked the grandmother of the three children, who were sitting ominously still, their jaws hanging loose.

"As soon as you left, the girl who was with you became terribly agitated. When the gentleman in the dark suit came in, she must have panicked, because she went out the rear door. She mustn't have known that it was the last carriage."

Isabelle had got onto the train through that door, so she must have known there was nowhere for her to go. Perhaps she thought she could lock the door from the outside. "Did the man follow her?"

"The man and then the guard." The grandmother stared at Grace with wide eyes and made the sign of the cross across her ample chest. "I heard the guard yell 'don't jump' when he opened the rear door, but that was all. After a moment, the guard came back in, yelled at us to sit down, then he pulled the emergency lever, before going back outside again."

Grace sprinted the rest of the way down the aisle, swerving like a drunk as the train slowed down in a squeal of brakes. She couldn't see any sign of people on the rear platform through the two narrow strips of glass in the door. Only when she opened it did she see the guard off to the side of the platform, operating the braking wheel.

"Get back in the carriage!" he yelled.

He followed her back inside, his face ashen and his body trembling. Grace's medical training overcame her desire to know what had happened. She rushed forward to help the guard as he slumped against the door, his breathing ragged. By supporting his weight on her shoulder, she managed to twist him sideways onto the bench seat. Grace eased his collar and tie away from the pounding pulse in his neck, watching closely as his breathing returned to normal.

"Thank you. I'm … I'm fine … the shock …," he mumbled.

"What happened?" Grace asked gently.

"I … I was too late. I thought she was going to throw herself off the train. When I got to the door, I could see they were struggling. At first I thought the doctor was trying to save her. But then …" He shook his head, as if he didn't believe what he had seen. "He pushed her. No, that cannot be … she must have fallen. She's gone … they're both gone. I tried to get to him …"

The train screeched its way to a juddering stop. The guard pushed himself to his feet as if the weight of the world rested on his shoulders. He restored his tie to the correct position and wobbled towards the door. "I need to attend to my duties. All the years I've worked this line and never had a single incident. Now, two deaths in one day."

He blew a short note on his whistle, although all the passengers were gaping at him already. "Everyone please stay calm and remain in your seats. There will be a short delay while I investigate an incident."

"An incident?" the grandmother gasped. "Two people disappeared over a cliff!"

"Please remain calm," the guard repeated. "I will be back as soon as I have determined their …" Words failed him. He set his cap straight and exited the carriage.

Grace followed him out, having to run to catch up as he strode rapidly up the length of the train. "I'm a trainee doctor. You might need my help."

The guard opened his mouth, but failed to form any words. Grace wasn't sure whether he was still stunned by what had happened or incredulous as to her qualifications to assist in what would surely be a double fatality. He whirled and strode off again, leaving her to hurry after him.

When they reached the locomotive, the grimy faces of the driver, stoker and brakeman were already leaning out. "What happened?" the driver asked.

"Two jumpers, lads," the guard reported. "I'm going back to check for survivors. Davies, come with me. McInnes, we'll need to be off as soon as I give the signal. Don't want the express butting us over the edge too. Plenty of leeway, but better safe than sorry."

A grease-smeared man, who looked as if a bag of coal dust had been up-ended over his body, jumped down from the loco. The three of them headed back along the track, hugging the inner edge of the cliff as the drop became steeper. Further along they could see a red flag waving in the wind.

As they got closer, Grace realised it was not a flag, but one of her most treasured possessions. "That red cloth is the shawl the woman was wearing."

"Did you know the girl, Miss?" the guard asked.

"Not at all. I just wanted to help her. She seemed so desperate. I feel terrible that I left her alone, but she was adamant that I should stop the doctor from coming to see her. I thought she might calm down if I stopped the doctor interfering."

They hurried along the track. As they got closer, Grace could see that the shawl had blown into a tree, which was clinging to the edge of the cliff with more hope than soil, well beyond their reach. The victims' bodies were nowhere to be seen, although Grace's plumed hat was caught on a scrap of vegetation that jutting out several yards down the cliff. The drop at that point was nearly vertical, with wave-lashed rocks below. By sheer bad luck, the two victims had gone over at the most dangerous point.

"No point looking further if she isn't trackside," the guard said. "They'll have to send a search team with ropes tomorrow, or maybe a boat."

They walked back along the track, peering down at intervals, until the guard spotted the doctor's body down a bank, right on the edge of the drop. The angle of his neck, where he had come down onto a boulder, confirmed their fears. His sightless eyes stared at them, sharing the horror of his final moments.

The stoker let out a heartfelt oath and crossed himself, while the guard looked as if he was about to throw up. Grace sympathised with both reactions, but held her own emotions in check. If there was one thing that medical school had taught her, it was to never show any hint of an emotion that could be seen as feminine frailty.

"There is no way to get down there safely," the guard said. "Besides, some of those express train drivers like to push their locos to the limit and I want to be having a stiff dram of whisky in Dunedin well before they come through."

Grace followed the two men as they hurried back along the track, looking behind her every now and then, in case the express train was early. If it was, there was not enough space to escape on the cliff side of the track. She would face the choice of being flattened by tons of steel, or leaping into thin air. Not a choice to dwell upon.

"Why do you think the woman ran away from the doctor?" Grace asked. "She was in no danger from him on the train, with other passengers around her."

"I couldn't say, Miss," the guard replied. "Lunatics don't think straight."

"Me mam reckons doctors what treat loonies is usually loony themselves," the stoker said.

"Have a bit of respect, lad. Those doctors have a devil of a hard job to do. Is it any wonder they turn to drink and morbid thoughts?" The guard mopped his brow with a handkerchief, before striding out for the train again.

By the time Grace caught up, the guard was standing by the rear door with a flag in his hand. He helped her to mount the steps, which were high off the ground without the usual station platform to assist.

As soon as she was through the gate, which he latched with exaggerated care, he waved the flag and they were off.

"Will you be all right, Miss?" he asked. "I have to man the rear brake for the downhill section. I expect one of the other passengers will take care of you, if you ask. Old Mrs Gallagher, with the children, is a kind woman."

"I'll be fine. Thank you for your concern."

The guard opened the door for her, leaving Grace to return to her seat. She ignored the looks of her fellow passengers, which ran the gamut from horrified to morbidly curious, and closed her eyes to the world.

The horror of what had happened began to take hold of her now that the urgency of responding to the crisis was over. Isabelle Forsyth had struck her as the kind of woman she could be friends with. When they had chatted together, she had seemed rational, albeit afraid of being caught. Not at all like a lunatic and absolutely not like a suicidal lunatic.

What could possibly have been so bad to terrify her to the point of rushing onto a part of the train from which there could be no escape? And why would a doctor, who had taken an oath to save lives, push a girl to her death? None of it made sense, unless it was a tragic accident involving an unstable girl and a rescue gone wrong. Goodness knows, she was painfully aware of how hard it was to remain upright on a moving train, even without the unbalancing effect of restraining an hysterical girl.

By the time the train emerged from a long tunnel and descended towards Dunedin's port, Grace had given up trying to make sense of it. The sight of dozens of masts rising up from the harbour usually left her feeling excited at the possibilities of travel to far-off destinations, but today she only felt miserable that, for one young woman, the future held no possibilities at all. She was left with the painful regret of having made a fatal error, by leaving Isabelle alone.

The platform at Port Chalmers was feverish with activity. Several groups of passengers disembarked the train, with baggage stacked around them, as porters worked to shuttle dozens of large trunks hither

28

and thither. As before, she marvelled at the disparity in the porters, from a swarthy giant with a long plait of black hair, who looked like he could balance a shipping trunk on each muscled arm, to a small, pale lad, with every type in between. Station attendants dashed between groups, pointing them in the direction of signs for exotic locales, such as London and Melbourne.

One day, she vowed, that would be her embarking on a voyage across the globe. But right now, she had a distressing interview with the police to face and her own guilt to come to terms with.

Lost And Found

The express train crawled around the edge of the cliff, slowing to a complete stop at one point. Charlie went out onto the platform between the carriages to see what was happening.

The guard pushed past him. "Go back inside the carriage please, sir."

He showed his badge. "I know a young woman who was on the other train. I want to help."

The guard swung the gate open. "Mind how you go on the steps, Constable, and for heaven's sake don't go near the edge of the cliff."

When they reached the locomotive, the guard called out, "Why have we stopped?"

"Red flag ahead. Or at least we thought it was, but it is only a red cloth flapping on a tree. Still, best be sure, given the two deaths earlier."

Charlie pelted down the track to where Grace's distinctive shawl hung from a branch, shouting her name into the chill wind.

Yelling for her was utterly pointless, but he couldn't stop himself. What if she was lying injured down the cliff and nobody had thought to look? He scrambled along the edge, peering down, but the cliff was in deep shadow, as the sun had already sunk behind the high hills on the other side. Loose rock dislodged under the pressure of his hands, skittering over the side and shattering on the rocks far below.

Stewart caught up with him as he was preparing to edge his way over the side. "Pyke, don't even think about trying to climb down there. The guard says it is far too steep and dangerous at this point for anyone to stand a chance."

He hauled Charlie back onto the track and kept an arm around his shoulders, as he guided him back towards the train. "It may not be Grace. Why would it be?"

"But the red shawl in the tree is hers. I should know, I gave it to her. What a fool I was to leave her behind in Dunedin."

"Enough of that. We're going to get back on the train. You'll find her safe and well at home, I know it."

"At least let me get her shawl."

"Don't be an idiot, Pyke. Look at that drop. If you fall off that sapling, or it snaps, you'll break your neck."

Charlie wrenched free of his grip. Nothing was going to stop him trying. He could always come back down if the tree wasn't strong enough to hold his weight. Besides, it was the only possible vantage point to look back towards the cliff.

The tree bent alarmingly under his weight, but at least he retrieved the shawl. There was no sign of Grace, but he did see the body of a man in the brief time he had had to scan the cliff before the tree trunk cracked under his weight.

The rest of the journey passed in silence. Stewart was fuming over his refusal to obey an order, while Charlie was too numb to speak. As the train pulled into Dunedin station, Charlie apologised and was forgiven for his foolishness.

They made their way through the crowd of disembarking passengers towards a burly man standing beside a train guard. The guard headed away along the platform as they approached.

Stewart slapped the burly man on the back. "DI Robbie Wallace, it's been far too long since we shared a fine Highland malt."

"DI Alistair Stewart, if my eyes aren't deceiving me. What sin have I committed to deserve a visit from you? Not come to stir up trouble in my patch again, I hope?"

"No need to worry, I'm on leave. Although I do need to speak to you urgently about the deaths on the earlier train. What happened, Robbie?"

"Seems fairly straightforward from what the train guard has told us. A young woman was in a distressed state and took fright when a doctor tried to help her. They struggled and both fell to their deaths. It is unclear whether her fall from the train was suicide or accident. The guard thought the doctor pushed her, but he is not sure. Seems unlikely. A bad business, either way. Constable Kelly is taking a statement from another witness in the stationmaster's office."

"The thing is, Robbie, we might know one of the victims. Do you have their names yet?"

"The man is Doctor Samuel Wilson, who works at an asylum up the coast. The woman was about twenty years old, slim with dark hair. We have a tentative identity, but we'd welcome your help if you can confirm who she is. Tragically, the woman was with child. As I said, a bad business – three lives lost in a single tragedy."

The two officers headed for the office, while Charlie lagged behind, despair turning his feet to lead. The description fit Grace exactly, right down to the distinctive shawl. But how could Grace be pregnant? Surely Aunt Lily would have told him if she had married, even if Grace had been unwilling to. Maybe that was why she wanted to meet him in Christchurch, to break her news to him in person? If only he had met her there, this tragedy wouldn't have happened.

Up ahead, Stewart stood at the door of the stationmaster's office, gesturing frantically at him. A flicker of hope lit a fire under his feet. He was at the door in a dozen long strides. Grace was staring in astonishment at them, while a man several years older than her rested his hand on the back of her chair.

"Charlie!"

The chair tipped over in her haste to get to him. She flung herself towards him, as he braced himself for the welcome impact of her embrace.

Unfortunately, the constable who had been taking her statement was far too quick on his feet. He stepped forward to stop them entering the office, putting himself between them and Grace. "Gentlemen, I have to ask you to stay outside. I am interviewing a witness."

Charlie side-stepped the constable, seizing both of her hands, feeling her fingers squeezing his through her soft kid gloves. "Grace. You're alive."

"Charlie. How do you always manage to appear just when I need you most?"

The constable and the other man both gaped at them, slack-mouthed. Grace blushed and stepped away to a more appropriate distance.

The local detective inspector exchanged a glance with Stewart. "Constable Kelly, this is Detective Inspector Stewart, Wellington Region."

"And Detective Constable Pyke," Stewart added. "Miss Penrose is an old acquaintance of ours, as you may have gathered. As soon as you have finished questioning her, we are eager to whisk her away for our own interrogation."

Kelly responded with a sharp salute. "I believe I have enough from the young lady for the moment, sir, if she is willing to come into the central police station tomorrow morning to sign her statement and answer any further questions we might have."

"Thank you, Constable Kelly," Stewart said. "You may be sure that she will be there tomorrow morning."

That was the last Charlie heard of the discussion between the other three policemen, as he led Grace into the far corner of the office. "They said a young woman fell from the train. When I saw your shawl hooked on a branch over the cliff, I was terrified it was you."

"I lent it to the woman who died, Charlie. I'm so sorry to cause you distress."

"You have no idea how relieved I am to see you alive." Charlie clutched her hands, as if she might vanish if he let go. "I hope the woman who died was not a friend of yours."

"I talked to her for no more than a few minutes, but that doesn't seem to have diminished the shock I feel at her death, especially as I could have stopped her."

Grace's companion appeared at her side, his lips pressed into a straight line that none would mistake for a smile. "It has been a trying day for you, Grace. Please allow me to escort you home."

33

Charlie registered his presence properly for the first time. Passably handsome and undoubtedly elegant, in a tailored suit and brocade waistcoat, with one of those annoying little moustaches, so thin that neither lips nor nostrils were acquainted with its slicked down bristles. The artist within Charlie ached to get his sketch book out. Add a top hat, monocle and a silver spoon and he could be a caricature of a toff straight from the pages of *Punch*.

Grace smiled at the man, who was resting his hand on her arm in far too familiar a manner for Charlie's liking.

"Thank you, Jamie. I appreciate your thoughtfulness at meeting me at the station, but may I beg your forgiveness for abandoning you? These men are old friends, who will see me safely home. I'll see you at work next week."

Charlie extended a hand to the man, which he shook after a momentary hesitation.

"Forgive me. I have completely forgotten my manners. Charlie, may I introduce the recently appointed police surgeon, Doctor James Cranston-Hartfield. I will be working for him over the summer break, until lectures at medical school resume next year."

"In town on police business, are you, Pyke?"

"I'm on leave." Charlie glanced at Grace. "Long overdue leave. This trip is purely for pleasure."

"What an extraordinary thought!" Grace teased. "Won't Wellington fall apart without you, DC Pyke?"

"I care not, Miss Penrose. Let it fall!"

"Goodness, how I have missed the company of my two favourite detectives. I thought your leave had been cancelled or I wouldn't have left Christchurch."

"It was, but we got a tip that allowed us to wrap up the case early. We made the steamer with seconds to spare."

Stewart joined them. "DC Pyke is being modest, as usual. The tip was thanks to his undercover work. He even had the honour of taking down the ringleader and saving a Chinese shopkeeper from a beating, or worse, into the bargain." He slapped Charlie on the shoulder, making him wince.

"Charlie, you're hurt. Don't give me that look. I know pain when I see it." Grace peered at the darker patch on the sleeve of his overcoat. "Blood?"

"Nothing to worry about, Grace."

Stewart took a step backwards under her glare. "Those anti-immigrant radicals can be a mite rough. I didn't know he was injured, I swear it."

"Don't fuss, Grace, it's clearly nothing serious," Cranston-Hartfield said. "Anti-immigrant sentiment is understandable, though it's unfortunate that a few rabble-rousers take it too far."

"Anti-immigrant sentiment is understandable, is it? Are we not all immigrants, Doctor Cranston-Hartfield?" Charlie drew out the syllables of his name, extracting verbal retribution, instead of flooring the idiot, as he deserved. He was Grace's boss, after all.

Grace eyes went wide. She knew him well enough to know the offence the remarks had caused, especially as he had a Chinese grandfather. She laid a restraining hand on the doctor's arm. "Jamie, I'm very grateful you took the trouble to meet my train, but I would like to go home with DI Stewart and DC Pyke. I haven't seen them in such a long time."

"Whatever you wish, Grace." Cranston-Hartfield looked like he was about to say more, but he only gave a sharp nod and left.

Stewart, with typical thoughtfulness, gathered up his valise and Grace's bag, leaving Charlie with a free arm to escort Grace. Charlie was a working man, through and through, who generally didn't think much of the so-called upper classes. Odd that he had never thought of it before, but Charlie had liked and admired Stewart from their first meeting, before he knew the man was one of the most respected police officers in the country, and despite his privileged background.

The three of them squeezed themselves and their luggage into a hackney carriage. Charlie noted that Grace grimaced as he handed her up. "Are you hurt too, Grace?"

"It's nothing. Just a minor collision with a rather hard shipping trunk." Grace settled into the seat with a wince. "Oh bother, I have forgotten to give Constable Kelly the victim's reticule."

"Tomorrow morning will do," Stewart said. "I don't wish to waste another moment getting you home, so I can hear your tale. And to see your great-aunt again, of course."

"And Lily, if she is home. Quite the gad-about, our Lily." Grace nudged Charlie, but relented at the sight of Stewart's crestfallen expression. "Between long hours at the women's refuge and her work for women's suffrage, she has no time for a social life. Does she know you two are coming?"

"I didn't get the chance to send a telegram that we were able to take leave after all."

Charlie was content with sitting silently next to Grace, enjoying the friendly banter as if they had only left Dunedin yesterday, not two years ago. Feeling the warmth of her arm against his, knowing she was safe and, for the next few days, that neither had any major calls upon their time. Perhaps it would be third time lucky after all.

Reunited

Grace banged open the door to her Great-Aunt Anne's house. "Anyone home? I have a surprise for you."

Anne and Lily were in the drawing room, reading by the muted light of a gas lamp. They looked up with mild curiosity, which instantly turned to delight.

Lily sprinted across the room in a flash of emerald silk. "Alistair! Why didn't you send a telegram to say you were coming after all? I would have come to the station."

"Lily, how well you look, my dear." Stewart was beaming from ear to ear. "We had a last-minute reprieve. We were lucky to make the steamer as it was." He looked over her shoulder. "Mrs Macmillan, lovely to see you again."

"Do call me Anne, please. Welcome home. Should I get our maid to make up two additional beds?"

"That is kind of you, Anne, but Charlie and I will be staying with a colleague of mine, who lives close by. My apologies for arriving unannounced so late in the evening, but our time in Dunedin is short and our desire for your company brooked no delay."

Charlie stood with his hands on his hips and a grin on his lips. "Well, Aunt Lily, can't you spare a single word of greeting for your favourite nephew?"

"My favourite nephew? Goodness, I hardly recognise you, Charlie. What are they feeding you up there in the North Island?" Lily wrapped her arms around his waist, her petite Chinese beauty appearing all the more delicate beside his solid-as-an-oak frame.

"Grace's family takes turns stuffing me like a prize turkey every Sunday, while my penny-pinching landlady starves me the remaining six days. Talking of food, I don't suppose ..."

"I set aside a meal for Grace and I'm sure I can find enough for Alistair, but I doubt there is a larder in Dunedin big enough for you." Lily swatted her nephew playfully. "I'll see what I can find. We expected you earlier, Grace."

"You won't believe what happened, but we'll save the explanation for later. I'll come and help." Grace got up, but Stewart beat her to it. Instead, she turned to Charlie. "If I can't help with supper, then it must be time for medical attention."

"Why does Charlie need a medical attention, Grace?" Anne asked. "And wouldn't it be more appropriate if I did it?"

"It's only his arm, Auntie. A minor injury thanks to a vicious thug who deserves to rot in gaol. No need for you to get up."

Grace dragged her reluctant patient down the hall to the kitchen. He protested that he was fine, but the extent of the damage was painfully clear when Grace rolled his sleeve up.

"The scar from your old knife wound has torn open across the bottom. Nothing major, but I'll clean and bandage it to ensure it heals properly. Does it give you much pain?"

"Not anymore."

She pushed his sleeve up higher, revealing an ugly bruise. "Charlie, just how far does this bruising extend?"

Lily came over to take a look. "Shirt off, now. Don't give me that look, Charles Thomas Lee Pyke, I can see by the way you are moving that you are in pain."

"I am not taking my shirt off in Mrs Macmillan's kitchen."

"Don't be shy on my account. I'll see to the food." Grace retreated to the pantry, leaving Charlie with his arms crossed over his chest and Lily with her hands on her hips. He didn't stand a chance.

"For heaven's sake Charlie, I bathed you when you were a baby. And Grace is a medical student. She's probably seen more shirtless male bodies than the rest of us combined."

"As if I needed reminding of that," Charlie muttered, as he stripped off his waistcoat and shirt.

Lily gasped. "Alistair, what in blue blazes have you had my nephew doing?"

Neither Stewart nor Grace could contain their curiosity. Both flinched at the sight of his muscular torso, which bore boot-shaped patches of livid bruising.

"I had no idea he was injured, honestly, Lily." The hardened detective cowered under her glare. "I lost sight of him in the middle of a riot. A mob was trying to torch Chinese-owned shops. You should be proud of your nephew for stopping them."

"What were they doing – dancing a jig on his body?" Grace ran her fingers over his ribs. It would be a miracle if none of them was broken. "Are you having any difficulty breathing? Not passing any blood?"

"I'm fine." Charlie winced. "Maybe a little sore. Nothing broken."

Lily tutted, but left the room without saying another word. By the time she returned with a large pot of arnica cream, Grace had washed the scar in warm water and applied a salve. The long, red slash was a painful reminder of how close he had come to dying on her behalf two years ago, when she had first met him.

Grace tied off the end of the bandage. "I suppose I should be relieved that you don't need any more stitches."

"I told you I was fine," the patient grumbled.

"Hmph." Grace slapped on the first blob of arnica a little more forcibly than ideal for a compassionate doctor. "Do you think you might manage a few days off from being a human punching bag?"

"I have every intention of it, as long as you can manage to stay clear of danger and death for more than five minutes. Two deaths at once this time – three if you count the unborn child. You have surpassed yourself, Grace. I swear I will have a stomach ulcer before I turn thirty at this rate."

Grace conceded the point silently and applied the rest of the liniment in gentle strokes. She was glad to see that he hadn't changed in character, although the intervening years had added a sharper edge to the boyish features she remembered. She could hardly be surprised

39

that he would no longer be the naïve young constable on his first posting, especially given all the undercover work he had been doing since then.

Two years of medical school had changed her as well. There was no room for ladylike modesty and reticence when surrounded by privileged young men who resented her presence. The only way to get through was to be thicker skinned than a centenarian rhinoceros.

"If my physician has finished her very thorough ministrations, perhaps I might get back to supper?"

Grace snapped back to the present, registering the amusement in his green eyes.

"Unless you would like me to tend to the bruise left by that trunk?" he added. "Don't think I didn't see you grimace when you sat down."

"You can wipe that smirk off your face, Charles Thomas Lee Pyke. I assure you that particular bruise will never see the light of day in public."

Charlie stretched his shoulders and back. "Feels better already. May I put my clothes on, doc, or are you so used to unclothed men that I need not bother?"

"Any more of your impertinence and my great-aunt will be adding to your haematoma collection with her walking cane. As if I don't get enough disrespect at medical school."

He pulled his shirt over his head. "It can't be easy being the first woman training to be a doctor."

"Nothing I can't handle. I've learned to check my seat before I sit down, as they seem to think it a huge joke to leave body parts in unlikely places. As long as I am faultless in my own behaviour and better prepared than they are, I'll eventually win over their objections to my presence. Sometime in the next century, if I'm lucky."

"Around the same time as I arrest the last criminal in the country, I expect. Shall we go? Supper left the room five minutes ago and I really am hungry."

"I read a scientific article about starvation being the best cure for severe bruising."

40

"And I read one about a hungry man being more dangerous than an injured wild tiger."

He adjusted the knot of his tie and was gone before she could think of a suitably cutting reply. As Grace tidied away her medical kit, she realised just how much she had missed sparring with him.

Lily had transformed the dining room into a candlelit feast. There was enough food to feed a platoon of starving constables, although the range of offerings was rather eclectic, as if she and Stewart had upended the entire contents of the larder onto the best serving dishes. Anne was busy handing out plates and cutlery, while Stewart poured wine. How good it was to hear their easy chatter, as if the gap since their last feast was days rather than years.

"How is the patient?" Anne inquired.

"In need of a medal and a few days of well-earned rest," Grace replied.

"Excellent. Then perhaps you might explain why the three of you look like little naughty children keeping a secret."

"First, a toast, to friends reunited." Stewart raised his glass. "With my apologies that it hasn't happened sooner."

When the ring of crystal on crystal subsided, Grace began her account of meeting Isabelle Forsyth on the train, finishing with the tragic death of both Isabelle and the doctor. "What worries me is the guard's initial impression that the doctor pushed Isabelle off the train, after which the doctor either fell or jumped."

"The incident must have happened very quickly, Grace," Charlie said. "It wouldn't be surprising if the guard was uncertain about what happened, especially if there was a struggle."

"It seemed to me as if he was uncertain only because he couldn't believe that the doctor could have done something so terrible as push her. The local police don't know whether to put it down to suicide, accident or foul play, but I suspect they will settle on accidental death for want of clear indication otherwise."

Stewart contemplated his wine, twisting the glass in the candlelight to admire the ruby glow. "An unstable young woman, who is unwed and with child, running away from a lunatic asylum in a clear state of distress. She had no reason to go out onto the rear platform of the train, as she would have been far safer staying where she was. On the face of it, suicide seems far more likely than murder."

"I talked to Isabelle and she seemed entirely rational once she had calmed down," Grace countered. "Why would she even board the train if she was truly suicidal? Far easier to stand in front of it."

"Disturbed minds don't necessarily apply logic in the same way we do," Stewart replied.

"Yet my instinct is telling me otherwise. Isabelle only became distressed when the train guard overheard us talking and went to get the doctor. She was terrified of what the doctor would do to her and her baby. Who's to say he didn't push her, to cover up whatever it was that frightened her?"

"Murder, Grace? Are you sure you haven't been reading too many novels?" Anne said. "We all know that people suffering from disorders of the mind can transition from rational to hysterical in an alarmingly short space of time for little obvious reason."

"I agree. But the step between hysterical and suicidal is a much larger one. I am absolutely positive that she was frightened rather than suicidal, which is consistent with the train guard's strong initial impression that the doctor pushed Isabelle off."

"There is nothing to be done about it now," Lily said. "You have done your duty by giving your account to the police. Perhaps it is best to forget it, Grace, if you can, and enjoy a few days off work. I'm sure both of you could use a rest."

"I trust Grace's instinct," Charlie chimed in. "It couldn't hurt to make a few discreet inquiries. If Miss Forsyth had reason to flee Stillwaters Sanctuary, then other women may be at risk."

Grace shot him a grateful look. "All we need do is to have a word with the local inspector of lunatic asylums. I should hate it if I said nothing, only to find out that something untoward was happening there. Do you know anything about the place, Auntie Anne?"

"From what little I have heard, I understand that Stillwaters is less a lunatic asylum than a sanitorium for wealthy young women of delicate sensibilities."

"All the more reason to believe Isabelle was not deranged." Grace picked up her knife and fork, having not yet had a bite to eat. "To add to my distress, I lent Isabelle my favourite shawl because she was cold and now it is gone forever."

"Oh no, not your beautiful red shawl? I believe you must have worn it every single day since–". Anne's eyes flicked to Charlie, who had given Grace the shawl as a parting gift.

Grace blushed as she caught him watching her. "You do exaggerate, Auntie. Besides, I happen to like the colour."

Charlie slipped away from the table and retrieved the rescued shawl from his bag, tucking it around Grace's shoulders with an inscrutable smile.

"How did you get this, Charlie?" She ran her fingers over the soft silk, which gave her so much pleasure. "Last time I saw it, it was in a tree, dangling over a precipitous drop."

"It would appear that my detective constable is part-monkey and entirely without a fear of heights," Stewart answered. "Fair gave me the vapours just watching him trust his weight to such a fragile sapling. Against my express orders, I might add. I thought we would have another death to report."

"Enough of our dramas." Charlie turned to Anne. "Mrs Macmillan, Aunt Lily says that Mr Kendall has been funding Lavender House. Is she pulling my leg or has he truly changed so much?"

His abrupt change of topic fooled no one, but Anne was willing to divert the conversation to the refuge's new roof, which meant they could dedicate their time to looking after women in need, rather than dashing around emptying buckets of water.

Grace took little part in the conversation, with the tragedy on the train still weighing heavily on her conscience.

Long Lost

Charlie knocked at their door at the unsociable hour of seven o'clock the next morning. "Not too early I hope? Your neighbour informed me that no gentleman would call upon a lady at such an hour."

"Ah, Mrs Patterson. You should recruit her to the police force. That woman's nose can detect a whiff of scandal at fifty paces, whether it is there or not. I hope you refrained from an unseemly response. We maintain a state of armed neutrality, as we have to live next door to her every day."

"I ignored the obvious response, that working-class scum like me don't live by gentlemen's rules, and wished her a good day. I may also have mentioned that a woman like you, who does so much good in the world, rises with the early birds and catches more than worms."

Grace laughed. "Never fear, the worms and I have been up for an hour. I thought you might have taken the chance to get some extra sleep, after two full days of travel on top of an intense undercover operation."

"Two days of sitting still was a nightmare. I need to be up and doing something useful."

Grace led him through to the kitchen. "Have you eaten? There's apple crumble left over from last night."

"All I've had is a plate of porridge and a couple of slices of toast and jam. Apple crumble would be most welcome. Pudding for breakfast is a concept I could learn to love."

"I expect there is a jug of congealed custard too, if you can stomach it." Grace poured two cups of tea. "I hope Detective Inspector Stewart is enjoying his rest."

"He had an early meeting at the police station. No peace for the wicked. Or, in his case, no peace for the officer who does not understand the concept of time off work." Charlie scooped crumble onto a plate and dolloped custard on top. "Should I save some for everyone else?"

"Safer for all of us if you have it, Charlie. I heard from a reliable source that a hungry man is more dangerous than an injured tiger."

"Never a truer word spoken." He slipped into his favourite spot at their table, with his back to the warmth of the range, feeling as content as a weary traveller returning to a familiar hearth. "Stewart said to meet him at the police station. He'll make arrangements for you to sign your statement and tie up any loose ends. What was your plan for the rest of the day, Grace?"

"I have sent a note to Doctor McLeod, requesting a meeting. What he doesn't know about disorders of the mind isn't worth knowing. He's sure to know the local inspector of asylums and any whispers of untoward behaviour at Stillwaters."

"Let's hope he says it is a paradise of healing. I could do with a break from bad tidings."

"Agreed. I promise to forget all about yesterday's tragic events if there are no issues at Stillwaters. Perhaps we might take the tram down to St Clair beach?"

"A day off work? Paddling in the sea? Ice creams on the promenade? How exceedingly decadent of you, Miss Penrose. How soon can we leave?"

Anne shuffled into the kitchen, her tall figure now stooped and leaning heavily on her walking cane. "It's like déjà vu seeing you two here, plotting who knows what dangerous scheme."

Lily appeared behind her, yawning. "What are they up to now, Anne? Do I need to get in an extra store of bandages and armaments?"

"I don't know Lily, but I dare not open the front door in case there is a pile of corpses outside."

Grace got up get them porridge, ignoring their mirth. "Sit down, both of you. Would you believe Charlie and I were planning a trip to the seaside?"

"No," said Anne and Lily, simultaneously and emphatically.

"It true, I swear it. Once we make sure there is nothing untoward going on at Stillwaters, we'll be on the first tram to St Clair. We could all go and make a picnic of it."

Charlie laid two extra places and took charge of pouring the tea. Grace's great-aunt was seventy-four now and needed a bit of discreet pampering, not that she would admit it. Anne's patience for fuss was as short as the fuse on a stick of dynamite, while her tongue remained as sharp as her mind. He liked her immensely and would be forever grateful that Anne had taken in his Aunt Lily when she was in need of shelter.

Grace put the plates down and resumed her seat. "Charlie, I almost forgot the tell you the other strange thing that happened on the train. When I offered her our help, Isabelle Forsyth recognised your name. Or rather, a friend of hers at Stillwaters Sanctuary knew of you. A woman called Charlotte."

"Not sure I know anyone called Charlotte who is living in a lunatic asylum." Charlie passed Anne a full cup and nudged the sugar bowl towards her. "Maybe she meant another Charlie?"

'No, it was definitely you and your father. Isabelle said if she managed to escape, she had promised Charlotte that she would try to find Charlie Pyke or Constable Pyke, from Clyde, and give them a message."

Charlie paused in mid-pour, hovering the teapot over the second cup. "Odd. Did she say what the message was?"

"Tell him that Amelia is still alive. And Josiah too."

Every muscle in his body ceased operating. The teapot bumped down onto the table, spilling a dark brew onto the white tablecloth. His lungs expelled pent up air in a whoosh, drowned out by a high-pitched squeal from Lily, before they both slumped to their seats like sacks of chaff.

"Charlie? Lily?" Grace said. "Whatever is the matter?"

Charlie couldn't find any words. Fortunately, Lily managed to gather her wits with an obvious effort of will.

"Amelia was a friend of our family in Clyde. We were all devastated when she disappeared in shocking circumstances six years ago. The whole town searched far and wide, but she was never seen again. Everyone thought she was dead, especially when her blood-stained shawl was found under the Clyde bridge, at the river's edge."

"But no body was found?" Anne asked.

"The Clutha River flows fast and strong. People who are swept away are often found miles away or not at all."

"But it is possible that she is still alive?" Anne persisted.

"Possible, but unlikely. The only man who might have taken her, as far as we know, was known as Doctor Josiah. He was seen driving a wagon along the Dunstan Trail, the mountain route from Central Otago to Dunedin. He appeared to be alone, although the wagon was laden, so he might have hidden her. But he had no reason to kidnap Amelia and every reason to leave Clyde as quickly and discreetly as possible."

"May I ask how old Amelia was?" Anne asked.

"Amelia was the same age as me," Charlie replied, his voice barely audible. "Seventeen at the time she disappeared. She would be twenty-three now."

Charlie could hear the strain in his voice, but his muscles refused to come under control. Grace had her head perked to the side and was eying him with that intense look that she got when she was thinking.

Lily rose and went around the table, so she could wrap her arms around him. "Amelia and Charlie had been friends since they started school on the same day. She was a timid slip of a child, who was teased for her pale skin and golden hair. Charlie took it upon himself to protect her. His mother despaired of all his bruises and black eyes, until she worked out why and sent his father to the school to sort it out."

"I remember that day. All the kids were terrified of my father. Constable Pyke as he was then, Sergeant Pyke now."

"They ought not to have been scared," Lily said. "Charlie and Thomas are peas in a pod. They might look big and tough, but they're both as soft as lambs' wool on the inside. After that, Amelia followed Charlie and his father around like a puppy."

"Aunt Lily, you make it sound so one-sided. Amelia helped me too. She was the sweetest girl you could imagine, my one true friend when other kids taunted me for being part-Chinese."

"Arrogant little sods. Most of the boys who were nasty to Charlie were the sons of failed gold miners and drifters, yet they held themselves above the Pyke family, who were pillars of the community. The same little guttersnipes were mean to Amelia. They changed their tune when she grew up into one of those fragile beauties, who make boys go weak at the knees."

"Forgive me if this question sounds harsh," Anne said, "but why do you think this Doctor Josiah would not have kidnapped a pretty, golden-haired seventeen-year-old girl?"

"He scarcely knew her," Lily replied. "Josiah Cowper was his real name, we found out later, although he called himself Doctor Josiah. He was a charlatan – a quack doctor and itinerant salesman of elixirs and snake oil, who came through Clyde on market days to hawk his patent medicines."

"Even if he knew her only a little ..." Anne was obviously reluctant to spell it out, but it went without saying that pretty girls were scarce compared to single men in want of company in the male-dominated goldmining towns of Central Otago.

Charlie had his head down, shredding a piece of toast into tiny slivers. "Cowper was on the run for murdering her father. Taking Amelia would have drawn attention to himself and slowed him down."

Grace and Anne exchanged horrified glances, looking to Lily for an explanation.

"Cowper robbed Amelia's family home while they were at church. Unfortunately, Amelia was at home, sick, and her father came back early to check on her. Josiah Cowper killed her father in cold blood. Mr Lawrence was the local bank manager, a man of standing in the community. To kidnap his daughter would have been foolhardy, as

Cowper must have known that every able man, woman and child would be hunting him down."

"Besides, we searched for her," Charlie added. "Not just around Central Otago. Every town in New Zealand was alerted. I was in Dunedin at the time, so I searched every single boarding house, hotel, tavern, stable, rough camp and hovel for them. Amelia's brother and my father did the same in the other towns along the way. But it was too late. We discovered that Josiah Cowper had hocked the Lawrence family valuables in a pawnshop and bought a single ticket on the first ship out to Australia. Every woman on that ship was part of a family or otherwise accounted for. None of them could have been Amelia. It's been six years now, with not a single sighting of her."

"Charlie, I am so very sorry for what happened." Grace's heart melted to think of Charlie as a child defending his friend, standing up to bullies even then. The loss of someone so close to him must have been devastating.

Charlie pushed his chair back and began pacing the kitchen. "Grace, tell me again exactly what the woman on the train said."

Grace paused to recall the exact words. "Isabelle said that she had met a woman called Charlotte at Stillwaters, when they both sneaked out at night. Charlotte helped her escape, in return for Isabelle delivering a message to you or your father. The message was: 'Tell them that Amelia is alive. And Josiah too.' That's all. Isabelle never said anything else about Charlotte and she had no idea who Amelia or Josiah were. There was no time for me to question her before she died."

Lily clamped her delicate hands onto Charlie's arms to stop him pacing. "Charlie, I can see that you want to grasp at any flicker of hope, but we have to remember that Isabelle Forsyth and this woman Charlotte, whoever she is, were residents of a lunatic asylum. It is possible Charlotte was remembering an old story about a lost girl called Amelia."

'Yet the request to tell me or my father that Amelia was still alive was very specific," Charlie countered. "And she mentioned Josiah too."

"Some people with mental disorders confuse past with present. Perhaps Charlotte lived in Clyde at the time and the kidnapping stuck in her memory."

"I suppose," Anne said, "if you wanted to hide a woman, what better place than an isolated institution. But why abduct her in the first place? And why would Josiah Cowper not just abandon her in Dunedin if he was leaving by ship, rather than going to the trouble of having her committed to an asylum?"

"I have to agree that the whole story seems improbable," Grace said. "If Amelia was there, why would she wait six years to tell someone who she was? The staff at Stillwaters would have to have been complicit."

"Not necessarily," Lily said. "If she was committed as insane, they might be inclined to dismiss her story of kidnap and murder as delusional. Witnessing her father's murder and being abducted might well have caused her to suffer a mental breakdown."

"Or she was too scared, or locked away or drugged," Anne added.

"It's probably all a misunderstanding," Charlie said, "but I need to be sure. I'll make inquiries about the asylum and send a telegram to my parents to see if they have heard anything. I suppose I should send a telegram to Amelia's mother too, not that she will thank me for it."

"Why on God's green earth would she not thank you for possible news of her missing daughter?" Grace asked.

"Because her mother blames me for Amelia's disappearance." Charlie tried to keep the pain from showing, but his words fell like daggers into the silence.

Grace gathered her plate and cup and took them to the bench he was leaning against, brushing her hand against his as she passed. "We will all do whatever we can to find out what happened to Amelia. I know you well enough to trust that you were not to blame."

"I don't know what I have done to deserve such loyalty, but thank you, Grace."

She looked into his eyes, no doubt seeing the glint of tears. He turned away to hide his anguish.

Grace busied herself with stacking dishes, clattering them together with uncharacteristically clumsy hands. "Charlie, I hate to dredge up painful memories, but it would be helpful to know the exact circumstances of Amelia's disappearance, when you feel ready to tell us. Even the tiniest clue might help, even now, after six years."

"My father will be the best person to ask about that, as he was in charge of the investigation of her disappearance. I wasn't even there when Amelia vanished. I was far away in Dunedin."

Charlie shrugged off the numbness holding his limbs captive. Action was what he needed. He strode to the door, stopping only to choke out an explanation in a voice that seemed to belong to another man. "I need to send a telegram to my father as soon as possible. I will meet you at the police station as soon as I can."

Official Duties

Charlie rushed out of the kitchen, leaving behind a half-eaten bowl of crumble and shocked silence. Despite the heat from the coal range, the room felt as cold as a tomb without him.

Grace emptied his bowl into the scrap bin for the chickens with unnecessary vigour, ignoring the clash of metal on porcelain. Her great-aunt would normally make a joke about scraping the pattern off the plate about now, but instead she came up behind Grace and kissed her cheek. Anne left the room without saying a word.

"Come and have a cup of tea with me, Grace," Lily said.

Grace sat down at the table, wondering whether it would be a breach of his confidence to ask Lily about the relationship between Charlie and Amelia and why he would be blamed for her disappearance.

Lily read her mind. "It's not what you think, Grace. Amelia was like a sister to Charlie. Unfortunately, her mother saw it in an entirely different light. Her daughter was no longer a little girl, but a pretty and vulnerable woman of seventeen. She didn't want their childhood friendship to turn into something deeper."

"She couldn't ask for a better man than Charlie. Although, I suppose I can see why Mrs Lawrence would think any young man might be tempted by a pretty girl who leaned on him for support."

Lily let out a delicate snort. "Charlie would never have been good enough for Mrs Lawrence. She wanted Amelia to marry someone with good prospects, like a banker, or a respectable man, like the local vicar. Certainly not the son of a half-Chinese woman and a policeman. She saw him as a man on the make, trying to lure a rich girl into a bad marriage."

"Charlie said he wasn't in Clyde when she disappeared."

52

"He was in Dunedin, applying to join the police force. I suppose I can see why Mrs Lawrence wouldn't want her dear, fragile daughter to marry a lowly police recruit, who would no doubt be assigned to a station far away from her family. Worse, I suspect she worried that Charlie would take advantage of Amelia's vulnerability without marrying her." Lily reached out for Grace's hand. "I meant what I said, Grace. The truth is, Charlie and Amelia were only ever friends. Mrs Lawrence was blinded by her prejudice."

"Amelia's mother must be an appalling judge of character."

"Her father was a moderating force. I know Mr Lawrence offered Charlie a position at the bank where he was the manager. He was always welcoming to the whole Pyke family. As you can imagine, Charlie was grateful for the gesture of support, but not interested in sitting behind a desk counting money."

"You say Charlie saw her as no more than a friend. But what about Amelia?"

"I honestly don't know, Grace. I was married and living in Dunedin at the time, so I hadn't seen them together since they were children. My sister Jasmine, Charlie's mother, said Amelia was behaving very oddly in the weeks leading up to her disappearance, on the few times her mother let her out of the house. Rumour had it that she was ill."

"Charlie must have known what was wrong with her."

"Jasmine said they wouldn't let him see Amelia. When she wrote a note to him asking him to leave her alone, he left for Dunedin early. The only thing I can say with absolute certainty is that Charlie would never have done anything to hurt her. For them to blame him for her illness was pure spite."

"But it still hurts him to be reminded of it, of course."

"No matter how blameless he is, Charlie will always feel guilt at her disappearance, if only because he wasn't in Clyde to stop it. I don't need to tell you how relieved he would be if she was still alive."

"Then I need to do whatever it takes to follow up this rumour and lay it to rest, one way or another."

53

"He would never ask for help, but I know your support means a great deal to him, Grace. Anne and I are committed to working at Lavender House today, but I'm sure we can find time to do whatever we can to assist."

"Thank you, Lily. Charlie and I can manage, at least until we know more about Stillwaters Sanctuary." Grace pushed her chair back with more force than she intended. "I should leave, or I'll be late for my meeting with the police."

By the time Grace had answered a few trivial questions and signed her witness statement at the police station, Charlie had returned from sending the telegram to his father, looking more composed than he had been earlier.

They found Detective Inspector Stewart with his local counterpart, chewing the fat over the successes and failures of their long careers. Grace felt her cheeks flush at being referred to as an up-and-coming assistant to the police surgeon and was even more thrilled to hear Stewart tell DI Wallace that Charlie was "the young man I was telling you about". Perhaps his hints about wanting a transfer to Dunedin were taking root at last.

"Might I ask why the three of you have such an interest in these deaths on the train?" DI Wallace asked.

"Only that Miss Penrose was a witness to it and has some concerns about the victim's state of mind," Stewart replied. "I would not have looked twice at it under ordinary circumstances, but Miss Penrose has an annoying tendency to be right."

"I would not wish to waste your time, Detective Inspector Wallace, or that of your men, based only on my strong impression that Miss Forsyth was frightened rather than suicidal. I have said so in my statement, for the record. My intention is to talk to an expert on local asylums, to reassure myself that all is well at the asylum from which Miss Forsyth escaped. After that, I am happy to leave well alone."

The local inspector stepped out of the room for a moment. They could hear a rapid bark of orders, then he returned. "I have asked Kelly to bring you up to date with developments." He slapped Stewart on the back. "Good to see you, old man. I hope you will find time to dine with me at my club while you are here. Tonight perhaps?"

"That would be splendid, Robbie, though I have other plans tonight. I'll keep you informed of any developments."

Constable Kelly, the man who had interviewed Grace yesterday and taken her statement this morning, appeared in the doorway, standing ramrod straight and perspiring freely. "Sir? You wished to see me?"

"Kelly, I want you to update Detective Inspector Stewart and his team on the train tragedy. Render any assistance they need, including full access to police files. He'll give you the details. I have already asked Peters to look up any past complaints against the lunatic asylum she escaped from."

Their meeting with Kelly was brief and uninformative. Doctor Samuel Wilson's body had been recovered and would arrive in Dunedin this morning. Isabelle's body had not been found and was presumed to have been washed out to sea on the high tide. "She'll be half way to South America by now," as Kelly put it. The only additional information he had was that a pair of women's shoes had been spotted on the cliff face.

"Was there much distance between the man's body and the shoes?" Charlie asked.

Kelly seemed stumped by the question. "His body was down a bank, near the tracks. The shoes were way down towards the bottom of the cliff, near the beach."

"Horizontal distance, I mean." Charlie gave Kelly a moment to respond before explaining. "If the doctor attempted to save her and they fell together in a struggle, then the bodies should have fallen off the train at the same time. If he pushed her off, then jumped when he realised the guard had seen him, they would be further apart."

55

"Oh, I see what you mean. I understand the doctor's body was further along the track. Perhaps he clung on a bit longer before he toppled off. The guard's evidence would suggest a gap."

"We are just trying to verify his account, Constable Kelly," Stewart said. "What else is being done?"

"Er, nothing, sir. The case is closed, unless the police surgeon finds new evidence during the autopsy. Accidental death for both victims. We suspect the girl committed suicide, of course, but her father is a highly respected member of the community, so we will give her the benefit of the doubt for the family's peace of mind."

Charlie studied his nails. "I believe the guard suggested that the doctor might have taken his own life?"

"Oh no, sir. A respected doctor is not the sort of man to throw himself off a train in a momentary pang of guilt. Unlike the woman, who was certifiably insane."

Annoyance surged within her, but Grace kept it suppressed. "In fact, I believe she was admitted to the facility for a rest cure during pregnancy. Bearing a child can be a challenging time, but it does not predispose a woman to insanity."

"I'm afraid I cannot agree, Miss. The woman's identity has been confirmed as Miss Isabelle Forsyth, a committed patient at Stillwaters Sanctuary. The asylum had already notified the police that she was missing. I communicated with them this morning and was told the woman was considered highly unstable due to deep-seated melancholia and episodes of hysteria and fantastical storytelling. They confirm she was pregnant and unmarried, which goes a long way towards explaining her suicidal behaviour."

Grace glared at him, but she could see his point of view, based on the evidence available to him. Besides, there was no point in arguing. "I stand corrected, Constable Kelly."

"I'd like to see the doctor's luggage, Constable Kelly," Charlie said.

"Luggage?"

"Doctor Wilson must have had some type of luggage with him. A doctor's bag or small valise."

Kelly's gaze swept the room, as if the bag might suddenly appear. "If there was such a bag, it was not found on the train. I understand that he was only at Stillwaters for the day. But, of course, I shall inquire at the station to be sure."

"And Miss Forsyth's bag?" Stewart asked.

Grace put Kelly out of his misery. "She was carrying only a reticule, which I have with me. There is nothing in it apart from a picture of an older woman, presumably her mother, along with a handkerchief and two pounds. She left Stillwaters without even an overcoat or hat, poor thing. I expect it would have been difficult for her to have escaped over the wall with any more."

"Do you have any background on either of the two victims?" Stewart clearly didn't expect an enlightening answer, but he was a man who never stopped questioning until he was sure he had squeezed out the last drop of evidence.

Kelly reached for a file and flicked through the few sheets of paper, most of which they recognised as the statements made by the train guard and Grace. "Doctor Samuel Wilson was the Visiting Medical Officer at Stillwaters Sanctuary, where he had worked for many years. He was on his way home, as he did not live on site and maintained another practice in town. The girl was the daughter of Mr Edward Forsyth, of Forsyth's Emporium."

An elderly man in spectacles entered the room and stopped a respectful five paces away. He waited for the end of Kelly's short summary before speaking. "I was asked to report back to you on any prior history of complaints pertaining to the Stillwaters Sanctuary or Doctor Samuel Wilson. Fortuitously, I have cross-referenced every complaint from all medical facilities and institutions in our region into individual folders for ease of access."

"Yes, Peters, very commendable," Kelly interrupted. "Any complaints?"

Peters held up a sheet of paper, which shook slightly in his aged hand. "Both the doctor and the asylum are duly registered as required under the relevant Act of Parliament. That would be the 1882 Lunatics Act, which encompasses all facilities admitting patients with disorders of the mind as certified by a registered practitioner. Annual inspections have been lodged as required under section—"

"Yes, yes, all very good. Just get to the complaints, will you, Peters."

"No actionable complaints. That is, nothing requiring the notification of a suspected offence to the police. I expect the local inspector of asylums would hold a long list of minor complaints about conditions – treatment, food, and suchlike."

Grace had a sudden vision of a golden-haired girl complaining about the porridge being too cold and the bed too hard, like the nursery story. She hoped, for Charlie's sake that they were not chasing a fairy tale.

"Excellent work, thank you, Mr Peters," Stewart said. "Efficient investigation relies on meticulous record keeping. It brings joy to my heart to have such ready access to information."

Peters glowed at the compliment, his hunched back becoming a little straighter as he snapped his heels together. "Thank you, Detective Inspector Stewart. I am honoured to be of service."

Charlie leaned across and whispered in Stewart's ear. Stewart called out after the retreating records clerk. "Mr Peters, might I request some additional information, please? Anything you have on Josiah Cowper would be most appreciated."

"He may be listed under his alias, Doctor Josiah, itinerant purveyor of patent medicines in the Otago region," Charlie added. "Age probably between thirty and forty."

Peters scribbled a note. "I'll find the rogue, don't you worry. Anything else, Detective Inspector Stewart?"

"It would be most helpful to know if there have ever been any criminal charges laid against the present staff of Stillwaters Sanctuary, especially those in charge of the asylum."

"It would be my pleasure, sir. As it happens, I have created an extensive indexing system cross-referenced by name, date and location." The records clerk romped out of the room like a terrier on a particularly delicious scent.

Stewart watched him go with paternal pride, even though the man had to be at least a decade older. "Unless you have any more questions for Miss Penrose, we will leave you to your duties, Constable Kelly. Thank you for your time."

Charlie paused at the door. "I take it that Miss Forsyth's parents have been informed?"

"Not yet. We had been hoping to find a body, so we could confirm her identity."

"Nevertheless, in the circumstances, perhaps sooner would be better than later," Stewart said. "Perhaps you might take Miss Penrose and DC Pyke with you. It may give her mother some comfort to hear about her daughter's final moments."

Kelly shuffled the papers back into the file with nervous fingers. "No disrespect to Miss Penrose, but would it be appropriate to allow a member of the public to attend while I notify the next of kin?"

"As you think best, of course. Although, I should note that Miss Penrose has a formal relationship to the police, given her current status as an assistant to the police surgeon. Do you wish to see her accreditation?"

Stewart might as well have said she was a performing elephant in a circus for the disbelief his statement generated. Kelly closed his gaping jaw. "I'll take your word for it, sir. It will have to be this afternoon, as Doctor Wilson's body is arriving at the train station soon."

Disorders Of The Mind

Charlie stopped on street outside the police station to check his watch. "We have an hour or two to spare. Any thoughts?"

"Doctor McLeod said to visit any time this morning."

"Perfect. It will be interesting to hear an expert opinion on Stillwaters. What's McLeod like?"

"Clever, energetic, committed to improving care for patients with severe disorders of the mind. He lectures medical students and advises the government on the topic, but he spends most of his time working with patients at Seacliff Lunatic Asylum. He specialises in the criminally insane, so he may not know too much about Stillwaters."

"An older, experienced man, then?"

"He wouldn't be much over thirty, I should think, but he does have a great deal of experience. He's an excellent teacher. He took us for our placement at Seacliff Asylum."

"I've had a few criminals committed there in my time, but I don't know much about Seacliff."

"Seacliff is the largest lunatic asylum in the country, a massive Gothic edifice north of Dunedin. The superintendent for the last three years, Doctor Truby King, has made a great many changes, with beneficial results. He believes in fresh air, exercise, a healthy diet and recreational opportunities for the patients, rather than the age-old practice of lock 'em and leave 'em. I was pleased to see that he discourages the use of physical restraints and drugs, where possible, although Seacliff still goes through large quantities of sedatives and the like."

By the time she had finished her explanation, they had arrived at Doctor McLeod's practice. To Charlie's delight, the doctor invited them to join him for morning tea, which included a plate of scones slathered with jam.

"I have an ulterior motive," Doctor McLeod explained in a thick Scottish brogue. "Miss Penrose shows promise of excelling in the care of mentally disturbed patients. I must admit I was unsure about accepting a woman as a medical student, but now I see the benefits. Female patients do seem to respond much better to one of their own."

"Very kind of you to say so, Doctor McLeod. I haven't decided what field of medicine I shall specialise in, if I am not to take up general practice. The need amongst women is so great, I feel pulled in a dozen different directions."

"You are working for the police surgeon over the summer, I understand. Your unusual choice has caused quite an uproar amongst the elder statesmen of the medical fraternity."

"You can blame DC Pyke for introducing me to the fascinating field of forensic pathology. Deceased victims of crime can have no qualms about being poked and prodded by a female doctor, unlike most living men, so I cannot see why that disapproving coven of fusty academics was so against it."

"Grace was instrumental in solving my first homicide case," Charlie added. "Her many admirers are keen to recruit her to our cause."

"I trust you will ignore them, Miss Penrose, for the living have much more need of your skills than the dead."

Charlie was not about to let that pass. "It is not only the victims of crime she seeks to help, Doctor McLeod, but the families left behind who seek justice for their loved ones."

"I concede the point. Now, would you care to tell me how I may be of assistance, as I imagine it is not my vocational advice you seek?"

"We hoped you might be able to tell us more about Stillwaters Sanctuary, out near Waitati, on the way to Seacliff. We hear mixed reports. One of our informants says it is a lunatic asylum, another that it is more of a sanitorium for wealthy young women of delicate sensibilities."

"They are both correct, Miss Penrose. Legally, it is classified as a lunatic asylum, as it is required to be, so they can take committals of

61

patients with mental disorders. In practice, it is one of only two private institutions in the country, and the only one specialising in the gentler conditions of young ladies. Melancholia, hysteria, anxiety and similar conditions, which benefit from a peaceful environment. You have spent enough time at Seacliff Asylum, Miss Penrose, to know that delicate ladies would struggle to cope in a public institution for the certifiably insane."

"Indeed. Five minutes there would be more than most could stand without resort to smelling salts or a large dose of medicinal brandy."

"Stillwaters came to our notice because of an incident involving a woman who was with child," Charlie said. "I don't understand how she could have been committed for care in an asylum."

"Ah, a delicate issue. I have noticed a few such girls getting off at Waitati when I have been on the train to Seacliff, so I am not surprised. This woman was unmarried, I take it?"

"Her father would not allow her to marry the baby's father," Grace replied. "I don't know for certain if she suffered any mental or physical health problem, beyond the stress of being abandoned in an asylum."

"Unfortunately, her father has authority to make those decisions, as long as he can persuade a qualified medical practitioner to agree that she was unable to look after herself or that she had a disorder of the mind, which is far less difficult that one might imagine. Many a father would consider her behaviour, in allowing her virtue to be violated, sufficient grounds for a diagnosis of hysteria. In such cases, I suspect shame often drives the decision. What better place to hide away from the world for a few months than a private sanctuary, far away from prying eyes? With luck, the gossip-mongers, and potential future suitors, might never find out."

"Is Stillwaters well run, in your view, Doctor McLeod?"

"I know only a little about the place. I have been there to carry out a routine inspection, when the usual inspector was laid low with a fever. I was impressed by the remarkably pleasant atmosphere, at least compared to other asylums. Stillwaters is privately run through a religious charity, the Magdalene Trust. Their mission is to help young woman onto a spiritual path back to wellbeing."

Hardly the type of place that would terrify a young woman into suicide, Charlie thought. "No complaints that you were aware of?"

McLeod shook his head. "I can give you the name of the current inspector of asylums if you wish. He would know of any official complaints or issues of poor practice."

Charlie picked up on his slight emphasis on the word "official". "Perhaps you have heard rumours?"

Doctor McLeod studied him over the edge of his teacup.

"I understand your commitment to maintaining confidentiality, Doctor McLeod, but if you have any concerns about the place, however vague, I would ask you to consider the young women who might be at risk within Stillwaters' walls."

The doctor took the time to wipe jam off his mouth with a napkin of snow-white linen. "Honestly, I don't know anything for certain. But I did sense a degree of tension between the doctor who acts as Visiting Medical Officer and the management of Stillwaters."

"Visiting Medical Officer?" Charlie asked.

"Smaller institutions, especially those without highly dependent or ill patients, have visiting, rather than resident, doctors. Doctor Wilson has a good reputation as a physician and sees it as his Christian duty to take on the role. Not a popular job, you understand, given the hours wasted travelling, when one could be tending private patients in the city."

Charlie and Grace exchanged a glance. He should have realised Doctor McLeod might be acquainted with Doctor Wilson. Was it possible he did not know of the doctor's death? Their pleasant meeting was about to take a turn for the worse.

Charlie pasted on his "delivering tragic news" expression. "Doctor McLeod, I regret to inform you that Doctor Samuel Wilson was involved in a fatal incident yesterday."

"Wilson is dead?" McLeod rocked back in his chair, clearly shocked by the news. "I cannot believe it. He was about the same age as me. A terrible loss for the medical community and his family."

"Would you like some time to come to terms with the news, Doctor McLeod?"

McLeod pushed his plate away. "I can see your inquiries are more than mere casual interest. With that in mind, I will give you all the assistance you need. I may not have known the man very well, but I know he was respected."

"Thank you. Can you tell us more about the cause of the tension?"

"Wilson and I happened to be talking after a meeting recently. He hinted that he was thinking of giving up his role at Stillwaters. A difference of opinion with the superintendent, I gathered. Just between ourselves, Doctor Wilson could be rather a cold fish. A good doctor, but a poor bedside manner."

"Forgive the indelicacy of the question, but do you think it was his desire to leave, rather than any suggestion that they were wanting him gone?"

"He suggested the former, but he would hardly admit to being pushed out."

Charlie cringed at the unfortunately choice of words. "Do you think his concerns were of a professional nature or due to personal differences?"

"I couldn't say. If I had to guess, I'd say he might have a had a different view about appropriate treatment programmes. When I was inspecting the place, my one concern was the imbalance between the medical and religious approaches. Nothing untoward, you understand, only … how can I put it? … the intensity of the religious fervour was rather startling."

"Who runs the treatment programmes at Stillwaters?" Grace asked.

"The superintendent himself. A man called Horace Gresham. I have met him several times and heard him speak. He is renowned as an orator and I believe he is well intentioned, though not a qualified physician, as far as I know. For those of a religious disposition, I imagine he may be inspirational. Finding spiritual comfort can be a powerful force for healing a troubled mind."

"And for those not religiously inclined?"

"In theory, listening to sermons should be harmless even for the agnostic, although one must be cautious not to overexcite fragile minds. Contemplation and prayer can be very calming for agitated minds, and potentially far less harmful than the medicines available to treat mental disorders. On the other hand, some of these religious men can be very judgemental. If the sermon extended to castigating fallen women for their sins, for example, that would most certainly be harmful."

"Do you know if Doctor Wilson had spoken of his concerns to anyone else?" Charlie asked.

"I couldn't say, but my sense was that he was gathering information, before taking any further action. He was not sure himself, I believe. I suspect he only talked to me after having a dram or two of whisky. Several hours of inter-departmental meetings on proposed legislative amendments can have that effect on the most sober of men."

"As it happens, he passed by me just before his death," Grace said. "I thought he might have been drinking. Only an impression, based on his slightly slurred speech. He may have just been tired."

"Working in an asylum can take a toll on a man. An off-duty dram now and then is to be expected, although one would not expect a physician to be the worse for alcohol in a public place. Although now I come to think on it, I have never seen Wilson touch a drop before. In fact, I had understood he was a teetotaller."

"I could not say for sure that he was the worse for drink. Certainly not anywhere close to inebriated, although he did push past me quite roughly."

"May I ask how he died?"

"A woman who had been at Stillwaters became agitated on the train journey back to Dunedin yesterday evening," Charlie said. "The circumstances are rather unclear, but it is possible that Doctor Wilson died trying to save her from falling from the train. Suicide, possibly, but I would appreciate it if you kept that to yourself."

"Good heavens, I cannot believe it. I was on that train myself, coming back from Seacliff."

"Did you not hear the commotion, Doctor McLeod?" Grace asked.

"I was sound asleep at the front of the first-class carriage. In my profession, one must take every possible opportunity to catch up on sleep, especially as I do a great deal of travel back and forth to Seacliff. I do have a vague recollection that we stopped for a while, but I assumed it was due to a signal issue or livestock on the track. Makes me feel sick thinking about it. Unless you have any further questions, perhaps I might cut our meeting short. I should inform the other staff members at the medical school."

Charlie reached out to shake his hand. "And we must get back to the police station, to accompany the local constable on a grim visit to inform the victim's parents."

Forms Of Grief

Constable Kelly jiggled nervously while they waited for the door to be answered. Grace wondered if this was the first time he had had to impart news of a loved one's death. Or perhaps it was the grandeur of the Forsyth's house that was intimidating him.

A butler answered the door, bestowing upon them a look that managed to convey his disapproval at their appearance during the luncheon hour, despite not moving a single muscle in his face.

Kelly didn't move, so Charlie stepped forward, showing his badge. "Detective Constable Pyke and Constable Kelly to see Mr and Mrs Forsyth on a matter of urgency."

Grace was intrigued to see that Kelly obviously expected Charlie to take the lead, even though it was his investigation, while Charlie took it in his stride, as if used to this level of deference. Again, she reflected on the change in him from when they had first met, when he was the most junior constable, on the verge of being dismissed by a corrupt superior.

The butler showed them into a library, which had the air of a mausoleum. He disappeared to inform Mr and Mrs Forsyth, closing the door firmly behind him. Charlie opened the door in time to hear the butler's discreet murmur on the upstairs landing. A short time later, a door banged open and a cantankerous voice drifted down the stairs.

"Of course I didn't leave them at my club, they're my favourite cufflinks. Solid gold, worth a fortune."

A female voice replied, too softly for them to hear.

"Don't shoosh me, my dear. Percival said they're only police officers, not guests. Perhaps I should get them to look for my cufflinks. Not that it would do an ounce of good. Damned police force couldn't catch a thief if they tripped over him coming out a window with a sack of valuables. A jolly good thrashing with a horsewhip is what the thief needs."

Footsteps clumped down the stairs. Charlie eased the door shut and withdrew across the room, taking up a nonchalant stance by the fireplace. A man with straining waistcoat buttons entered the library, followed by his thin, over-dressed wife.

Grace took one look at the man's puffy, flushed face, complete with deep scowl lines, and prayed that hearing the news of his daughter's death wouldn't be the trigger for Mr Forsyth's inevitable heart attack.

Charlie introduced himself and gestured for Isabelle's parents to take a seat. Grace stayed in the background, taking a peek at the portraits on the wall. Mrs Forsyth had been a beauty in her day. Isabelle was the youngest of her children by a wide margin, featuring in more than her share of the family pictures. The older children must have left home some time ago. She didn't blame them.

"What is this all about then, constable?" Mr Forsyth demanded. "I'm a busy man."

Charlie remained calm in the face of his aggravation. "Mr and Mrs Forsyth, I regret to inform you that I am the bearer of tragic news."

"Isabelle!" her mother wailed. When everyone stared at her, she blanched. "I knew in my heart that something had happened. Didn't I tell you last night, Archie? A mother knows."

"Don't be ridiculous, woman, let the constable speak."

"I'm afraid your wife is correct, Mr Forsyth. There was an unfortunate incident on the train into Dunedin last night and it appears your daughter has been fatally injured."

Mrs Forsyth sniffed into a handkerchief, but her husband was not the sort to let emotion get in the way of indignation.

"Appears?"

"Her body has not yet been recovered, Mr Forsyth, but we know she was on the train and fell at a particularly dangerous cliffside section of the track. There can be no doubt that she would not have survived the fall. My sincere condolences to you both."

"But how could she have been on a train?" he demanded. "She was committed to … she was placed in the care of an expensive sanitorium for her health. Always a delicate girl, Isabelle."

Grace was astounded at his apparent failure to grasp the most relevant detail – that his daughter was dead. She had the strongest sensation he was about to say something even more inappropriate, such as threatening to sue Stillwaters for losing one of his prized possessions, just like the missing cufflinks. But Mr Forsyth collected himself.

"Dead you say? Isabelle was our only daughter. I cannot believe it. How could she fall off a train? It is preposterous."

"The details are unclear, Mr Forsyth. It would appear that she became upset and went outside onto the rear platform, perhaps to take some air."

Isabelle's father sank back into the chair. "My dear Isabelle – she's really dead?" He appeared stunned for a full minute, then belligerence bubbled to the surface again. "I blame that wretched man for taking advantage of an innocent girl. She wouldn't have been there if not for him. I was forced to separate them, of course. One would think she would be grateful for my protection, but she showed every sign of hysteria. He was a tradesman, for heaven's sake."

From the tone of his voice, one might be excused for thinking a tradesman akin to a mass murderer.

Mrs Forsyth twisted her bare fingers at her husband's tirade. "Otto was an apprentice watchmaker, Archie, and a very good one," she said, too quietly for him to register.

"Isabelle was determined to bring scandal to her family, with no thought to her reputation or mine. I only hope we can convince the coroner to bring in a verdict of accidental death, not suicide."

"Archie!"

Mr Forsyth recollected that they were not alone. One did not air one's dirty laundry in front of the lesser ranks of the police force. "By which I mean, naturally, she doubtless slipped by accident and I should hate to have any unfounded gossip that there was more to it than that."

Charlie took pity on him. "We understand she took fright when a doctor from the sanitorium tried to help her. He was trying to get to her, to calm her down, when the accident happened."

Mrs Forsyth clutched the armrest of her chair, her face deathly pale, her eyes unfocussed. Grace feared she was on the verge of fainting.

"Perhaps a breath of fresh air and a cup of tea, Mrs Forsyth?"

Grace threaded her arm under the mother's elbow and guided her out of the library, leaving Charlie to deal with the odious father. The butler was standing by the door, either waiting for orders or eavesdropping.

"Could you show me to the drawing room, please? Mrs Forsyth will require a cup of tea, as she has had some dreadful news."

The butler opened the door across the hall and waited for Mrs Forsyth to enter. Grace sat Isabelle's mother in a seat by the window, with a stunning view across the harbour and out to the Otago Peninsula. The butler ignored the request for tea, instead pouring her a stiff brandy, which he delivered to her on a silver salver. Mrs Forsyth clutched the glass like a life preserver, dismissing the butler with a wave of her hand.

Grace gave her a moment to settle. "May I express my condolences too, Mrs Forsyth. I do have some questions for you, and perhaps you have questions for me, but I can come back later, if you would prefer."

Mrs Forsyth drew her shoulders back, until she was sitting so upright, she could have balanced a Bible on her head. A product of an excellent finishing school or a strict governess, no doubt. She kept clutching at her throat and hands. Their arrival must have disturbed her while she was dressing for luncheon, before she reached the jewellery stage.

"I will assist you in any way I can." Mrs Forsyth took a gulp of brandy, knocking back half a glass. As the colour seeped back into her face, she registered the lack of a glass in her guest's hand.

Grace realised she was trying to work out her guest's status and thus whether the offer of refreshments was appropriate. "My name is Grace Penrose. I work with the police, but I am also here because I happened to meet your daughter on the train. I only talked to her for a short time, but I could tell she was a lovely young woman."

"Thank you, Miss Penrose."

Isabelle's mother seemed to be at a loss for words, so Grace continued. "I don't wish to cause any further distress, but can you tell me why Isabelle was staying at Stillwaters Sanctuary and whether she was content to be there?"

Grace expected weeping incoherence or sugar-coated prevarication, but Mrs Forsyth was made of sterner stuff than first impressions had indicated.

"Isabelle was with child. The young man was eager to marry her, but Archie – Mr Forsyth – wouldn't hear of it. Otto Jensen is a lovely man. Kind, clever, hard-working and very much in love with my daughter, as she was with him."

"May I ask if you have Mr Jensen's address? If he loved her, he has a right to know of her passing."

A red flush spread across Mrs Forsyth's cheeks. "When Mr Forsyth committed Isabelle to that place, Otto's heart was broken. I understand he has left Dunedin permanently."

Heart-broken? Or making a hasty escape from Mr Forsyth's vengeance? "Did you receive any letters from your daughter?"

"Her one letter was no more than a short note, stating that she was being well looked after. They read the letters before they are sent, Miss Penrose, so I cannot vouch for the truth. Her writing was firm and the sentiments cheerful enough, if rather bland compared to her usual lively style, but she imparted no further information."

"What sort of place is Stillwaters Sanctuary?"

"They shelter respectable young women who find the strain of life's expectations too much to bear. Not only girls who have found themselves compromised, but also those suffering melancholy. Not the

71

truly insane, you understand. We would never expose our daughter to any such vulgarity."

Mr Forsyth's bombastic voice penetrated the thick walls of the drawing room, causing his wife to wince and Grace to feel sorry for Charlie. Her sympathy for Isabelle and her mother rose with every strident decibel emanating from the library.

"Stillwaters restricts admission to the daughters of gentlemen and prides itself on providing a serene, devout sanctuary in the peace of the countryside, near the sea." Her words trailed off into a sigh. "I must admit that I have, on more than one occasion, been tempted to join her."

Grace hid the smile that tugged at her lips. Mr Forsyth might note his wife's absence at any moment, so there was little time to waste. "May I ask how you heard of Stillwaters?"

"Our family physician recommended it. In fact, he arranged the meeting with Superintendent Gresham and provided the medical certificate they required to admit her. Doctor Wilson is an excellent physician. He wouldn't have recommended the establishment if he had any concerns."

Mrs Forsyth showed no sign of knowing that her caring family doctor had died alongside her daughter and Grace certainly wasn't going to be the one to tell her. "Was Isabelle meant to stay there until she had her baby?"

"I … I don't know what Archie arranged. He had to sign the documents to commit her, of course. I made it very clear to my husband that I wished to raise the child myself, until Isabelle could … find her place in society again. He was vehemently against the idea, of course, but I believed he would have agreed eventually. My eldest son would have taken the child if necessary. He and his wife have three girls, so he would have been eager to do so if Isabelle had a son."

"She never mentioned any concerns about Stillwaters or the care she received there? Did she mention any friends she had made there?"

"Nothing like that. She had only been there for two weeks."

"Thank you for your time, Mrs Forsyth. Isabelle was fortunate to have a loving mother to support her."

Isabelle's mother dabbed at her eyes with a handkerchief. "I was the lucky one, Miss Penrose. My daughter is … was … the light of my life. Clever, amusing, loving, level-headed. I shall be lost without her."

Grace patted her arm, for want of any better means of consolation at so overwhelming a loss. Mrs Forsyth was handling the news far more calmly than expected, which probably meant she would be lost to grief as soon as she was alone. She had probably had a great deal of experience of being stoic in the face of challenging circumstances.

Grace extracted Isabelle's reticule from her own and handed it over. "This is all Isabelle took with her on the train."

The mother cradled it in her hands, running her fingers tenderly over the intricate beading, before holding it to a flushed cheek. "You have been very kind, Miss Penrose. I'm glad she spent her last minutes in your company."

Grace left her at the sideboard, refilling her glass to the brim with brandy. Poor woman. Grace hoped she would find another outlet for her love, before the brandy became an unbreakable habit.

The rest of the house was silent. The library door stood open, but no one was within.

Charlie was waiting out on the street by himself. "Kelly had other work to attend to. Isabelle's father had a great deal to say, but none of it useful. Suffice to say, there will be strongly worded letters written to the superintendent of Stillwaters and the Minister of Railways on their lax standards of safety. I shouldn't wonder if Forsyth sues for compensation."

"What a pompous boor. He seemed to be more concerned with the loss of his cufflinks than his irreplaceable daughter."

Charlie took her arm as they walked down to the city. "If I hear he has beaten some poor servant for stealing those cufflinks, I'll personally go up there and shove that horsewhip up–"

"Charlie! Pity the poor doctor who would have to extract it. Didn't they teach you how to lick the boots of the upper-class oppressors at police training?"

"I must have been asleep for that session." A grin flashed across his lips and faded again. "Did you manage to extract anything beyond grief from Mrs Forsyth?"

"Away from her husband, she showed herself to be a woman of sense and compassion, as well as a devoted mother. She was definitely on Isabelle's side, but unable to sway her husband's decisions. It does sound as if Stillwaters is nothing like the usual lunatic asylum, but rather a place of quiet reflection for young woman who wish to retreat from society. A pleasant place to hide from the shame of a pregnancy out of wedlock."

"And a convenient place for those whose guardians wish them to disappear from polite society?"

"Exactly so. Her entry to Stillwaters was arranged by Doctor Wilson, the Forsyth family doctor."

Charlie's arm jerked against hers. "Is that so? How strange that Isabelle would react so violently on the train to a doctor she knew well."

"Perhaps her reaction stemmed from knowing him all too well."

Body And Clyde

They walked in silence down the steep street leading back to the city. Charlie's thoughts drifted between the dreadful Forsyth and the dubious doctor, before circling back to the uneasy feeling that his precious time with Grace was slipping out of his grasp. Remarkably, she seemed to be tackling the situation with her usual combination of good humour and astute observation skills. He might almost imagine she was relishing the investigation.

Grace must have read his mind. "Call me crazy, but I've missed the thrill of working with you. Makes a change from sitting in a freezing lecture theatre or having my head down amongst a pile of medical text books."

"I hate to disillusion you Grace, but I spend endless hours immersed in a mountain of paperwork, when I'm not experiencing the joy of having the stuffing kicked out of me by a band of ruffians. Not very glamourous work, being a detective. And far less enjoyable without you by my side."

"I am happy to leave the paperwork and the ruffians to you. How is your bruising today?"

"Fading from purple to a delightful shade of sickly yellow, thanks to your ministrations." He stopped at an intersection, waiting for a laden cart to amble past. "What now, Grace? I suppose an excursion to St Clair beach is out of the question?"

She glanced up at him with those all-seeing blue eyes. "And have you spend the rest of your life wondering if Amelia Lawrence is still alive?"

Charlie grunted. "I suspect you harbour some doubts about what is happening at Stillwaters Sanctuary too."

"You're right, as usual. I cannot rid my thoughts of the train guard's initial impression that she was pushed. Whatever the local police think, that is grounds for keeping our minds open to the possibility that she was murdered for what she knew about the doctor."

"A doctor in a position of complete authority over a large number of vulnerable young women does suggest a range of unpleasant possibilities. This case is making the hairs on the back of my neck stand up. And don't say that a respectable doctor would never take advantage of his position, Grace."

"I wasn't about to, I assure you. Doctors are by no means exempt from the many forms of disrespect which flow from a sense of entitlement. Not as bad as some of the patients though."

To Charlie, that sounded uncomfortably like the voice of experience. "Has it been very difficult for you, Grace?"

"Mostly the harassment is subtle, rather than blatant. But don't you worry, I give as good as I get. A sharp rap on the knuckles with my reflex hammer works wonders on wandering hands and Tiny Tim showed me a few tricks for disabling anything more serious."

"Glad to hear it." Charlie pushed aside the surge of protectiveness within him that she neither wanted nor needed. He just wished he had been here to help her, instead of Tiny Tim, who was a former bouncer at a gambling den and now helped to get incapacitated patients to Lavender House. "I've arranged a telephone call to my father to discuss Amelia, but we have some time to spare beforehand."

"Perhaps a visit to the police surgeon to view the corpse, since we are so close to the mortuary? I'd like to see if Doctor Wilson has any defensive wounds. If Isabelle was pushed, rather than falling accidentally or jumping on purpose, her struggles should have left a mark."

"Ah yes, the charming Doctor Jamie Cranston-Hartfield. I trust he hasn't been the recipient of your reflex hammer? Or worse?"

"Not at all. Do try to be nice to him, Charlie. I need the work for both the money and the experience, even if it is mostly cleaning up bodily fluids and handing over scalpels and saws."

"Why did you choose to work with corpses, Grace? As Doctor McLeod pointed out, you have many other options open to you."

"Perhaps because I find myself in need of the skills, every time you are around. Besides, it's interesting work, though mostly rather routine. As you are only too aware, most deaths the police deal with are not exactly mysterious. The average murderer appears to have an extremely limited imagination."

"Thank heavens for that, or the constabulary would never cope. A handy chunk of stone applied to a skull in a drunken fight, a knife grabbed from the kitchen table during a marital squabble, a creditor strangled, a rival drowned, rat poison in the morning porridge. I have not had a single death from the venom of a rare type of snake found only in the depths of a tropical jungle on a remote island."

"Ah, but would you recognise such a cause of death if you saw it? I suspect the clever ones get away with murder without any of us realising it. A doctor might well sign off a death from snake venom as heart failure, without ever informing the police. After all, with no snakes in New Zealand, no doctor would even think of it."

On that thought-provoking note, they arrived at the mortuary. Charlie held the door open for her. "Not much likelihood of a mystery cause of death in Doctor Wilson's case. Falling from a train is not exactly as difficult to identify as snake venom."

Grace kitted them both out with protective gowns. Doctor Cranston-Hartfield was in the autopsy room, with Doctor Wilson's body already on the slab.

"Morning, Jamie. Hope you don't mind if I poke my nose in."

"Morning, Grace," he said cheerfully, as he prodded at the black-and-blue epidermis of the victim. "Thought you might be along." He looked up. "And DC Pyke. I wouldn't have thought the Wellington police would be interested in a Dunedin accident."

"Good day to you, Doctor Cranston-Hartfield," Charlie replied, ignoring the implied question. "You're sure it is an accident then?"

The police surgeon gestured at the corpse, which was lying face down. "My initial examination indicates the cause of death to be this jagged penetration of the posterior of the cranium, along with ruptures

77

to C6 and C7 of the spinal cord." He turned to Charlie. "To put it in layman's terms, he hit his head on a sharp rock and broke his neck."

Layman's terms? Did this idiot really think this was his first autopsy? "Miss Penrose, would you care to examine the anterior surface of the corpse? I would like to establish if there are any lacerations to the epidermis, especially in the buccal area, suggestive of pre-mortem trauma from the distal end of the phalanges."

Grace stifled a grin and examined the front of the body. She turned back to him with twinkling eyes in a straight face. "No sign of defensive wounds made by Miss Forsyth's fingertips, DC Pyke, on the cheeks or anywhere else."

Charlie tried to concentrate on the evidence, rather than the way she was looking at him. "So, if Doctor Wilson he did push Isabelle Forsyth off the train, it must have been too fast for her to react or he was gripping her too tightly for her to fight back."

Jamie let out a dismissive sniff. "Despite what the train guard said, I feel it is far more likely that the doctor tried to stop her jumping, rather than pushing her. I suspect he must have overbalanced in the struggle and went over himself."

Charlie stooped to examine the doctor's clothes. "There's a smear of grease across the back of his jacket. Probably leaned on the railings around the rear platform at some point."

"Not much evidence of grazing or bruising to the limbs," Grace noted. "Must have fallen straight from the train onto the rock, rather than tumbling down over the ground and vegetation. Not surprising, as it was very steep where he went over."

"At least it saved his face from excessive damage," the police surgeon added. "In my experience, it is always difficult for the next of kin to cope with a mangled face."

"Will you include the possibility that Miss Forsyth committed suicide in your report, Jamie?" Grace asked.

The surgeon pulled the sheet back over Doctor Wilson's body. "Insufficient evidence. I like to be absolutely sure, given the enormous anguish a verdict of suicide would cause to her family."

"Quite right," Charlie agreed. "Grace, we should go or we will miss my father's call. Thank you for your time, Doctor Cranston-Hartfield."

"Always a pleasure to be of service to Miss Penrose. I will see you on Saturday night, Grace. Reserve a few dances for me, if you would."

"Saturday night?"

"The Christmas Ball? I happened to see your friend, Miss Sugden, in town. She invited me to join your party."

"I haven't seen Molly for a few days, as I've been away. I must admit I had quite forgotten about the ball. I'm not sure whether I'll be able to go. But do enjoy yourself, Jamie. I shall see you next week, if not before."

"You're still friends with Molly Sugden?" Charlie asked, when they were back out on the street, hurrying across town. "How is she?"

"As well as could be expected. We often go out with a group of like-minded women, mostly to suffrage meetings, but sometimes on picnics or to dances. I cannot think why she invited the police surgeon to join us."

"I wouldn't want you to miss the Christmas Ball on my account, Grace, especially not if the dashing Cranston-Hartfield wishes your presence."

"Perhaps you would care to come too, if our investigations are completed by then. I expect I could manage to find a space on my dance card for you, if you ask nicely and behave yourself. If memory serves, your dancing skills are more than acceptable."

"How kind of you to remember. I do enjoy a good waltz." Charlie would never forget their first dance as long as he lived. From the smile that flitted across her lips, she hadn't either.

"So my cousins keep telling me. It seems that you have become the escort of choice for the entire Penrose clan. My ratbag brothers are delighted to have been released from the task."

"Your parents and aunts and uncles have been very kind to me, since I arrived in Wellington knowing nobody. I'd do anything to repay the favour."

Grace sighed. "My family adores you. Every letter I get is 'Charlie said this' or 'Charlie did that'. Sometimes they get through a whole letter without asking after me."

"Shall we declare a truce? I only have a few days at most in Dunedin and I don't want to spend all of it debating our respective social lives. Or chasing a phantom murderer for that matter."

"But you do need to find out about Amelia. I know enough about your loyalty to understand that it must be your first priority. I will do everything in my power to assist you."

"My dear Grace, how I have missed having someone around who knows me so well. I am more grateful for your support than I can possibly express."

"Come on. Let's go and find out if your father has uncovered any recent evidence about Amelia's disappearance. I'm rather thrilled by the opportunity to witness a telephone in operation. I still find it hard to believe that two people can talk to each other from as far apart as Central Otago and Dunedin."

"Who knows, one day there may be a device in every home."

They were directed to a booth and told to wait for the telephone to ring. The sense of excitement grew as they stared expectantly at the oddly shaped instrument in front of them. When the bell rang, both of them jumped.

Charlie lifted the handset from the cradle with more confidence than he felt, but it didn't give him the electric shock he had feared. After a series of buzzes and clicks, he heard the voices of the two operators. Grace perched on the edge of her seat, pencil at the ready to take notes.

Finally, Charlie heard his father's voice yelling "Hello? Hello?"

"No need to shout, Pa, I can hear you fine. How's Ma?"

"She's right here, trying to grab the instrument from my hand." There was a voice in the background. "She says she loves you and when are you going to visit."

"As soon as I can get more than a few days of leave, I promise."

"I know how it is, son. The police force is a hard taskmaster. Now, you wanted to know about Amelia Lawrence's disappearance. May I ask why?"

"All I have is the faintest of leads, based on a short conversation with a woman from a lunatic asylum who later died. I don't want to raise any hopes until I have made further inquiries." The line echoed with crackling and whooshing. "Hello? Can you hear me?"

"I hear you, Charlie."

"I wanted to ask you whether there have been any new developments on Amelia's disappearance from your end. Reported sightings, deathbed confessions, that sort of thing."

"I've been through my notes of the case. Not a single potential sighting in six years."

"Does the Lawrence family still live in Clyde?"

"Only Violet Lawrence, Amelia's younger sister, who is now Mrs Violet Duggan. I went to see her when I got your telegram to get her mother's contact details. Mrs Lawrence lives in Milton now, with her son Albert and his wife. Randall Barclay, the vicar who always hung on their coattails, is in Milton too. What? Hold on … Your mother is reminding me that Mrs Lawrence has three grandchildren already and she wants to know when it will be her turn."

Charlie rolled his eyes at the familiar question. "I wish you hadn't brought Violet into this, Pa."

"I'm sorry all the painful memories have been dragged up again, Charlie, but I know how important it is to you too. And my visit to Violet paid off, because she made a confession about information she had previously kept quiet–."

His heart beat faster as the static on the telephone line swallowed the rest of the sentence. "What information did she give you, Pa?"

"You remember how Amelia had been unwell in the weeks leading up to her disappearance? Violet has now admitted why that was. Mrs Lawrence had been giving Amelia a tonic from a quack doctor – the one we think was responsible for her disappearance. Violet thinks Amelia's strange behaviour started after she took the tonic, but her

81

mother told her not to tell me about it at the time. Violet was only fifteen then and did as her mother told her. Mrs Lawrence convinced Violet the tonic was to cure Amelia's illness, not cause it."

"I would love to know what her mother was giving her."

"I have the bottle in my hand. Violet saw her mother hide all the bottles after Amelia vanished. We found them in the back of the shed, exactly where she said they were."

"All the bottles? How many were there?"

"We found nine. Violet thought there might be more. The label on the bottle is discoloured, but clear enough to make out. It's called Doctor Josiah's Miraculous Elixir. I can't read the small print. Hold on a moment."

The line crackled with faint voices.

"Charlie? My eyesight is better than your father's."

'Hello, Ma. Can you read out the label slowly. I have a doctor on hand who will know what it is."

"That will be Miss Penrose, I hope. You won't be putting her in any danger this time, will you, Charlie?"

"Yes, it's Miss Penrose and no, I won't. The label?"

Charlie relayed his mother's words to Grace. "The label says the tonic can cure every disease known to mankind, from headaches to cholera, including 'feminine ailments and hysteria'. It is a ten percent extract of *Papaver somniferum* with herbs, honey, cinnamon, and cloves in ethanol, and some other ingredients that my mother can't make out." He glanced at Grace, who nodded that she had what she needed. "I'd better say goodbye now, Ma."

"Promise to come and see us soon, Charlie. We miss you."

"I will as soon as I can get enough leave. Love you, Ma."

Charlie replaced the chunky handpiece on its cradle with a sigh. "I do wish I could see my folks more often."

"Why don't you invite them to come to Dunedin next time you are here? I'd love to meet them and they would be welcome to stay at Anne's house. I'm sure they must miss Lily too."

"What, drag my father away from the police station in Clyde? The town would go to rack and ruin." Charlie picked up her notes. "So, what is *Papaver somniferum*. The rest of the ingredients sound delicious, rather like mulled wine."

"Far from it, I assure you. The honey, cinnamon and cloves will be there to disguise the bitter taste of the medicine. Essentially, that so-called tonic is laudanum, an extract of opium poppy in alcohol, and whatever else was unreadable. It would have caused Amelia to feel sleepy, unwell and increasingly dissociated from reality. It is also extremely addictive. If Amelia had been given several bottles of it over a few weeks, she would have been in a very serious state and suffering terrible cravings for more of it."

Charlie muttered an oath under his breath. "That interfering cow of a mother was poisoning Amelia, probably at the behest of Randall Barclay, the local vicar who was always hanging around like a bad smell. And they had the gall to blame me!"

"That's not quite what I meant, Charlie. Mrs Lawrence's intentions may have been honourable, if she didn't understand how potent the elixir was. In my limited experience, naïve folk are willing to accept without question anything sold to them by a person who calls himself a doctor."

"You think that charlatan, Doctor Josiah, deceived her?" He turned over the evidence, considering it from all angles. "I wonder if Josiah Cowper had his eye on Amelia all along and wanted her drugged and under his power?"

"That would be a big leap based on what we know, Charlie. You have to understand that laudanum is widely available at reputable apothecaries and used for a vast range of conditions. In my opinion, it is scandalously overused, but the fact remains that there may not have been any malicious intent in giving the tonic to Amelia. If she was anxious or not sleeping well, due to being sick, laudanum might well have been prescribed by a legitimate doctor."

In truth, Grace thought it possible that Mrs Lawrence and her vicar had resorted to desperate measures to subdue Amelia, to keep her under control and away from Charlie. But it would have been both tactless

83

and upsetting to mention that possibility to Charlie, especially as they had no proof. Besides, it seemed inconceivable that a mother would give her daughter such a harmful drug as a tonic if she understood what was in it and what its long-term effects would be.

"Regardless of intent, from what you have told me it seems fair to assume that Amelia would have been in no condition to fend off an attacker and may even have sought this Doctor Josiah out, if she craved more of the opium."

"That's a definite possibility," Grace agreed. "A slim young woman with no prior experience of opium might well have become addicted very quickly."

"I know one can't change the past, but I would give anything to go back to that time and rescue her. I was a fool to believe that Amelia wrote that note telling me she didn't want to see me. Without it, I would not have left for Dunedin."

Grace's Plan

Grace woke up the next morning to bright sunlight and the sound of a blackbird singing in the garden.

Last night, she had twisted the bedsheets into a tizzy, haunted by the death of Isabelle and her unborn child. Not just because of the guilt Grace felt at not preventing her death, but for the crawling dread that other women might also be at risk, including Charlie's missing friend. This morning, she was determined to take action.

Anne had a pot of tea ready in the kitchen. "Thought I heard you thumping around up there at last. I was about to come up to see if you had expired in the night."

"Every now and then a lady needs her beauty sleep. Given the hour, I thought I might have missed you."

Despite her advancing years and stiff hips, Anne rarely missed a day at Lavender House, the women's refuge she had run for decades. For her to still be at home, at the outrageously late hour of eight o'clock in the morning, was cause for concern.

"Are you feeling well, Auntie?"

"Fit as a filly. I was waiting for you to drag your bruised rump out of bed. You wish to discuss the matter with me, do you not?"

"You should apply for a position as a police interrogator. Nothing gets past you. I was hoping you could use your contacts to find out about Stillwaters Sanctuary and Doctor Samuel Wilson. Any rumours or opinions – good or bad."

"Already done, my dear. Don't look so surprised, your ancient auntie isn't completely doolally yet."

"Doolally? You? I'd sooner believe you had invited Henry Fish to share crumpets by the fireside."

"Pray never mention that odious man's name in my hearing. Without Fish and his brandy-soaked liquor barons manipulating their pet politicians, women would have had the vote years ago."

"We'll beat the fiends soon, I'm sure of it. So tell me, what have you found out?"

"I myself have had dealings with Doctor Wilson, who has helped us out at Lavender House on occasion. He was one of the few doctors who didn't turn up his nose at unwed mothers. My assessment is that he was a competent doctor, who acted, rather than just talked, with genuine Christian charity. His manner was rather gruff, which did not appeal to those who like to have their every whim pampered, but he and I rubbed along well enough. I am not in the least surprised that he was the one to refer Miss Forsyth to Stillwaters. He will be missed."

"Your opinion brings me comfort, Auntie. Perhaps the discord at Stillwaters is simply a matter of differences of temperament. Do you know the superintendent there, Horace Gresham?"

"I have crossed paths with him at various charitable meetings. He does strike me as the opposite of Wilson. Gresham is a compelling orator, beloved by the twittering classes of charitable ladies who have more money than sense. I have heard more than one lady whisper that his spiritual healing has saved their daughter from disgrace."

"What exactly do you think they meant by that?"

"At the time, I thought Stillwaters took in cases of mild hysteria and melancholia. Spiritual healing might therefore be simply a matter of providing a calm retreat to restore their daughter's mental health. At worst, I thought that being shut away in a religious asylum might have been awful enough to inspire some of the patients to see the error of their ways and thus learn to conform to social expectations. But now that I know they also take in unwed mothers-to-be, I wonder if pregnancy was the disgrace to which they were referring."

"And how would spiritual healing cure that particular disgrace?"

"Perhaps merely a coincidence. I wouldn't put it past Gresham to claim he had 'cured' those who have miscarried naturally. Miscarriage is not uncommon, as you know."

"Not common enough to claim a fair chance of a successful cure. Is there any suspicion that Stillwaters is taking such treatment beyond the spiritual?"

"Terminating pregnancies, you mean? It would be illegal. And utterly immoral to impose without consent upon a woman held against her will."

"But highly lucrative. As we well know, back-alley terminations are readily available in the poorer parts of town. Imagine how much a service catering to the daughters of the wealthy might charge, in such an attractive and private location, with no one the wiser. One which didn't kill their patients at the alarming rate back-alley patients suffer. I bet the likes of Mr Forsyth would leap at the chance to have the shameful problem removed."

"If so, they have managed to remain extremely discreet about it. Even with all my years in the medical field, albeit amongst the poor, I had heard no more than I told you."

Grace lapsed into silence. The possibilities for wrongdoing were many, when vulnerable young women were gathered into an enclosed community, losing what few rights they had in the outside world. The only way to find out for sure was to get inside Stillwaters. Equally obviously, as the only young, female, single, well-to-do woman available, she was the only person able to do the job. But she owed it to Anne to be honest with her plan.

Anne pre-empted her. "You mean to get yourself committed to Stillwaters, don't you, Grace."

"Only with your consent. I cannot see any other way."

Anne let out a heartfelt sigh. "It's what I would do if I was fifty years younger, so I suppose it would be wrong of me to refuse. However, I must insist we put some precautions in place. Alistair Stewart would be the best person to advise on that."

"The very man I had in mind, if he is willing."

"Alistair will jump at the opportunity to impress Lily. It's Charlie you'll have to worry about. He nearly lost you once, Grace. He won't be happy risking it again, especially now we know about the anguish he suffered after Amelia's disappearance."

"I know, Auntie. But what could go wrong in a place known for its serenity?"

"For heaven's sake, Grace, it's a lunatic asylum not a health spa. I suppose you want me to pay the admission fee too?"

"Oh dear, I haven't thought through all the details. May I borrow the money and repay the debt from my summer earnings?"

"Don't be silly, Grace. I'd be proud to fund your investigation. I must admit, I am intrigued by what goes on there myself."

The first step in the plan Grace had formulated was another visit to Doctor McLeod. Not unexpectedly, he reacted as if she had suggested a foray into the depths of the Amazonian rainforest armed only with a silk parasol.

"You want me to give you a formal referral to Stillwaters, attesting that you are with child and in a unbalanced state of mind? Miss Penrose, are you insane?"

"Well, yes, Doctor McLeod, that is the general idea. Insane and abandoned by my callous lover. And please, can we keep this confidential?" When he continued gaping, she added, "It's a cover of course. I'm not really pregnant. But I do have a very compelling reason to get into Stillwaters undetected, which I cannot share with you at this moment."

"You realise you will need a father or guardian to commit you into their care?"

"I have it in hand."

"And the approval of another doctor and magistrate?"

"Not if I agree to be committed as a voluntary patient."

McLeod fiddled with the stationery on his desk for a full minute, nearly knocking over an inkpot in his distraction. "I suppose I must trust your judgment, as I know you are working with the police, but only with a strong recommendation that you reconsider this folly. I should hate to feel responsible for any harm that might befall you."

"I will be under the protection of the two men I trust more than any other to ensure my safety. I presume we'll have to arrange a meeting at Stillwaters to apply for admission?"

"As it happens, I was called into the police station this morning to give a statement. Not that I could say much, as I was asleep for most of the train journey. The superintendent at Stillwaters, Mr Gresham, was there for the same reason. He mentioned he had further business in Dunedin today. With luck, you might catch him at his hotel, the Imperial. I'll send him a message to expect you, if you are determined to go ahead."

"Thank you, that would be most helpful, Doctor McLeod."

McLeod shook his head, but got out the required referral documents. "I'll put you down as suffering from mild melancholia, brought on by finding that you are with child. I refuse to imply a more serious form of mania, as you might be subjected to increased oversight or even physical or chemical restraint."

Grace shuddered at the thought of it. "Mild melancholia it is."

"I assume you wish to enter under a false name?"

How could she have failed to think of that? Put on the spot, it was impossible to come up with a name. "Er … what about Jane Smith?"

He raised his reading spectacles, giving her a stern look. "Suspiciously common, don't you think?"

"My mind is blank. How about Atropa Belladonna?"

"Deadly nightshade? Really Miss Penrose, hardly likely to be a parent's first choice of name, unless they wished their daughter to grow up to be a poisoner." McLeod shook his head again, but this time his eyes were smiling. "You need something ordinary, but not too common. Best to choose a name you will respond to, rather than something completely made up. Perhaps the name of a character in a book or a favourite cousin?"

"As it happens, I have a cousin called Jane Bennet, a name which fits into both of those categories."

"That will do. I've never heard of her."

Grace was about to say it really wouldn't do, as *Pride and Prejudice* was far too well known, when McLeod's assistant chose that moment to knock on the door to announce the next patient. McLeod scribbled furiously and handed her the completed referral document.

"I trust you know what you are doing, Miss Penrose. I should hate to hear that you ended up going insane inside a padded cell. Waste of a promising doctor."

On that sobering note, she thanked McLeod and departed for step two of her plan.

Grace found Detective Inspector Stewart at the police station, poring over files with Mr Peters. She waited until the filing clerk had departed before confessing her plan to Charlie's boss.

"You want me to commit you to Stillwaters? Grace, are you insane?"

"Indeed I am. I have the medical referral to prove it. You must see that it is the only way to find out what is happening inside Stillwaters. I'm sure I won't be in any danger."

"It's not the danger to you that worries me. Pyke will throttle me when he finds out. Even if he lets me live, he may never forgive me if I put you in harm's way again."

"I'm doing it for him and his family, so they don't spend the rest of their lives in torment over Amelia. Surely Charlie will see that."

"He will appreciate the thought, but not the very real risk to you. I dread to think what Lily will say."

"You are being remarkably calm about it, Detective Inspector Stewart."

"I cannot fault your logic and I know you well enough to see that you will go regardless of what I say. All I ask is that we have a plan in place to communicate with you and get you out if there is any doubt as to your safety."

"I hoped you would say that, though I hate to ask you to give up your precious time with Lily."

"She will thank me for it in the end, if she ever forgives me."

90

"You will have to pretend to be my father, in order to commit me. Can I ask whether you were present at the interview of Superintendent Gresham this morning? My plan will fail if he has met you as a policeman."

"No, I wasn't there. The local team is handling the case."

"Excellent. Would you be able to go now? With any luck, Gresham went back to his hotel after his police interview."

"After you, dearest daughter. You will not go under your own name, I trust."

"I am to enter under the name Miss Jane Bennet."

Stewart looked at her sideways with a grin. "Perhaps Lydia Bennet might have been a better choice for a wild young woman who has gotten herself in trouble."

"My dear Mr Bennet, it is not I who caused my troubles, but the vile cad who coaxed me into surrendering my honour, on the promise of his hand in marriage. I am laid low with the shame of it."

"Have you ever thought of writing novels, Grace? Far less blood and disease than being a doctor. And far less risk than being an undercover detective."

"I only hope Superintendent Gresham isn't a reader of Jane Austen." Grace had the feeling she would regret not making the effort to think of a better false identity. "I expect the superintendent will wish to speak to you alone. Ask about their plan for having the child. And you might inquire about the details of the treatment programme they provide, if any, at Stillwaters. Sign me up for anything that sounds dubious."

"Indeed I shall not. You will be there to observe, Grace, not to put yourself at risk by taking part in any treatments. On that, I must absolutely insist."

When they arrived at the Imperial Hotel, they were shown into a small sitting room, where a slim man was already seated. He rose from his chair, smoothing a burgundy silk cravat with one hand, while extending the other manicured hand to Stewart.

"Mr Bennet, delighted to make your acquaintance. Doctor McLeod's note reached me just in time." After a fractional pause, he dipped his head in Grace's general direction without meeting her eye. "And Miss Bennet."

"Mr Gresham, how good of you to meet with me on short notice. It was fortuitous indeed that McLeod was able to inform us of your visit to Dunedin."

"Please, take a seat." He waved Stewart to the armchair standing close to his own. "Perhaps Miss Bennet would care to avail herself of the ladies' waiting room?"

"Don't mind her," Stewart replied, directing Grace to a seat in the far corner. "She'll do as she's told. She needs to accept responsibility for the trouble she is in."

Grace slunk to the indicated hard-backed chair, keeping her gaze on the floor and her posture penitent. McLeod was right. Gresham did have a lovely rich voice, even if his manner irked her. He kept stroking his meticulously trimmed goatee beard, presumably to project the impression of a great thinker.

"May I inquire as to the nature of the case, Mr Bennet?"

Stewart handed over the medical referral. "We brought our daughter up to respect God and her parents. She gave every indication of being a credit to her future husband, yet moral corruption has sought her out and stamped her with the shame of sin." He leaned forward in his chair, lowering his voice. "She allowed herself to be taken into the gardens during a house party, by a young man who professed an earnest desire to marry her, but … Well, I'm sure you do not wish to hear the sordid details. I blame her governess for allowing her to read inappropriate novels."

Grace struggled to keep her face straight at his amateur dramatics. She drowned her snort of laughter in a pathetic sob, muffled by a lace handkerchief.

"My dear Mr Bennet, hers is precisely the type of feminine disorder we pride ourselves on alleviating at Stillwaters Sanctuary. Our facilities and care are the very best you could wish for. The families who seek our help praise our discretion, which has allowed many a young lady to return to society unblemished, so that her life is not ruined by a single foolish indiscretion. We allow only the best class of patients to be admitted, of course. The delicate sensibilities of your daughter will rest easy within the calming atmosphere of Stillwaters."

"Excellent. I cannot tell you how relieved I am to discover a solution to this calamity that avoids public disgrace. Naturally, we will say she is making an extended visit to distant relatives. How I wish the problem would vanish without such subterfuge, but one must face reality."

Gresham shifted in his chair, rubbing his hands together in a way that was oddly suggestive of both prayer and avarice. "We have an exceptional programme of spiritual healing, run by myself, which has shown excellent results. If the young lady is truly repentant and opens herself to God's blessing, we find that miracles can occur. No expense is spared. We even provide holy water from the most sanctified springs of Europe."

Stewart gave a discreet cough. "One hates to raise the matter of money, when the reputation of one's daughter is at stake ..."

Gresham passed a sheaf of papers across the space between the two men, as if bestowing a gift. Grace noted the momentary flaring of Stewart's nostrils. Clearly, the fact that Stillwaters was run under the name of a charity did not preclude the charging of an exorbitant fee.

Stewart folded the documents into an inner pocket after the most cursory glance. "Excellent. When might one hope for a place to become available?"

Gresham allowed himself a benevolent nod. "Fortune smiles upon Miss Bennet today. A place became available only yesterday. Indeed, if you wish it, you may visit tomorrow morning, on the early train. Once you have viewed the facility and completed the admission procedures, Miss Bennet may join us immediately. You will find all the information in the documents."

"Marvellous." Stewart rose and shook the superintendent's hand. "I will look forward to meeting again tomorrow morning."

"You will be met at Waitati station. We look forward to welcoming Miss Bennet to our place of sanctuary."

Stewart walked to the door without turning his head towards her, leaving Grace to slip out after him like an obedient shadow. By the time she reached the street, Stewart had secured a hansom. He handed her in without a word and directed the driver to take them back to Anne's house.

When they were clear of the hotel, he released a pent-up breath. "I could do with a whisky, though I suppose a strong cup of tea would be more appropriate, given the hour."

"You were magnificent. I am sorry to put you through that charade."

He leaned back on the hard leather seat. "I had no idea that being a father would be so demanding."

"You sound just like my real father. I'm afraid I have been even more trouble to him that the fictional Lydia Bennet, though for entirely different reasons of course."

"In my view, he is a fortunate man indeed to have a daughter like you."

Grace was taken aback at his words, which were spoken softly, without a trace of flattery. "May I ask if you have children, Detective Inspector Stewart?"

"Sadly, my wife was ill from an early age, which meant we never had children of our own. No need to look so distressed on my behalf, Grace. I wouldn't exchange my years with her for anything in the world. I have been a widower for the last fifteen years."

He helped her down from the cab. "You know, meeting you all has given me a new lease on life. I see in young Pyke the eager young copper I used to be, before I got old and cynical."

"Don't tell him I said so, but Charlie worships the ground you walk on. And Lily wouldn't care for your company so much if she thought you unworthy. Come on, let's have that whisky. I suspect I may need it when I read through that document and find out what is in store for poor, melancholic Jane Bennet. From the look on your face when he showed you the fees, Anne is going to have an apoplectic fit when she hears how much I will need to borrow from her."

Stewart poured the drinks, while Grace settled down to read. The fees ranged from pulse pounding to heart stopping. The base fee covered accommodation, food and sundries, payable monthly, with additional fees depending on the diagnosis and specific requirements, such as medications, spiritual healing, birthing and infant care. The last appeared to be a carefully worded allusion to finding an alternative home for the child, should the birth family not wish to take it.

Stewart handed her a glass with an appropriately medicinal dose of liquor. "I will be paying the fee. Amelia's disappearance has obviously taken a toll on the Pyke family. I want to have the opportunity to show them my support."

Grace opened her mouth to protest, but Stewart cut her off. "I must insist. I have an independent income far in excess of my limited needs. I want to do this, for Lily and Charlie." He took a seat beside her and ran his gaze over the papers, which she had spread across the table. "Look at all these rules and requirements. I'm reminded of my old boarding school, which was little better than a military camp operating under the pretence of an educational institution."

"It's not so bad. I can cope with the minimal list of allowed possessions, while the draconian dress code is not so very different from my usual clothing. Practical, plain and modest – just the thing for medical training or entering an asylum."

"This daily schedule makes army training look lackadaisical. I'm not sure you will have much opportunity to investigate, Grace."

"But see here, large portions of the day are devoted to quiet contemplation and refreshing outdoor diversion. I may even have the opportunity to improve my woeful croquet skills. Sounds positively delightful, after a busy year of study and work. Although I hope I will only be there for a few days at most."

"I wish we had more time to reconnoitre the place, before entrusting you to their care. We will need a way to communicate. At the very least, we need to establish an emergency signal."

"Perhaps a white handkerchief dangling from the bedroom window? Rather a cliché, but less conspicuous than a skull and crossbones flag."

"As good as any, I suppose. The cavalry will descend as soon as it appears, I assure you."

"Cavalry? How many men are you thinking of recruiting to this mission?"

"Pyke and I ought to be enough to keep watch, assuming you will be there for no longer than a few days. One hopes the authority of my position will be enough to avert the need for actual troops and weaponry, should we need to raid the place. We can set up a plan for scouting the grounds once we see the layout. I assume it will be fenced, but no doubt young Pyke will be able to get in and make contact with you during your afternoon sessions of outdoor activities."

"Agreed. Stillwaters Sanctuary is hardly likely to be as well guarded and fenced as the average gaol. I am truly grateful to know that you two will be keeping watch over me, even though I suspect that I will be entirely safe. You never know, I might even enjoy it."

Charlie's Plan

Charlie spent the morning wallowing in paper. The man on the street might think a detective spends all his time chasing criminals through back alleys, if he gave any thought to the matter at all, but the reality was rather more prosaic. No investigation could succeed without the help of the Mr Peters of the world.

He lifted his weary eyes from the scrawl of the last inspection report for Stillwaters Sanctuary. Pages of potentially useful information filled his notebook, from the names of the key staff, to the details of the charitable trust, and notes from the inspection itself. The Magdalene Trust meant nothing to him, other than the connection between the name and the objectives of the sanctuary, to resurrect fallen women and drive the seven demons out of them.

He gave his writing hand a vigorous shake, wishing himself anywhere else but the basement archives, redolent with the smell of old parchment and dust. Outside, the day had promised to be a scorcher, perfect for a paddle in the ocean.

What would Grace be doing this morning? She had been withdrawn last night, presumably due to the distress caused by recent events, not helped by frustration that their time together was once again derailed. He could hardly blame her if she had decided to give up on him and go to the seaside with her friends. He only hoped Cranston-Hartfield hadn't invited himself along.

An energetic patter of feet on the stairs alerted him to the return of Mr Peters, no doubt with another armload of musty documents for his perusal. Charlie gathered his notes together for a hasty exit.

"Detective Constable Pyke, I see you are preparing to leave."

"I have another appointment to attend, Mr Peters."

"Can you spare a minute?"

Charlie pulled his watch from his waistcoat pocket. The hands had moved around the dial with all the speed of an inebriated slug. His appointment was still half an hour away. He sighed. "What have you got for me?"

"I have a colleague who works as an archivist at the city council. He has managed to track down an original plan of the building that now houses the asylum." Peters unrolled a scroll of paper across the table, pinning the corners with assorted stationery items.

"Mr Peters, you are a miracle worker. I owe you a pint of best bitter."

"An occasional small sherry is my one indulgence. The pleasure of a job well done is enough for me."

"This is marvellous. Do you have a large piece of paper so I can make a copy?"

"No need, DC Pyke. My colleague trained in technical drawing. It did not take him long to make this copy, for you to keep."

Charlie could have embraced him, but he contented himself with a gentle pat on the back. "I am most grateful for your diligence. I will be sure to ask DI Stewart to pass on our appreciation to DI Wallace." He rolled up the scroll again and tucked it under his arm. "I must be going."

The sunshine blinded him as he emerged onto the street. He sucked in a lungful of fresh air – if air laced with the smell of tobacco, horse droppings, burning coal and sundry other city aromas could be called fresh. Paperwork was all very well, but it was action he craved.

The only logical way to find Amelia was to infiltrate Stillwaters Sanctuary, which meant his only option was to get a job as an attendant. If they didn't have a position open, then he wouldn't hesitate to resort to a bribe to create a position, even if it drained his hard-earned savings.

First, he must have a reference. He had sent a note this morning to Doctor McLeod, requesting his help. Asking a reputable professional to fake a reference was likely to see him thrown out onto the street, but he was desperate and too short of time to find another way. Ordinarily, working his way into an undercover role took days or weeks of subtle machinations.

As Charlie knocked on the door to the doctor's office, he hoped that McLeod's goodwill towards Grace might extend to him. Surprisingly, Doctor McLeod seemed amused, rather affronted, by the request. Before Charlie could explain, McLeod waved his concerns away.

"You start tomorrow morning. I hope that is all right. Your note did indicate that the matter was urgent. You will be met off the early train."

"You astound me, Doctor McLeod. How you worked this miracle I cannot begin to imagine."

"I sent a telegram asking if they had any staff vacancies, saying that one of our attendants at Seacliff Asylum wanted to work closer to home. Your name is Charles Pearce, by the way. I hope that is suitable."

"Wonderful. What a stroke of good fortune that they had a vacancy."

"Not really, Detective Constable Pyke. The matron jumped at the chance to take an experienced male attendant. Indeed, her thanks to me were about as profuse as one could get, given the brevity of a telegram. An asylum is not an easy place to work. Out in the countryside away from the diversions of the city, always on call, doing tough and often dirty work with some of society's most difficult characters. It is far easier to get female attendants, as there is always a supply of women who are grateful for any roof over their head. Spinsters with no one to support them, or women who have been widowed or abandoned."

"I have no experience. Is there anything I need to know about the work?"

"Being firm and kind goes a long way. Staff are expected to set a good example by their behaviour, and above all, accept that you will have unpleasant tasks to perform, such as cleaning up after those who cannot or will not control their bodily functions. If you do exactly as you are told, you won't go too far wrong. And, of course, do not turn your back on the violent ones. Although, my understanding is that Stillwaters Sanctuary takes only low risk patients, so you should make it out with all your limbs intact."

"Sounds an awful lot like being a policeman." Charlie unconsciously reached up to the bandaged scar on his arm. He really hoped that this time he would make it through without adding to the injury count. At least he wouldn't have to worry about Grace being at risk this time. "To be honest, I wasn't even sure they had male staff, given the delicacy of the patients."

"Even the most fragile woman can be a handful if they have manic tendencies. They would need one or two strong men around to call on. Besides, Stillwaters does take male patients, although they live separately for the most part. They tend the gardens, which supply the vegetables and fruit for the meals. All sons of wealthy men, naturally, and not at all the usual run of deranged inmates one might see at a public asylum. I expect most are feeble-minded or melancholic. You may encounter a few of the more effeminate types, who find normal life a challenge. I trust you can handle that without resorting to abuse."

"Of course. Sounds a lot better than most of the criminals I deal with. I am exceedingly grateful, Doctor McLeod."

"I hope you remain grateful once you have spent a few days incarcerated with the inmates of Stillwaters. I would be interested to hear what this is all about, once your investigations are completed."

"To be honest, we are clutching at smoke. If it wasn't for Miss Penrose's intuition, which I have learned not to ignore, this elaborate charade would not be considered."

Charlie saw a tiny tic around the doctor's eye at the mention of Grace, triggering an all too familiar sensation of apprehension. "Has Miss Penrose been to see you again too?"

"I'm not at liberty to say."

As if the rueful quirk at the edge of the doctor's lips wasn't answer enough. Charlie wasn't the least bit surprised. He waited out the silence, a trick that worked in the vast majority of interrogations.

McLeod gave in after a few seconds. "When Miss Penrose started at medical school, we had a small wager on how long she would last. Guesses ranged from hours to days. I chose a month, but only because I knew Professor Scott had no doubt that she would last the distance. He was right. Despite all the unpleasantness she has had to cope with, she never once wavered."

"I don't doubt it, Doctor McLeod. How have the other medical students treated her?"

"Appallingly at first. After two years she has subdued them into three groups – those who are devoted to her, those who secretly admire her from afar, and the majority, who are terrified that she will show them up. I will not ask you which of the three groups you would fall into, DC Pyke."

"All three groups on a rotating basis, but mostly all three at once."

"Wise man. Take care of her. I worry that her tenacity might come with a streak of recklessness."

"Thank you for the warning, Doctor McLeod. Believe me, I am all too aware of it."

They met back at Anne's house in the late afternoon. Despite liberal amounts of sherry, the conversation remained subdued, as each person appeared intent on keeping their thoughts to themselves. Grace was uncharacteristically silent, running her fingers absent-mindedly over her silk shawl, as she sipped at a glass of water. Charlie would have given far more than a penny for her thoughts.

Lily sat down beside her. "I'm pleased you like the shawl, Grace. I helped Charlie choose it. If it had been left to him you'd have ended up with something entirely unsuitable as a farewell gift."

"Do tell me, Lily, what unsuitable options were considered?"

"Oh, I don't know. Considering the events leading up to his departure, I wouldn't have been surprised if he had given you a throwing knife or a pistol."

"Or a cage, to keep my niece out of trouble," Anne suggested.

"Laugh if you will, but I assure that you none of those items crossed my mind," Charlie retorted, not entirely truthfully. "Although I wish I had thought of the cage."

"Better yet, install a cannon by the front door to keep the villains at bay. Or a moat of–"

The rest of Lily's suggestion was interrupted by the clang of the doorbell. A few seconds later, a strident voice silenced their merriment. A middle-aged woman, with lemon-sucking lips and a fierce frown, barged into the drawing room, with Anne's maid hot on her heels. Two young men trailed in her wake, one looking apologetic, the other haughty.

"I beg your pardon, ma'am–" the maid began, but the woman cut her off.

"What's all this I hear from my Violet? Who is stirring up trouble again?" Her ice-blue eyes scanned the room, stopping at Charlie. "Pyke. I might have known. You caused my daughter's death and now you don't even have the decency to let her rest in peace."

Charlie stiffened in disbelief at his old nemesis. Damn and blast it – after six years, could the old harpy not manage a civil word, especially in such company?

Both Anne and Stewart rose from their chairs at her cruel words. Anne thrust out her walking cane to hold him back. She stalked over to her uninvited caller, stopping right in front of her.

"This is my house and I will thank you not to come barging in like a pack of ill-mannered hyenas. Detective Constable Pyke is acting on credible information, in the interests of your family, and I will not allow him to be so unfairly berated in this appalling manner."

The younger gentleman went bright red from the roots of his hair to the nape of his neck. "I do beg your pardon, Madam. May I introduce my mother, Mrs Lawrence, who is a trifle upset, and our vicar, Mr Randall Barclay. I am Amelia's brother, Albert Lawrence."

"You may take a seat, if you promise to behave. I am Mrs Anne Macmillan and this is my great-niece, Miss Grace Penrose. Detective Constable Charlie Pyke and his aunt, Mrs Lily Wu, you already know.

And this gentleman is Detective Inspector Stewart, one of the most experienced detectives in the country."

"Well, I never," Mrs Lawrence said, "I'm sure Pyke had no need to request the help of so eminent a police officer."

"I am honoured to count myself a friend of the family, Mrs Lawrence." Stewart resumed his seat beside Lily, taking up her hand and holding it conspicuously in his own.

Mrs Lawrence looked scandalised by this overt display of affection, but she settled herself into the best available armchair nevertheless. Albert Lawrence remained standing beside her, looking embarrassed, with Mr Barclay on the other side, looking everywhere but at his hosts.

"If I might explain," Grace began, "it was me who raised the issue. I was talking to a young woman on a train and happened to mention Charlie – that is, Detective Constable Pyke. She recognised the name and asked me to pass on a message to tell him that Amelia was still alive. Tragically, the woman delivering the message met with an accident before I could question her further."

Albert leaned forward with an expression halfway between hope and anguish. "I always had a strong feeling that my sister was still alive, despite the evidence to the contrary. Did this woman say where Amelia is living?"

"Not precisely, but she had just left an institution which specialises in caring for young women with … delicate sensibilities."

Randall Barclay swivelled his head and examined her with his markedly protruding eyes, which made him look like a fish, especially combined with his long, thin nose. "Why would Miss Lawrence not have contacted her own family if she was safe?"

"You must understand that we intended to find out more before distressing you with this news," Grace replied, with forced civility, "but we needed to request information from Sergeant Pyke in Clyde."

Mrs Lawrence let out a huff between pursed lips. "So you weren't planning to inform me that my dear daughter could be alive."

103

"It was a matter of ascertaining the facts first, Mrs Lawrence," Stewart said. "The correct procedures must be followed."

The vicar steepled his hands in front of him and stared down his hatchet nose as if he was addressing a rag-tag bunch of children at Sunday school. When he opened out his hands, every ear in the room waited for the coming sermon. Instead, Barclay addressed Stewart as if he was alone in the room. "We do not want Pyke anywhere near this investigation."

"Steady on, Mr Barclay," Albert said. "Charlie was a good friend to Amelia and me. Amelia was terribly bullied before he stood up for her. Besides, he had nothing to do with Amelia's disappearance. He wasn't even in Clyde at the time."

"And who was it who drove her to the edge of madness with his constant pestering?" The vicar let his harsh words sit in the air, festering. When Albert opened his mouth to reply, Barclay cut him off, his eyes bulging all the more in his wrath. "If Pyke hadn't made her so ill by threatening to leave, she would never have met that awful quack doctor and none of this would have happened. If she hadn't been under his thrall, she would have been happily married to a suitable husband."

Anne, Grace and Lily all broke into outraged protests, while Charlie sat silently hunched in his chair, staring at the fire, with his hands balled into tight fists. All the old agony of Amelia's disappearance flooded back on the wave of vitriol spurting from Barclay's mouth. At least Albert was still loyal.

"Enough." Stewart's sharp command demanded and got silence. "I will not have my investigation dictated by someone who has no authority over me. DC Pyke is an exemplary policeman and my inquiries so far indicate that Mr Lawrence is correct – there is no reason to lay any blame whatsoever upon his shoulders, broad as they are. Moreover, the message specifically requested his help, not yours." He turned to Anne. "Mrs Macmillan, may I commandeer a room to question these people?"

"By all means, Detective Inspector Stewart. You may use the library."

104

Judging from her flushed skin, Mrs Lawrence's blood pressure had risen to boiling point. "Question *us*? What possible reason could you have for such an outrageous action."

"You may recall information of significance, Mrs Lawrence. Often perspectives change with the passage of time. Besides, I need to satisfy myself about exactly what happened in the lead up to Amelia's disappearance. Shall I start with you? I wouldn't want to inconvenience you by making you wait."

Mrs Lawrence sat back in her chair and crossed her arms, but Albert levered her up and led her up the stairs after Stewart. The vicar followed close behind, after sending a fierce glare in Charlie's direction.

Lily crouched down by her nephew and held his hands in hers. "What a nightmare of a mother. Was she always that bad?"

"She got worse after Randall Barclay returned to Clyde. You had left town by then, Aunt Lily. That so-called man of God encouraged her to believe the worst of me, due to my wicked Chinese blood. Excuse me, I need some fresh air."

Charlie was up and out the door before anyone could stop him.

Compromise

Grace sat seething at the gall of Mrs Lawrence and her ungodly vicar, until she couldn't stand the strain any longer. Seven seconds, to be exact.

She found Charlie sprawled in a patch of herbs, which had escaped the vegetable patch at the bottom of the garden. The smell of crushed thyme rose up around him in the warmth of the late afternoon sun.

Without saying a word, she sat on the adjacent garden seat. A long silence followed.

Butterflies flitted amongst the flowers.

Small creatures rustled in the undergrowth.

A dog barked across the valley.

Slowly, the sun sank towards the hills, extending a long shadow up the valley towards them.

When the shadow had enveloped them, Grace shivered. "Charlie, if you ever want to talk, I want you to know that I am always here for you."

"My talking skills are rather rusty. Much like my letter writing. I blame it on the police code of silence."

She nudged him with her foot. "A poor excuse, DC Pyke. Talking is simple. Take what is in your heart and let it out your mouth." Grace touched her hand to her heart, then to her lips. "A year or two of practice and you'll get the hang of it."

Charlie repeated the heart to lips gesture with a flourish. "You do realise that policemen are reputed not to have hearts?"

"As a student of anatomy, I must beg to differ."

"All right. Here goes. Grace ..." He paused, as if building his courage to let out his innermost feelings. "I think it is time to go back up to the house."

"Does that mean that you are ready to discuss the situation with our investigating team?"

"No, but I am hungry. Lily's mutton stew smells wonderful and she's made dumplings."

Grace threw her hands up in despair. "Honestly, Charlie, how can you think of food at a time like this?"

"Perhaps because I do not wish to think of anything else." Charlie didn't move. "Grace?"

"Yes?"

"Thank you for sitting with me."

"If I had stayed with that Lawrence woman one more minute, I would have impaled her with a sharp object. Such a pity you didn't get me a nice throwing knife instead of that ghastly shawl."

He started to laugh. Which made her laugh. It must have been a good five minutes before they had fully recovered their composure.

"Mrs Lawrence I can cope with," Charlie said, as he wiped the tears from his eyes. "She's only trying to protect her daughter. It's that sanctimonious vicar, Randall Barclay, who winds me up, until I have to leave the room or lash out. His 'holier than thou' sneering, pretending he was protecting Amelia, when he was really looking out for himself."

"He has certainly taken Mrs Lawrence under his wing. Personally, I should hate to have to listen to Barclay's sermons every Sunday. He gives me the creeps."

"Keeping a wealthy family like the Lawrences on his side is very much in his best interests. I suspect he was angling to make Amelia his wife, hence his desire to blacken my name."

"Can I ask how Amelia felt about him?"

"She hated him at school. He pulled her hair and taunted her, even though he was a couple of years ahead of us. He was sneaky about it, never getting caught. I nearly got expelled for teaching him a lesson. Just one of the many reasons Barclay loathes me."

"Amelia was lucky to have you on her side, Charlie."

"I sometimes wonder if I shielded her too much. Maybe if I hadn't, she would have become independent and capable, like you, instead of relying on other people."

"Independence comes from within. If she wanted it, she had every chance to show it. Did she still dislike Barclay later?"

"When he came back from his religious training, everything changed. She thought he could do no wrong. The Lawrence family are the sort who believe in blind faith to their church, no matter who is standing in the pulpit. Even so, I know Amelia never liked him as a person."

Grace shivered again. "Shall we go back to the house? I expect they are long gone by now. With any luck, we'll never have to see them again."

She stood up and shook flakes of lichen from her skirt, then brushed sprigs of thyme from Charlie's back. She was aware of his eyes on her, but she couldn't guess what he was thinking from the serious expression on his face. Without warning, he pulled her to his chest, embracing her tightly for long seconds, before striding up the path, leaving her to hurry after him.

The others were in the dining room, about to start the evening meal, with no sign of the Lawrence family. Stewart rose from the table and pulled out a chair for Grace, while Charlie slid into the seat between Lily and Anne.

"Alistair was about to recount the results of his inquisition of the infidels," Lily told them, as the maid laid steaming plates of stew and dumplings in front of them. "A shame he didn't think to bring his instruments of torture."

"I can't honestly say I found out anything much. Mrs Lawrence admitted purchasing the tonic for Amelia, having been told it was a perfectly safe remedy to calm her anxiety."

Grace was in no mood to allow a claim of good intentions. "By sedating her daughter and turning her into an opium addict?"

"She denied knowing what its effect would be," Stewart replied.

"Maybe at first, but she should have stopped giving her daughter the tonic as soon as she saw its adverse effects."

"She is far from the most sensible woman I have ever met," Stewart agreed. "I won't offend you by sharing the rest of her sentiments. The brother, Albert Lawrence, seems a decent fellow. He is the only one of them who expressed guilt and regret, although his only fault was not to question his mother as to why his sister was unwell. He recalled being alarmed by Amelia's odd behaviour, moving between episodes of lethargy, to bouts of hysteria, then anxiety. He knew nothing of the tonic."

"Those are exactly the symptoms one would expect from too much opium. Amelia would have been even more distressed if her mother stopped dosing her, as she would have craved it by then." Grace sent an apologetic look at Charlie, but he was bending over his plate, hiding his eyes and shovelling stew with ungentlemanly haste.

"The brother insisted on helping. He said he would do anything he could to get his sister back." Stewart waved away her unspoken protest. "He's genuine, I believe, and it would be useful to have another recruit."

"He did speak in support of Charlie, I suppose," Grace said. "What about the vicar, the obnoxious Randall Barclay? Did he have anything useful to say?"

"Barclay said he was trying to protect Amelia. In that I believe he was genuine, if misguided. He must have realised she was in a fragile state, but it is not clear if he knew why. Naturally, he claimed that anything she confessed to him would have to remain confidential, which suggested she had spoken to him about something that was troubling her."

"This is all very aggravating and not very helpful," Lily said. "I vote for direct action to find out whether Amelia is still alive. Alistair, can you not use your police powers to search Stillwaters Sanctuary?"

"I'm sorry, my dear, but there is no evidence that a crime has been committed by anyone at the asylum. At best, I could ask for their cooperation in providing additional information on Isabelle Forsyth, but I expect they would want to protect the privacy of their patients. I have even less cause to ask about anyone named Amelia who might have passed through their care any time in the last six years."

"Then we will have to investigate from within," Grace said, "using a person who can discreetly mingle with the patients to see if Amelia is there. As Stillwaters is an institution for young ladies, I believe the best candidate is obvious."

"Absolutely not," Lily said. "For all we know, Amelia's abductor might still be in contact with her. Charlotte's message was that Doctor Josiah is alive too. Let's not forget that Josiah Cowper murdered Amelia's father in cold blood in order to steal the family valuables. Besides, I will not allow Grace to risk herself in an institution for the insane, especially not on the slightest of evidence. Charlie has already lost too much to risk another person dear to him."

"I am grateful for your concern, Lily," Anne said, "but we all know Grace is not one to turn away from a challenge. I doubt we could stop her, unless we confine her to a strait jacket at home."

"Alistair," Lily said, "Surely you would not want Grace to risk herself? Can the police force not send a battalion in to storm the place on some pretext?"

"Unfortunately, that might put Amelia at greater risk, if she is there," Stewart replied. "I hate to say it, but the best approach is always to scout the enemy, before engaging them. And Grace is right. The only way to get inside information is to send in someone of the same age and background. The critical thing will be to make sure she has outside support and an escape plan."

"I believe the risk is being overstated," Grace added. "The sanctuary is supposed to be a place of quiet contemplation, designed to sooth those of a nervous disposition. I have to say, it sounds like a lovely rest from my studies."

"Don't try to fool me, Grace, I wasn't born yesterday. If it is so charming, why was Isabelle Forsyth so desperate to escape that she was willing to throw herself off a train rather than be forced to return there?" Lily looked to Charlie for support. "Surely you cannot countenance putting Grace in such danger?"

110

"Of course I don't want her put at risk," Charlie replied. "But Grace makes her own decisions. I may not always agree with them, but I must respect her choices."

Grace was momentarily silenced by his response. She caught his eye and tried to convey her silent gratitude, which he acknowledged with a fleeting elevation of one eyebrow.

"I'm inclined to agree with Grace," Stewart said. "The small risk is worth it if Amelia is there."

Charlie cleared his throat loudly. "As I was saying, I am grateful for Grace's kind offer to help. However, it is not necessary, as there is a better option. I will go undercover as an attendant at Stillwaters Sanctuary. Thus, there is no need for me to throw Grace to the lions."

Grace reached out to pat his arm, which was folded across his broad chest in a gesture that brooked no opposition. "As it happens, I agree with you, Charlie."

"You do?" His eyes narrowed as he tried to figure out where the unexpected checkmate might be sprung upon him.

"I agree it would be best if you were not the one to take me there, so as not to risk compromising your cover and mine. I have arranged someone else to accompany me to Stillwaters."

Grace waited for the steam to burst out of Charlie's ears, but he maintained a state of glacial calm that was all the more terrifying for its cold intensity.

"And what idiot has agreed to put your life at risk, Grace? Please, for the sake of my sanity, tell me you haven't got Jamie Cranston-Hartfield playing the role of your repentant lover."

"Unfortunately, I never thought of that option. Perhaps it is not too late to ask."

Anne tapped her fork on a glass. "Do stop winding each other up, you two. Without doubt, it would be best if you were both there, as a patient and an attendant will be able to investigate different parts of Stillwaters Sanctuary and look out for each other as well. Anyway, we have time to think through the best approach, as it will take several days to make the necessary arrangements."

Charlie rocked back in his chair with a smug grin. "Too late. I start tomorrow."

"As do I," Grace replied. "The Sanctuary has an available space, I have a doctor's signature to support my committal for care, and my father has completed the paperwork and agreed to pay the appallingly large fee, bless his kind heart. He is taking me there by the first train tomorrow morning."

Anne, Lily and Charlie looked at her in astonishment.

"But your father is in Wellington," Anne said.

"Grace Penrose's father is in Wellington. But the father of Miss Jane Bennet, my melancholic alter-ego, is right here." She nodded to Stewart. "Aren't you, Papa dearest?"

Stewart bowed to his startled audience, conveniently avoiding the searing glare of his detective constable and the shocked disbelief of his beloved Lily.

Lily raised her hands in surrender. "I hope you weren't thinking of leaving me out of this plan, Mr Bennet?"

"As I see it, we might all play a role," Stewart replied. "Charlie and Grace inside, with me on lookout, ready to assist as needed. Lily and Anne, would you agree to stay in Dunedin to conduct further investigations on Stillwaters Sanctuary and to liaise with the police here? Albert Lawrence has already agreed to help us by arranging a means of transport and communication. He'll follow us up on the afternoon train. The only problem is that we don't have a great deal of information on which to base a plan."

"On the contrary, I spent the morning entombed with Mr Peters. He even came up with an architectural plan of the building. The rooms will have changed in function, of course, but at least we will have a general idea of the layout."

"How did I ever manage without you, Pyke?"

Grace pushed her chair back. "Now that we are all in agreement, I shall go and attend to my packing, while you form a plan. I wonder what the well-dressed lunatic is wearing this season?" She stopped beside Charlie and whispered in his ear. "Might I have a word?"

Charlie passed his notebook to Stewart and caught up with her at the bottom of the stairs. "I'm beginning to think you are mad enough to be in an asylum, Grace. I know that nothing I say can sway your decision, but I hope you will promise me not to take undue risks."

"I won't find anything if I take no risks, Charlie, but I'll try to be sensible." She hesitated to ask the next question, but it had to be done if she was to have any chance of success. "I'll need to see a picture of Amelia. Do you have one?"

"Not with me. But I can sketch her for you, as she was at seventeen. Meet me in the drawing room after you have finished packing."

Grace didn't need long to pack, as the list of what was permitted was far shorter than the list of prohibited items. Simple, modest, drab clothes – that was easy, since she lived in a succession of sober grey skirts, with white shirtwaists, topped with a dark jacket tailored for easy movement. Even with all the other minor items required – undergarments, nightdress, brush, combs, hair pins, hat, handkerchiefs, and so on – everything fitted into a single valise.

The hair pins might be a problem, since sharp items were prohibited, but she left them in anyway, as her long hair would be uncontrollable without them. The hat pins were set aside, along with her lovely red shawl. Anything bright and cheerful was discouraged, which seemed rather counterintuitive when so many of the women would be suffering from melancholia, but Grace wasn't about to risk losing the shawl again.

She hesitated when it came to choosing titles for her small allocation of reading material. While it would have been useful to use the time to revise her anatomy and physiology, that would not fit with her cover story. Reluctantly, she opted for a collection of worthy poetry and a dull novel with a morally uplifting theme.

Finally, Grace slipped a photograph of her family into the depths of her valise and added a notebook and pencil, being careful to ensure than no item was labelled with her real name or other identifying information. Without a doubt, her possessions would be searched for prohibited items. With that in mind, she discarded the lock picks and small, folding knife, which were bound to be discovered.

Lily knocked on her door as she was squeezing the valise shut.

"I thought this might be useful, Grace." Lily held out what appeared to be a pouch with long ties. "I use it when I wish to carry my valuables safely. It ties around your waist and sits under your skirt at the front, where a pickpocket cannot get to it."

"Ingenious. With a little padding, it might make me look pregnant. I had planned to say I was less than three months gone, so there is no chance of my deception being discovered, but a little roundness wouldn't go amiss even so."

"If they find the padding, won't that make them suspicious?"

"Surely they wouldn't make me strip off my clothes in front of them?" Grace pondered the options, before concluding that anything was possible in an asylum. Privacy was not a commodity they would set much store by. "I have the very thing!"

She rummaged in the back of her bottom drawer, pulling out a small, padded circle of material, embroidered with "By Grace Are Ye Saved". Their kindly neighbour, Mrs Patterson, had made it for her, but she had never found a use for it before. If she had been a better person, she would have displayed it on her dressing table, but the colour put her in mind of festering wounds. If she unpicked the side seam, she might even be able to slip the knife and lock picks inside it.

Lily stuffed the padding into the pouch and tied it around her waist. "Perfect. Just the right amount of bulge."

"And if it is found, I can claim that I am wearing it against my belly to seek divine help for my predicament."

"Dearest Grace, please take care." Lily embraced her with more wiry strength than Grace could have imagined from one so petite. "We are humbled by your courage, especially in the circumstances, when you have little to gain by it."

"I will be fine, I promise. Shall we go back downstairs and see what the others are plotting?"

114

Down in the drawing room, Charlie greeted her with a sketch of a girl with smiling eyes, a heart-shaped face, and long, flowing hair. "Her hair is her most distinctive feature. Lily, what colour would you call Amelia's hair?"

"I'm not sure what the correct word for it would be. Pale red-blonde or light auburn?"

"More or less the same colour as your cousin Elizabeth's hair," Charlie added.

Lucky Amelia, Grace thought. Elizabeth had pale golden hair, with strands of darker red-gold, which was much admired by men and envied by women. "Distinguishing features? Eye colour? Height?"

"Bright blue eyes, pale lashes. About your height. Thin build, rather fragile looking. I suppose one would call her small-boned and delicate. I don't recall any moles or scars or anything like that. She used to wear big hats and clothes that covered as much as possible, to protect her pale skin."

"Voice? Mannerisms?"

"She had a soft voice and a sweet laugh. Educated – nice round vowels – not like some of the children from the rougher end of town. Ladylike mannerisms, I suppose. Not one to burst into raucous laughter or prop her elbows on the table. Honestly, I cannot think of anything else that was distinctive."

He might as well have said that Amelia was everything that she was not. "Thank you, Charlie, that's a good start. She will no doubt have changed over six years." She didn't add "especially after all she has been through", but she could tell he was thinking it too.

Without doubt, Charlie had shared a strong bond with Amelia, his pretty, sweet-natured, devoted friend, but she wasn't about to let that stop her from helping him when he needed it, regardless of the consequences for herself if Amelia was alive. Besides, if he really preferred golden-haired, fragile, ladylike women, then he would never see Grace as more than a friend and fellow sleuth.

"Have you changed much since then, Charlie? I mean, would she recognise you now?"

115

He appeared startled by the question. "I don't know. Aunt Lily, have I changed much since I was seventeen?"

"My dear nephew, I hardly recognise you myself and I saw you two years ago. No one would mistake you for a callow youth anymore and I expect few would wish to risk taking you on in a fight." Lily turned to Grace to explain. "Charlie was as skinny as a fishing pole when he was a lad and not too much taller than me until he was about fifteen. But, my goodness, how he made up for it after that."

"Aunt Lily, I'm sure you're exaggerating. I haven't changed that much, have I, Grace?"

"Not in character or fundamentals, but I have to agree with Lily that you have gained an air of authority that few would care to argue with. Not surprising, given the company you keep."

Stewart looked up from his perusal of Charlie's notes. "I will take that as a compliment. It's been my honour to push Pyke to the limit and beyond. Very character building."

Charlie grunted. "I'm sure nothing builds character like going undercover amongst violent agitators and anarchists."

"Would you prefer to go back to your days of breaking up drunken brawls under your old sergeant?" Stewart sat back, twirling his moustache with a satisfied smirk. "Or perhaps you would prefer a job as a desk clerk, taking statements from little old ladies who have misplaced their handkerchiefs?"

"Gentlemen, if I might interrupt, I believe we still have work to do." Grace filed the picture of Amelia into her memory and handed the original on to Stewart. "Charlie, do you have a description of the kidnapper – Doctor Josiah, alias Josiah Cowper? The message Isabelle passed on to me said he was still alive, which suggests he has been seen in the vicinity recently."

Charlie shrugged. "I never met Cowper. The description I was given when we were searching for him could have applied to a large proportion of the men in Dunedin. Brown hair, blue eyes, average height and build. He would be somewhere between about thirty and forty years old by now."

"Not much to go on. After six years, Cowper could be grey-haired, fat, bearded and unrecognisable."

They spent the next hour memorising the layout of the asylum and discussing contingency plans, until Grace was ready to collapse into bed.

Charlie followed her to the base of the stairs, out of earshot of the others. "I have a bad feeling about this case."

"What is worrying you, Charlie?"

"I'm not sure. Perhaps it is just that we have so little evidence to work with, along with the fact that I haven't been thinking clearly since I arrived in Dunedin. Missing you in Christchurch, then thinking you were dead and now … everything else."

"I'm sorry if I have stirred up a fuss over a straightforward accident, when you are so in need of a few days of rest and recuperation. Hearing that Amelia might be alive must have been the final straw."

"Grace, I lost one dear friend when I failed to read the evidence correctly. I could not bear to lose another. This entire plan seems overly hasty. I am concerned that I might have missed something crucial."

"What is it about the evidence that is prickling your instincts?"

"It's the little things, I suppose, such as the discrepancies in reports of the doctor's character and the fact that his bag was not found on the train."

"I wish I had taken more note of my surroundings when I went into the first-class carriage. Doctor Wilson was already standing when I came through the door, so I never got close enough to his seat to see if he had a bag. I tried to stop him, but he told me to step aside so he could do his job. He pushed past me quite roughly. That's all I recall."

"You didn't see him when he got on the train?"

Grace closed her eyes and visualised the stop at Waitati station. "You're right, I did! I recall thinking that he must be a professional man, as he was carrying an expensive-looking leather case."

"If the train guard didn't find it at the end of the journey, someone in the first-class carriage must have taken it."

117

"I don't like where this is heading, Charlie."

"We must face the possibility. The most likely candidate is Doctor McLeod. I fear I have just made a terrible error of judgement, relying on him to get me a position at Stillwaters."

Grace felt a dreadful sinking feeling in her gut. "McLeod was the one who gave me a referral to Stillwaters too. We had better hope that he is on the side of the angels, or our cover will be in tatters before we step through the gates."

"What do you know of McLeod?"

"He is well regarded, an excellent lecturer and practitioner. I believe he trained in Edinburgh, or perhaps I am making assumptions based on his accent. I cannot believe he would have any reason to take Doctor Wilson's bag. He hardly knows the man and only has the most tenuous of links with Stillwaters. Far more likely that nobody thought to look under the seat or someone else took it, meaning to hand it in at Dunedin station."

"We only have McLeod's word for his relationship with Wilson and his links with Stillwaters. I wish we could have questioned the other first-class passengers, to see if the two talked to each other on the journey. I'll have a word with Stewart. Don't be surprised if we decide to postpone the mission until we have checked McLeod's background."

Into The Unknown

Charlie watched Jane Bennet and her father board the first-class carriage of the early train. Uncertainty nibbled away at his intestines at the thought of how vulnerable she would be at Stillwaters, especially if her true identity was known. For the hundredth time, he wished he hadn't let Stewart and Grace talk him into proceeding with such a reckless plan.

As he settled onto the hard bench seat in second class, he had to admit that Grace looked the part. She had worn sombre clothes, with a high-necked shirtwaist and drab jacket, even adding a veil to her hat to cover her face. One might have assumed she was in mourning, had not shame oozed from every pore of her body, from the slumped shoulders, to the hanging head, to the slight bulge at her slim waist. Even if she had been a stranger, if he hadn't known of her inner courage, his heart would have gone out to her the instant he saw her being dragged up the steps into the first-class carriage by her hard-faced father.

The train pulled out right on schedule. Time to focus on his own role. It was all very well to pretend to be an experienced asylum attendant, but the reality was likely to be less straightforward. He hoped that, as a new member of staff, he would be told exactly what to do. Surely he would not be trusted to administer medication or treatments in his first few days? If they hadn't found any trace of Amelia by then, he would have Grace and himself out of that place before they could notice anything amiss.

"Sir? What station, please?"

The train guard leaned forward, as if he was about to shake him. The volume of his question and the pursed lips under his bushy moustache told him that it wasn't the first time the guard had asked for his destination.

"My apologies. I must have been daydreaming. I'm going to Stillwaters Sanctuary. Would that be Waitati station or do they have their own stop?"

"Waitati. It's not but a couple of miles away from Stillwaters." The guard took his money, rustling in his satchel for the correct change. "Normally it's only young ladies and their fathers who get off there." He sized up Charlie with world-weary eyes. "Are you sure you have the right place?"

Charlie nodded. "I'm about to start as an attendant. You must have seen a good many young women stop there in your time."

"More than I can count."

"Do they ever give you any trouble?"

The guard handed him a ticket. "Most of them are timid as lambs going to the slaughter, if you'll pardon the expression. The occasional loony one kicks up a fuss, but never anything I can't handle. Not like some of the crazies we are forced to transport to Seacliff Asylum, wrapped in those restraining jackets. That lot come with police guards, of course, or we wouldn't allow them on board with decent folks."

When the guard passed on down the carriage, Charlie closed his eyes to avoid any further conversations while he was thinking. He jerked awake again at the squeal of brakes. After a moment of disorientation, he spotted the station sign and scrambled to pull his bag from under the seat. He was in such a hurry to disembark that he knocked into a man wheeling a trolley that rattled with bottles. The man gave him a disgruntled scowl, before heading towards a cart emblazoned with a Saratoga Hotel sign.

For a small station, it seemed a hive of activity. Sacks of flour and oats, casks, crates of bottles and boxes of foodstuffs were being wheeled to an unmarked cart, outnumbering by far the items of luggage for the few disembarking passengers. A woman in a dark grey outfit, tailored to fit her sturdy figure, was ticking items off as they were unloaded.

The train guard walked across the platform to her. Their greeting was brief but cordial. The guard handed her a package, flicked his head towards Charlie, and pointed to where Stewart was helping Grace out of the first-class carriage. Then the guard hurried about his business, while the woman headed towards Mr and Miss Bennet with a purposeful stride, causing poor little Miss Bennet to startle and grip even more tightly to her father's arm.

Meanwhile, the milling crowd trickled away, as the guard shouted "All aboard" and chivvied the last of the passengers onto the train. With a blast of his whistle and a wave of his flag, he leaped aboard as the locomotive belched its way to life. It picked up speed gradually, chugging along the seaside causeway, so close to the mirror of the sea that it appeared as if there were two trains.

When Charlie approached Grace's group, he heard the woman introduce herself to Stewart as Matron Roberts, using the brisk tone of a woman who is sure of her place in the world. However, her voice was warm and caring when she addressed Grace.

"You must be Miss Bennet. Welcome to Stillwaters Sanctuary, my dear. We pride ourselves on being a place of calm contemplation for young ladies who seek to restore their spirits in times of personal challenge. Come, our buggy awaits." Matron turned and caught Charlie's eye for an instant.

A blink was all the sign of recognition he got, but he nodded his head politely in return. "May I take the young lady's luggage, sir?"

Stewart inclined his head the slightest amount possible to indicate his assent and walked past Charlie without a word. Grace's veil twitched, but she gave no other sign of recognising his presence. As a policeman, he had become used to expecting a modicum of respect, or at least grudging attention. This new role seemed more akin to servitude. Nevertheless, he picked up the valise and followed the party to the waiting buggy, where he deposited the bag on the luggage rack.

When Stewart tried to give him a coin, he said, "Oh no, sir, that is not necessary," and moved a few respectful paces away.

"I will be with you in a moment," Matron said to Stewart, before shifting her attention to Charlie. "You are the new attendant, Mr Pearce?"

121

"Yes, Matron." He found himself slipping back into the role of a third-class constable on his first posting, standing to attention, awaiting orders, although Matron struck him as more of a strict motherly type than the institutional equivalent of a sergeant-major.

"You'll do well here, Pearce. We value good manners and a professional attitude. You were at Seacliff Asylum?"

"Yes, Matron."

"You will find Stillwaters a great deal easier. We have no violent lunatics here, only young ladies and a few gentlemen who struggle to cope in the outside world. Our young ladies are vulnerable and prone to flights of fancy. You will treat them with absolute respect at all times. Any untoward behaviour will not be tolerated. Do you understand?"

"Perfectly, Matron."

"Then I welcome you to your new role, Mr Pearce. Please go with the cart and present yourself at the staff entrance. Ask for the Head Attendant, Mr Quigley."

Charlie helped load the last of the supplies into the cart. The buggy was already well ahead of them, throwing up dust on the narrow road, which meandered around the inlet. Matron had the reins, thereby reinforcing his view of her as a competent woman who did what was needed to get the job done. The sort of person he would find easy to work with, especially given her kindness to the new patient.

He climbed up beside the driver, an older man with weather-hardened skin. "Charlie Pearce, new attendant." He extending his hand, which the driver shook with a calloused paw.

"Bartholomew Yates. Call me Bart. The only person who calls me Mr Yates is my mother-in-law, and only when she is in a temper. I'm Head Groundsman, which means stableman, gardener, odd jobber and general lackey."

The driver's words might have been self-deprecating, but his tone was cheery. "Is Stillwaters a decent place to work then, Bart?"

"Better 'n most, I dare say, so long as you follow the rules and keep your nose clean. I have the groundsman's cottage and a couple of lads to help me, which is more than other positions would offer. The inmates – that is to say, the patients – are supposed to help, but most of them are worse than useless."

"All part of their treatment regime, I expect. Do the women patients help too?"

"Not sure you could call it help exactly. They gather flowers for the indoor arrangements mostly. One or two are keen gardeners, who know their weeds from their perennials. Not that I have anything to do with them, mind. The women have set hours in the gardens and none of the male staff are allowed to be there when they are let loose. One of my cheekier lads got caught peeking once and he was out on his ear in a minute flat."

"My great-aunt asked me to look out for a patient. Her whist partner's second cousin's daughter, or some such obscure connection. Amelia, her name is."

"Don't ring no bells with me, lad. But then it wouldn't."

"I tried to tell my great-aunt that I would be unlikely to see any of the women patients, let alone speak to them. But, great-aunts are not put off by practicalities, are they?"

The driver let out a bark of laughter. "Indeed not. One might sooner stop a bull by waving a red rag at it."

"I'd take the bull any day," Charlie agreed. "How many do they have on staff at Stillwaters?"

"Well, I couldn't rightly say. Outside, there is the farm manager and a couple of lads, to look after the dairy and livestock. We produce as much of our food as possible. Inside is not my place. There's Superintendent Gresham, Matron Roberts, the Head Attendant, Quigley, and not more than a dozen attendants at a guess, plus the laundry maids, cook and scullery maids. I know the laundry maid and she told me the patients were expected to help with the chores, so the staff is not as large as you might expect."

The road had left the flats and was winding around a hillside. Soon, they parted way with the public road, which itself was not much more than a broad track leading to a scattering of fishermen's cottages.

A sign warned them that they were now on private property, trespassers prosecuted.

Amongst the trees, Charlie could see the eaves of a large building, which had the look of a grand mansion. Probably the former home of one of the many wealthy men whose fortunes had suffered during the depression. Plenty of fancy homes to be had at a good price now that wool prices were so low.

Before they could emerge from the trees, Bart turned the cart onto a track leading around the back of the property.

"Tradesman's entrance for us, lad. The inmates may be crazy, but they still get to go through the front door. Best not forget that."

A high wall surrounded the house. The track led to a tall, spiked gate, no doubt matched by an equally formidable gate at the main entrance. Even with his climbing skills, he would struggle to get over the wall without help, with so few toeholds on the smooth surface. He would have to scout for overhanging trees. Otherwise, there would be no way out if things got rough, except to get a message to Stewart.

The gate opened as they approached, revealing the high façade of the mansion beyond. Two storeys of grey brick, rendered almost black by the accumulated moss and rampant ivy flourishing in the deep shade. The house must have been designed to face the sun and the sea view, while the gloomy rear side was strictly utilitarian.

"Looks more like a house of horrors from this side, but she's a right grand old dame from the front." Bart said. "Shame I couldn't take you in that way."

"Must have been quite something in its heyday. Too good for an asylum."

"Best not use that word around here, lad. They prefer to call it a sanctuary."

Charlie's eyes were drawn to another substantial building in the rear corner of the walled area of the sanctuary, barely visible over the high hedge around it.

"Coach house and stables," Bart said. "Off limits to everyone except authorised staff. The orchard, farm and farm buildings lie

124

beyond, on the other side of the wall, which you can get to through the back gate."

"I've seen less security in some gaols. Is the front gate manned all the times?"

"Night and day. The guard patrols the grounds too. It's not so much that they are worried about patients trying to escape. Patients who aren't right in the noggin tend to wander if they're not kept under tight control. Wouldn't want them fancy moppets coming to harm. Years back, before the place was secure, one of them drowned in the sea and another stepped in front of the Christchurch express."

"What happens if somebody arrives at the gate while the guard is patrolling?"

"Never happens. Everyone who comes here arrives by train and is picked up at the station at a set time."

Bart pulled the horse to a halt near the rear entrance to the main building. Two men in farm clothes knocked out their pipes and stepped forward to unload the provisions from the cart.

Charlie touched the brim of his cap. "Much obliged for the grand tour, Bart. Hope to see you around."

"A pleasure. You'll do well here, lad. I could tell that Matron approved of you."

"I hope the Superintendent and Head Attendant feel the same."

"Quigley's a decent enough chap." Bart leaned closer to Charlie, making sure the other two men had gone inside the house before he spoke. "Gresham's a couple of pints short of a gallon, if you ask me, but don't worry, you won't have much to do with him. I'd advise you not to get on the wrong side of him though. He may look as if he is away with the fairies, but don't be fooled by appearances."

Charlie shivered in the cool shadow of the house. He jumped off the cart with his canvas bag over his shoulder, grabbing a sack of oats off the back of the cart as he went.

Bart got down too, to help with the unloading. "Wipe your boots before you go in or Matron will have your guts for garters."

125

Charlie wiped his boots twice and entered, his pulse kicking up a notch at the thought of what lay on the other side. Charlie pictured Grace walking through the front door, her countenance projecting her usual quiet confidence, while her gut churned with nervous tension. He would never forgive himself if any harm came to her.

Sanctuary

Miss Bennet and her father journeyed in silence to the front entrance, where a discreet plaque set into the stone gatepost simply said "Stillwaters". A trespasser, had there been one in this secluded spot, would have no idea that this was a registered lunatic asylum, albeit a private establishment catering to a better class of troubled patients.

Grace knew the building would be large, from her glimpse through the trees from the train. What she hadn't expected was the imposing majesty with which the building rose above them. While it was nothing like the enormous Gothic splendour of Seacliff Asylum, it definitely projected an air of stately home rather than institution.

The carriageway looped around a landscaped knoll to a set of steps, leading up to a terrace set between the side wings of the main house. Two storeys of elegant grey brick dwarfed the massive arch of the central door, with the grandeur heightened by large bay windows on the end of each wing and the steep roof rising behind the gothic arches of the upper windows.

If it wasn't for the intimidating walls and the guard at the gatehouse, she could almost imagine that she was visiting a country estate for a few days of social flummery. Not that she ever attended such frivolous diversions.

Matron Roberts smiled with proprietorial pride at their wide-eyed gawking. With an expert touch on the reins, the buggy slowed to a halt beside the broad steps up to the entrance. A young lad took hold of the horse's bridle.

"Please be ready to take Mr Bennet back to the train, Zachary." Matron took Grace's arm and guided her up the steps. "Miss Bennet's valise will be collected momentarily, Mr Bennet."

Stewart had been waiting by the buggy, unsure whether he was expected to carry it himself. With a grunt, he followed the two women.

Once they reached the terrace, Matron turned Grace to face the view, lifting her veil with all the gentleness of a mother soothing a frightened child. "You have no need to hide here, Miss Bennet. Let the walls be your veil. Open your heart to beauty."

Grace absorbed the sweeping view across the lawns, to the flower-laden shrubs shielding the tall wall, which no longer seemed a prison to keep her in, but a barrier to keep the world out. Beyond the wall, she could see the sparkling waters of the inlet, framed by trees, with not another dwelling in sight.

The tranquillity of the place made her forget her melancholic role. Her shoulders straightened as she took in a breath of nature's air, fresh with the scent of flowers and the tang of salt water.

Matron stepped back, casting a satisfied glance at her newest patient. For one panic-filled moment, Grace wondered if Matron knew she was a fraud, but Matron was smiling.

"I can tell that your daughter is already feeling the powerful healing properties of Stillwaters Sanctuary, Mr Bennet."

"It is a fine prospect, I grant you, Matron."

The door opened as they walked up the steps, suggestive of an arrival at an exclusive hotel. Grace doubted such hospitality would be extended to any patient attempting to exit the door in the opposite direction.

Once they had passed over the flagstones of the lobby, a great hall opened out before them, with polished parquet floors and glowing wood panelling. While the hall looked grand enough for a ball, it was set with long tables and benches, of the functional type found in all institutions.

"What a splendid hall, Matron," Stewart said. "One might almost use the floor as a mirror."

"Beeswax and turpentine is the secret, Mr Bennet. We pride ourselves on maintaining a superior standard at Stillwaters."

Matron dropped her cloak into the cloakroom off the lobby, retrieving a chunky set of keys on an iron ring from a locked cabinet.

On the other side of her belt, she fastened a chatelaine, dangling what appeared to be a set of large silver charms.

Grace edged closer and realised they were all practical items: a whistle, a watch, a number of smaller keys, and two small containers. In an ordinary household, these boxes would be for sundry small items, such as matches or a needle and thread. Here, Grace imagined they might contain anything from pills to miniature thumbscrews. Best to not let her imagination run riot, she decided.

With all that weight of responsibility, it was just as well Matron was a sturdy woman with a rigid spine, although she was not much taller than Grace. She was younger than Grace would have expected for such a role – probably not much more than thirty years old, which suggested that she was highly competent, or ambitious, or both. A woman to admire, but at the same time a woman to watch, despite the evidence of her compassion. With all those keys, one could at least hear her coming – something Grace felt sure that both the patients and staff appreciated.

The few visible members of staff straightened up and stood to attention as Matron passed. She gave each of them a fractional nod. She lingered for a moment at one man, lifting her finger briefly to the base of her throat. Instantly, he straightened his tie, before clicking his heels. Her own attire, of course, was perfectly pressed, with not a stitch out of place.

Matron waved her hand at the cavernous space which opened out before them on the other side of the lobby. "The great hall is used as dining room, meeting hall and church, as well as for occasional entertainments. My office and the library are at the rear of the building, while Superintendent Gresham's office is at the front." She turned to Grace with a tight smile that did not reach her eyes. "You will notice two sets of stairs, Miss Bennet. The one to the right is for women only, the one to the left is for men."

"You have male patients here too?" Stewart allowed a tremor to creep into his voice.

"Only a small number of carefully selected men. It is useful to have men to tend to the work in the kitchen garden."

"But they are suffering maladies of the mind?"

"They are all well behaved, Mr Bennet, I assure you. None have violent tendencies. Indeed, our men tend to suffer from undue meekness, which leads them to struggle with the rigours of colonial life."

"Are all the patients expected to work? My daughter is used to having a ladies' maid to tend to her needs."

"We find patients fare a great deal better when they are kept occupied, Mr Bennet. The ladies, naturally, are not expected to undertake manual labour, although we do encourage healthful fresh air. Some of our ladies are fond of flower gardening and that is encouraged, along with needlecraft and the like."

Matron raised an eyebrow at the open door of superintendent's office. "It would appear that Superintendent Gresham wishes to greet you personally." She directed them into a large office with a view over the terrace. "Mr Bennet and Miss Bennet have arrived."

Gresham rose from behind a vast desk to shake Mr Bennet's hand. "Welcome, welcome. I knew as soon as we met in Dunedin that our services were the perfect match for your needs." He turned to Grace with a disconcertingly intense stare. "I have every confidence, Miss Bennet, that you will return to society refreshed and reborn from your stay here."

His words struck Grace as odd, but they were strangely compelling delivered in his rich baritone. The real question was whether the words reflected the genuine enthusiasm of a believer or the honeyed deceptions of a first-class charlatan. Time would tell. Hopefully, not too much time. Her acting abilities were insufficient to maintain the façade of a repentant fallen women for more than a few days.

She wasn't sure what to reply, but Matron stepped in with brisk efficiency.

"Quite so, Superintendent Gresham. We won't take up any more of your time." Matron herded them towards the door.

"Matron, if I might have a quick word?"

Her nostrils flared for an instant, before she turned with a pleasant smile to the Bennets. "Do excuse me for a moment. Perhaps you would like to look around the great hall and library. I will be back with you shortly."

They exited like obedient sheep, but circled back to linger by the door.

"What can I do for you, Horace?" Matron's voice was tight with suppressed frustration, as if dealing with a fractious child.

"Bertha, I hope you have remembered that the ladies from the Magdalene Charitable Mission have their monthly visit next Monday. Please ask Cook to provide tea and cakes. If they ask about the incident on the train, you must reassure them that the girl had been discharged as expected at the end of her stay and that her death was a tragic accident with no connection to Stillwaters."

"Yes, Horace. Might I suggest that you take charge of them. They won't ask questions if you flatter them with your charms and allow them to practise their philanthropy. I will gather a few of the less excitable patients for a lesson in flower-arranging, followed by a hymn or two. That usually does the trick."

"Excellent idea, Bertha."

"The Trustee's meeting is scheduled for next Thursday," Matron Roberts continued. "I will prepare the agenda items for their approval. We simply cannot continue without an additional trained nurse. The matter of the replacement doctor is even more urgent."

"We must pre-empt the Trustees by having a candidate selected and ready to start. Let us hope we can find a doctor more suitable for the role than the last one."

"I have already attended to it. The letter is in your basket, ready for your signature. Can I remind you that there is a new male attendant arriving this morning, who will no doubt be eager to hear your thoughts on the philosophy of Stillwaters. I have great hopes that he will be better than the last one. He appears to have a pleasant, helpful attitude, which makes an agreeable change."

131

Matron lowered her voice, so that Grace could only just make out the words. "He has a physique well suited to restraining difficult cases. But be sure to tell Quigley to keep him away from our lady patients. The last thing I need is a dozen silly girls swooning and hitting their heads."

Grace stifled a laugh and noticed Stewart doing the same. They slunk away to examine the paintings in the great hall – a row of starchy men depicted by a competent, but uninspired, artist. Past trustees of the charity which oversaw Stillwaters, in all their bewhiskered pomp.

"Shall I take your arm, Miss Bennet," Stewart whispered, "in case the new attendant appears and you feel the urge to swoon?"

Grace smothered a chuckle, just as Matron came up behind her. Right on cue, Charlie and another man appeared from the opposite direction, from the men's entrance to the great hall.

Charlie nodded politely as he passed, but otherwise gave no sign of recognition, beyond a glance that lasted a fraction of a second too long. Grace forced herself to pretend he did not exist, in that haughty way she imagined young ladies might use in the presence on a lowly servant one wished to ignore.

Philosophy

Charlie had been directed through a maze of utility rooms to the office of Mr Quigley, the Head Attendant, a middle-aged man with the face of a bloodhound. Morose eyes registered his presence, but the effort of smiling appeared beyond the capability of his facial muscles, which were working hard to keep his jowls from dragging on his neck.

"Pearce, is it? I'm told you came from Seacliff Asylum. Thanks heavens for small mercies, for I have no time to train another useless young wastrel." He eyed Charlie up, then opened a cupboard and flipped through a rack of uniforms. "Biggest we've got. Change next door."

Charlie donned the dark blue serge jacket and trousers over his own plain waistcoat, white shirt and dark tie. The jacket was rather tight across the back, but he could always undo the buttons if he needed to flex his muscles. The trousers needed hitching in at the waist and letting down at the ankle, but they were good enough for the short time they would be needed. He tugged on the peaked cap, feeling more like a tram conductor than a lunatic asylum attendant.

Quigley inspected him with a murmur of approval. He held out a set of service keys, flipping through them at speed. "Side exit, men's dayroom, door into the great hall, men's dormitory, bathroom, secure cells, your room. If you need any other key, see me or Matron. Any questions? No? Super wants to meet you. Follow me."

Charlie followed in silence, resisting the overwhelming urge to reach out and touch Grace as he passed the Bennets in the dining hall. How did she manage to look so serene? And that wickedly haughty dismissal of him, offset by a wink so subtle it might have been an ordinary blink. He clamped his lips together and hurried after his supervisor. Just as well he did, with Matron's eagle eyes on him. He had little doubt that she had sharp talons to match.

133

Superintendent Gresham was far from the impressive figurehead he was expecting. A little below average height, with pale blue eyes, brown hair and a forgettable face, wearing a neat, sombre suit. His little pointed beard was marred by a dribble of egg yolk. He might have been a senior clerk within an important but obscure branch of government, but for the touch of drama from his colourful cravat. The upward tilt of his nose hinted at more than a touch of vanity.

Like Matron, he was younger than Charlie had expected, which suggested either a high degree of competency or an exceptional ability to fake it. When he opened his mouth, Charlie realised why this unprepossessing man had done so well for himself. His voice was like liquid honey, seeping into the listener's ear and compelling their attention.

"Welcome to Stillwaters Sanctuary, Mr Pearce." Gresham waved both arms, like a conductor directing his orchestra. "I like all new members of my staff to understand the philosophical underpinnings of our mission here at Stillwaters. Moral management of patients, Mr Pearce, with the very highest standard of care. The families who entrust their sons and daughters to us expect no less than the best. We base our patient care on the Truby King model, which you will be familiar with, having worked at Seacliff, although I flatter myself I have made refinements that set my establishment above the rest."

"Yes, sir." What was it that Grace had said about Seacliff? "Fresh air, productive work and a nourishing diet, combined with respectful treatment."

"Precisely. Lunatics should be regarded as objects of tender solicitude, who lack the mental acuity to manage in the outside world. The patients will rely upon you and the other attendants to present a perfect role model of good sense, proper routine, cleanliness, sobriety and strict morality, Mr Pearce. At Stillwaters, we particularly value to power of Our Lord to guide patients to a better life, to the extent that their mental infirmities allow."

"It will be a privilege to serve, Superintendent Gresham."

Charlie wondered if he was laying on the flattery a little too thickly, but Gresham was nodding and smiling. Although he must have

134

given the same speech innumerable times, he made it feel as if it was a gift just for Charlie. The man had missed his calling – he should have been a preacher. Although, given McLeod's comments on the religious focus of the sanctuary, perhaps he was more of a preacher than a doctor. Charlie noted the framed certificate from a foreign university on the wall, but Gresham didn't use the title "doctor".

Having been dismissed with a regal wave, Charlie returned to Mr Quigley's office.

"Glad to see you're still here, Pearce. Just as well, as we're short-staffed, as usual. Superintendent Gresham likes to run a tight ship. Tends to scare off the folk who think working in a lunatic asylum will be an easy ride. Your role is to remain strictly within the men's section of the house and the kitchen garden the men work in during the day. That rule is broken only in emergencies."

"Yes, sir. Do you have many such emergencies?"

"Occasionally one of the women patients will have a grand mal seizure or a sudden rage resulting in a paroxysm of violence, requiring strong male attendants to prevent injury to the woman and those around her. Fortunately, a fairly rare occurrence here. I hope you will be up to the task, Pearce."

"I am well used to it, Mr Quigley. Such events are commonplace at Seacliff."

"Good. As you are experienced, I will give you a quick tour and set you to work, for I have little enough time to spare. Please familiarise yourself with the Rulebook as soon as possible. I have had a copy placed on your bunk."

Quigley only got as far as the corridor, which was filled with a savoury aroma drifting down from the kitchens. "It would appear that it is almost dinner time. Let's put you to work and see how you go. The male patients will need to be supervised while changing out of their boots and washing up before they eat. A couple of them are feeble-minded, but usually the other patients help them if need be."

Reality

Matron took Grace and Stewart into a long, high-windowed dayroom running along the west side of the building. The room glowed with the light flooding in through a glass conservatory, which jutted out from centre of the dayroom. A broad bay window on the north side provided a glimpse of the sea, proving that Stillwaters Sanctuary was aptly named. The room was decorated with plants, flowers and framed samplers, embroidered with scripture verses, which gave it a homely feel.

The unexpected sound of laughter greeted them, coming from a group of women rehearsing a play in the centre of the room. Scattered around the rest of the dayroom, young woman were reading, sewing, mending clothes and linen, or simply sitting, contemplating the vibrant flower gardens.

Three dozen eyes flicked in her direction. Although the chatter died away, the rules of good breeding were maintained. Nobody stared, nobody rose to examine the new patient more closely, nobody spoke loudly at her or to each other, and nobody showed the least sign of hysteria.

Matron took in the tranquil scene with a satisfied smile, further convincing Grace that she took pride in running the sanctuary with gentle efficiency. The remaining tension in Grace's body dropped away. So much for Charlie's concern that she might be in danger. From what she had seen so far, the only danger was that she might never wish to leave this haven, to return to the hectic world of medical training.

"Charming," Mr Bennet conceded. He leaned closer to Grace. "And no wonder it's so lovely, with the fees they charge. You won't forget what you are here for, will you Jane?"

"Not a chance, unless they have us all so heavily sedated that I cannot recall the mission."

Grace scanned the room for a fragile young woman with golden hair. Unfortunately, the Scottish heritage of the local populace presented her with a frustratingly wide selection, ranging from red to auburn to blonde, most of whom also had pale skin and delicate bones.

"May I see where my daughter will be sleeping? She is quite sensitive, you understand, and would prefer a quiet room."

"I'm afraid men are not allowed into the dormitory area, not even family. I assure you, Miss Bennet will be entirely comfortable."

"Dormitory?" From Mr Bennet's tone, one might think Matron had said dungeon.

"Nobody has their own room, Mr Bennet. We could not care for so many young women in need if that were so. But you will find that our young ladies come to prefer the company of others. The women's wards are all on the west side of the building, above this dayroom, with a lovely view over the garden. The gentlemen, naturally, are segregated behind locked doors on the other side of the building."

"I should hope so. Well, Matron Roberts, I declare that I am impressed by the pleasant situation you have created here. Might I ask when one may visit?"

"Visiting is by appointment only. Saturday afternoon is the accepted time, although we can be flexible if the situation warrants it. But I would ask that you do not visit for the first month, Mr Bennet, to allow your daughter ample time to settle in to her new routine."

Grace caught the flicker of surprise in Stewart's eyes, but he continued as if unperturbed. Indeed, he managed to look a little relieved, as if a burden had been lifted from his paternal duties.

"She may correspond with her family, I trust? And receive letters from us?"

"Naturally. We suggest new patients write a note at the end of the first week to reassure their parents that all is well. We do reserve the right to monitor the contents of the patients' letters, for their wellbeing." Matron flipped open the silver watch on her chatelaine. "I'm afraid it is time to complete our business here, Mr Bennet, if you wish to catch the train back to Dunedin."

Matron's index finger curled ever so slightly towards a tall, thin woman in the attendant's uniform of a white pinafore over a dark dress, with a starched white collar, cuffs and cap. The woman's sour face tightened at the summons, but she came over promptly.

"Miss Dalloway is the ward sister in charge of supervising your care, Miss Bennet, as she does for all the girls in Dormitory One. Do as she says and all will be well. Mr Bennet, if you would accompany me to my office to finalise the admission documentation."

Mr Bennet patted Grace's shoulder with a complete lack of fatherly love, though Stewart's eyes met hers with a more heartfelt sentiment. "Farewell, Jane. Make your mother proud."

"Farewell, Father. My love to all the family."

Stewart allowed himself a last, regretful look at his sinful daughter, before following Matron to the door without a backward glance, to bestow upon Stillwaters a sinfully large sum of money.

"I do hope you are a sensible girl, Miss Bennet," Miss Dalloway said in a high-pitched, grating voice, dispensed through downturned lips. "All we ask of you is that you pray for forgiveness and adhere rigorously to our rules. Do so and your time will pass without trouble. I advise you not to test my patience with girlish foolishness or unruly behaviour. I assure you that you will not care for the consequences."

"Yes, Miss Dalloway," Grace replied meekly. She gave no sign of objecting to being labelled a foolish girl, at the age of twenty-two, by a woman no more than a decade older. The malicious glee with which Dalloway has emphasised the word "consequences" had Grace imagining manacles and medieval racks.

Grace followed her warder up the stairs and down a short corridor.

"Facilities to your left. Dormitory One to your right. My room is here. I should warn you that I leave the door open and sleep lightly. Girls are not allowed out of the dormitory after bed time. Naturally, I will not countenance any shenanigans or pranks."

Miss Dalloway selected a large key from her collection and opened the door to the dormitory. A row of six narrow beds marched along each of the two long walls, with a narrow aisle in between. The warder stopped at the fourth bed against the inner wall. She made a note in her daybook, before straightening the near-perfect line of the sheet against the counterpane, tucked without a trace of wrinkles. Grace's valise sat, open, on the bed.

"This is your bed, Miss Bennet. You may unpack your valise into the drawers later. I am pleased to note that you followed our guidelines for packing."

Grace was startled that her warder didn't bother to disguise the fact that she had searched the valise. The message could not be clearer – privacy and self-determination were rights she had abandoned at the spiked gate.

"The Rules and Daily Schedule are posted on the dormitory wall by the door. Please read them until you know them by heart. After a day or two, it will seem like second nature." She drew her watch out. "The gong for midday dinner will sound any minute. Time to go back downstairs, Miss Bennet."

Grace trailed after her like a well-trained Labrador, pausing only to glance at the Rules. Within a long list of dos and an even longer list of don'ts, she read "bath once a week, change bath water after no more than four uses" and suppressed a groan. She was inordinately fond of a hot bath at the end of the day. Whatever happened to the concept of cleanliness being next to godliness?

She had no sooner returned to the dayroom when a gong sounded.

Miss Dalloway commandeered a young woman with dark hair and lively eyes, who had been drawing in a sketchbook. "Miss Trelawney will take you to the dining hall."

The Power Of Magic

When the gong for the midday meal sounded, Charlie was told to go and stand by the servery.

In a perfectly choreographed sequence, the servery hatch into the kitchen opened, revealing a tray of spoons and a line of salt and pepper pots, while the door swung open to disgorge two kitchen maids, each wheeling a trolley with two steaming pots and a pile of sliced and buttered bread. Half a dozen women appeared from the other side of the dining hall, led by an attendant. Without a word, they began setting the tables.

The moment the last spoon was placed on the table, a stream of men appeared at one end of the hall and women at the other, taking their places at the tables. The only sound was the hypnotic shuffling of their feet in soft indoor shoes, followed by the scrape of bench legs on parquet. There was no discussion or jostling, leaving Charlie with the impression that the patients sat in the same seat every day. Perhaps such monotonous routine helped them to cope. As for himself, it would drive him mad to do this every day.

Quigley pointed out the empty tables between the male and female patients. "As an attendant, you will supervise and make sure there is no trouble. Once all the meals are served, you may eat at the table closest to the men. The female attendants take the other empty table, thus keeping a degree of segregation between male and female patients. Super, Matron and I, of course, have a separate dining room."

He nodded towards another trolley being wheeled towards a side room. The crystal glasses and fine china, surrounding a dome-topped silver platter, were as clear an indication of the privilege of rank as a row of stripes on an officer's uniform.

Quigley beckoned to another attendant, whose heavily lined face and weary eyes gave the impression of a man who had seen it all and

140

not enjoyed the experience. "Walker, would you show Pearce around the upper floor after lunch."

"Supposed to be my half day, Guv'nor."

"I've no one else to spare, Walker. Make it a quick tour, then you can be off. Once Pearce proves his competence, you may leave early on your next half day."

At a signal unseen by Charlie, the first table of women stood up without a word spoken and formed an orderly queue in front of the serving station. Each woman got a dollop of stew, topped by a spoonful of mashed potato and a slice of bread, thinly spread with butter. As soon as they began shuffling back to their table, the next table rose, including Grace. The various degrees of rounded belly left him in no doubt that this was the group of fallen women.

The third group seemed to hum with supressed energy, like bees trapped in a hive. The final group of women to be served, at the furthest table, were even further along towards the manic end of the scale. Unlike the first three groups, these women were closely escorted by two attendants. Two of the women stayed behind at the table, facing away from the other patients, and had their food brought to them.

The queue shuffled forward with such a mindless sense of humdrum habit that Charlie's mind drifted to other thoughts, as he kept an eye out for golden hair.

Which made it all the more shocking when chaos erupted in the blink of an eye. One second, the kitchen maid was taking a carving knife through to the separate dining room. The next, she was looking down at a bloody hand, while a wide-eyed girl with a crazed grin was left holding the knife. She waved the knife around vaguely, as if not sure what to do next.

One of the female attendants edged towards her. "Beatrice, dear, put down the knife."

Beatrice swung the knife around, stopping the attendant in her tracks.

While her attention was diverted, the other male attendant moved up behind her. With lightning speed, she pirouetted and sidestepped, grabbing him around the throat with one arm, while holding the knife to his throat with the other.

Silence reigned for a fraction of a second, then the captive attendant swore. That set his captor off, spewing forth a string of obscenities that would have made a dock worker blush. A wave of shrieks and gasps and nervous giggles spread across the dining hall, rising to a high-pitched frenzy.

"Quiet!" Quigley yelled. "Sit down, all of you."

The uproar cut off instantly, leaving a subdued hubbub of nervous whispering. The woman holding the knife had nicked the attendant's chin, leaving a trail of blood trickling from his jaw to his collar. The knife wavered perilously close to his jugular.

Quigley touched Charlie's elbow and they stepped forward together.

On the other side, the female attendant tried again to break the stand-off. "Now, Beatrice, Mr Bevan has done nothing to harm you. Why don't you let him go, so you can have your dinner. I'll bet there is apple pie for dessert, your favourite. You wouldn't want to miss that, would you?"

The woman considered it, but the knife stayed within an inch of the death zone. "You're lying. We had apple pie two days ago. I wouldn't feed this slop to pigs."

"Cook could make a pie just for you, if you put down the knife."

Beatrice stamped her feet, causing the knife to jerk up. Another drop of blood formed under the attendant's chin. He looked ready to faint.

Charlie could see that this was not going to end well, unless they could distract Beatrice from whatever was upsetting her. In desperation, he tried an old magic trick that he used on little children when they were playing up.

He took a shiny coin from his pocket and flipped it a few times in the air, until he was sure that Beatrice's eyes were following it. The clamour in the dining hall dropped away. Charlie flipped the coin again, but his time he palmed it, so it appeared to vanish in mid-air. The knife dropped away just a little, as Beatrice's mouth sagged open.

"I'll bet Mr Quigley has a spare coin. What do you think, Beatrice?" Charlie didn't wait for an answer. Instead, he reached behind Quigley's ear and drew out the shiny coin. Then another from the other ear. "Maybe you have a shilling in your ear too, Beatrice."

The knife hand dropped to her side as Beatrice reached behind her ear with her other hand. Charlie stepped forward and pushed the shocked attendant aside, as he produced a coin from her other ear. "Well, look at that, you do have money coming out of your ears."

He waved the coin in front of her, then clasped both of her hands between his, with the coin between them. The knife clattered to the floor, where Quigley scooped it up.

When Charlie opened up her hands again, the coin had vanished. "Money is a bit like that, isn't it Beatrice? It comes and goes. Better to stick with things you can rely on, like a nice plate of stew and potato. Shall we get some?"

Beatrice took the arm he was holding out to her and stepped forward to the servery, as the rest of the patients and staff let out a collective exhalation of breath. The female attendant deputised Beatrice's neighbours at the far table to take her back to her place.

Quigley stepped around the male attendant, who was still sitting on the floor, dripping blood. "Who is saying grace today?" Quigley asked in a commendably calm tone. Nobody answered. "Shall I then?"

By the time they opened their eyes after an extended version of grace, during which thanks was given for the many benefits they enjoyed, the attendant had been taken away for medical attention and calm had been restored, more or less, aside from a minor dispute resulting in an overturned plate.

Across the far side of the hall, a woman in a nurse's uniform returned to her place and resumed her task of filling a row of medicine glasses. The attendants collected these and watched as each patient drained the glass, before returning to their meals.

Beatrice was given a larger dose of whatever it was and drank it down without a qualm. By the time she got to the tapioca pudding, her head was sagging towards the plate. Walker and Pearce were ordered to take her away.

To Good Health

Grace watched the scene unfold from her allotted spot at the dining table between Miss Trelawney and a cheerful woman with hair like teased lambswool. Her training urged her to help the bleeding male attendant, but Miss Trelawney pulled at her arm as soon as she rose from her seat.

"Best to stay out of it. Come on, sit down before you're noticed."

Grace was about to say she wasn't likely to be noticed with all the commotion, but, looking around, she could see it wasn't true. The attendants must have been trained to keep a roving eye on all their charges, no matter what crisis arose to divert their attention.

When Beatrice was subdued, routine was reimposed with startling efficiency, as if such ructions were everyday events. Following the lead of the women at her table, Grace picked up her spoon and dipped into her stew. Although it was a far cry from Lily's delicious stew of the previous evening, it was palatable enough, if rather overcooked and oversalted. Only two patients at the far table required help with feeding, the rest managed well enough on their own.

Meanwhile, the nurse prepared medication, which the attendants carried on silver trays to each table, as if distributing drinks at a soiree. Several of the woman at the table furthest away from the men got a small dose of rust-coloured liquid, with a double dose for Beatrice. All the patients dutifully drained the glass. However, the moment the attendant turned her back, a copper-haired woman spat the liquid out into the remnants of her stew and pushed the plate away with a smug grin.

Every other patient received a dose of another liquid, which was the colour of lemon juice but moved in the glass with oily viscosity. Grace was hoping that her table would be exempt, but a small glass of

145

pale chartreuse liquid was soon plonked in front of every patient at her table, in addition to the oily one.

"You're the new girl?" the attendant asked, as she held out the second glass. "Dorm one, bed four?"

"Yes." Grace was the fourth bed along the back row, so that made sense, although it vexed her to be referred to by number rather than name. "What is this?"

"Just you drink it up and stop asking silly questions."

"Please, I am not trying to be difficult. I'm new here. I don't want to take anything that might harm my baby."

The attendant rolled her eyes. "One's a tonic to build up your strength, the other is castor oil to facilitate the digestion."

Under the unwavering gaze of the attendant, Grace had no choice but to drink the foul duo down, although she came within a whisker of bringing them back up again. One could only hope Stillwaters had an adequate supply of lavatories if they dispensed castor oil regularly, regardless of need.

The pleasant sense of being in a sanctuary was evaporating rapidly, as the harsher side of life inside Stillwaters became apparent. She wondered if they had made the dayroom such a lovely space to impress the fee-paying guardians, who would go home blissfully unaware of the realities of their daughter's incarceration. No wonder Isabelle had been so desperate to get herself and her unborn baby away.

By the end of the meal, the purpose of the medication was obvious, as Beatrice's head sagged ever closer to her pudding. As Grace had suspected, the rust-coloured liquid was laudanum. She stifled her outrage that several women at that table were being given a sedative, when only one had shown signs of needing calming. No doubt the resulting tranquillity made life easier for the attendants, but what of the long-term harm to the patients?

Beatrice was taken away by Charlie and another attendant.

"What will happen to her, Miss Trelawney?" Grace asked her neighbour.

"Do call me Lizzie. Miss Trelawney belongs to another girl in another life."

The woman on the other side of Grace answered her question, despite her mouthful of tapioca. "They'll put her in a padded cell to teach her the error of her ways. I'm Fluff, by the way."

"It's unusual for Beatrice to act up," Lizzie added. "Perhaps she missed her medication this morning or spat it out. Don't try that by the way, as the attendants keep a close watch and you will be in big trouble if you are caught."

The mix of castor oil, stew and tapioca sat uneasily in Grace's stomach as her mind churned with her first impressions of the sanctuary. The sooner she found out what she wanted to know, the sooner she could be home again. She pushed down the regret that, had she taken the express train, she would now be spending the day paddling in the sea and eating ice cream in the sunshine with Charlie, none the wiser about any of it.

After today's display of gentle persuasion via magic, she suspected half the women in Stillwaters would be dreaming of him tonight. Indeed, Charlie was the sole topic of conversation as they finished their meal. With the segregation of men and women, there was little chance she – or any of the other women – would be able to talk to him, unless she took drastic action with a knife. Always good to know there was a last resort to get his attention, if a dozen other women didn't think of it first.

When the meal was over, she joined the line to wash her bowls and spoon, noting that all the cutlery was carefully counted. Grace wasn't sure what damage she could do with a spoon, but apparently they weren't taking any chances.

"This way, Miss Bennet." Miss Dalloway chivvied her up the stairs. "Don't dawdle, girl, it's time for your health check."

Grace was of the firm opinion that medicine was far more agreeable for the doctor than the patient, but, whatever the health check involved, she was unlikely to have any choice in the matter. Finally, two days too late, the enormity of what she had let herself in for hit home. As an asylum patient, she had few of the rights she could expect in ordinary life. Her mind and body were now ruled by the holders of keys, who may or may not have ill-intent.

Miss Dalloway ushered her into the medical room, closing the door behind her, leaving Grace alone with the nurse who had been in the dining hall. She was busy removing bottles from a dumb-waiter and stacking them in a cupboard. A selection of spoons, droppers and measuring glasses sat by the sink.

"Take your clothes off, please. There is a gown on the bed by the window." The nurse's voice was brisk, but by no means harsh. "Excuse me, I will be back in a moment."

As soon as the nurse disappeared into the office attached to the medical room, Grace took the opportunity to inspect the open cupboard, identifying such large quantities of castor oil and Epsom salts that her bowel went into an involuntary spasm. There also appeared to be gallons of a patent tonic, which was a combination of herbs and mineral supplements. The highest shelf contained enough bromide, laudanum and chloral to stupefy half of Dunedin.

Grace palmed a couple of items that might prove useful later, before undressing quickly, being careful to fold the padded pouch and stolen items within her skirt.

The nurse reappeared with a file clutched in her hands. She was wearing a similar uniform to the female attendants, but with a light blue dress in place of their severe black, under a white pinafore. She put the last of the bottles on the shelf and locked the cupboard, pulling on the handle to ensure it was properly secure. Cupboards ran all along one side of the room. Stillwaters appeared to be as well stocked as a small hospital.

"Now, who do we have here?" The nurse opened the file. "Miss Jane Bennet, age twenty-two, coming up for three months gone. Is that correct?"

"Yes, nurse." Grace was reassured by her competent manner, despite her youth. With a sweet smile and rosy cheeks, there seemed no reason to be afraid.

"I am Sister Jones. I will deal with all your medical needs and assist the midwife at your delivery. Any serious complications will be seen by the visiting doctor." A frown tugged her eyebrows together for a moment. "But you seem like a healthy young woman, so I am sure you will get along just fine. Lie on the bed, please."

The nurse gathered a few instruments together and came over to the window. In the sunlight, her blonde hair gleamed with a few threads of gold.

"Have you been here long, Sister Jones?" Grace asked.

"Some days it seems like forever, but I suppose it is only a few years. Let's have a look at you, shall we?"

The nurse took her pulse, examined her eyes and skin tone, and palpitated her abdomen. "Too early to feel the baby. Are sure you are pregnant, Miss Bennet?"

"Yes, Sister Jones. I haven't had my monthlies since … since that man forced me …"

A flicker of sympathy passed over the nurse's face. "Yes, I understand, my dear. Have you noticed changes in your body or felt unwell at all?"

"My corset is too tight. I think my …" Grace swept a hand vaguely above her chest area. "They seem to have grown. And they ache."

"Nothing to worry about. That is perfectly normal. Any nausea?"

"A little, but only in the morning. I feel hungry, but I cannot stand the smell or taste of some of my favourite foods. I was ill in the drawing room after taking a sherry, in front of guests. Mother was very cross, but I couldn't help it."

"Mothers sometimes forget what it was like for them. All women go through a similar phase. It will get easier as the child grows."

"What will happen to my baby when it is born?"

"That will be for your family to decide. I advise you not to worry about such things. Your role is to concentrate on keeping yourself and your baby healthy. Proper eating, a little gentle exercise, and plenty of rest. Above all, you must maintain an untroubled mind."

Little chance of that, Grace thought. No wonder only novels with gentle, uplifting themes were allowed. She wondered what would have happened if she had tried to sneak in a copy of *Dracula* or, worse still, a copy of the book that had so scandalised England last year, *Tess of the d'Urbervilles.*

"I'm scared. I never wanted to have a baby. I just wish it would go away."

"Hush now, Miss Bennet. That is up to God. But know that the power of prayer is strong here at Stillwaters Sanctuary. I advise you to attend the sessions conducted by Superintendent Gresham. You will be amazed and uplifted by his ability to direct the benevolent gaze of our Saviour upon our humble souls. Knees apart, Miss Bennet. We must attend to the physical as well as the spiritual, must we not?"

Fortunately, at that moment the door swung open and two women staggered in, saving Grace from further indignities.

One of the women was clutching her massively swollen belly and moaning. The other was a plump woman in an attendant's uniform, with a sallow face and wispy white hair, as if she had seen hard times.

Sister Jones helped her get the pregnant woman onto the other bed. "Miss Thomas, go and find the midwife. Miss Bennet, back to the dayroom please. Quickly now, both of you."

Mind Your Manners

Mr Walker left Charlie with the burden of getting Beatrice's limp body up the stairs, while he went ahead to unlock the women's secure ward.

"Put her in the second cell, lad. What was your name again?"

Charlie almost said Pyke, but slurred it to Pearce with the help of a timely intake of breath. "She's not heavy, but she's not exactly helping either. Do they always sedate the patients so much?"

"Only the troublemakers. Teaches them to mind their manners. She'll not come to any harm in a padded cell."

"Are there many secure cells here?"

"Half a dozen. Not much call for it, though there's often one or two in use. Problem is, if one of the girls throws a tizzy, it often sets the others off. Supposed to be a load of fancy ladies, but that don't stop them getting hysterical when they feel slighted."

Walker locked the door behind him and peeped through the slot to check that Beatrice hadn't fallen off the padded platform she was laid out on. Charlie had been hoping to check the other secure cells, but Walker had other ideas.

"Best not to disturb them, Pearce. Come along, I'll show you the rest of the upstairs."

As soon as he had locked the outer door behind him, Walker swept an arm around the wide lobby in the centre of the house, speaking at a rapid clip. "At the front you have the Super's chambers, then Matron's, the women's dormitories along the west side, the medical rooms and maternity wing, with storage rooms and secure cells along the back. The most important rule is that you never, ever come up the stairs to the women's side of the house without explicit instructions to do so. Right, let's move on."

He hustled Charlie back to the east side of the house, through another locked door. "Men's wing. Dormitory at the front, bathrooms

151

and staff rooms adjacent. Head Attendant's room at the front of the house, by the stairs. Secure cells at the back. I presume you will be in the previous attendant's room. Lazy sod that he was, better off without him."

"I have a room to myself?"

"Room might be too grand a word." Walker opened a door into a narrow cell, which was as spartan as a monk's quarters. "We have a small staff here, especially on the men's side, so it is difficult to cover all the shifts. As there is always a man trying to get some sleep after night duty, it's best to have your own space."

"Looks fine to me." Palatial, after the cramped row of bunks in the police barracks. Someone had even brought his canvas bag up. A slim book, labelled "Rules", was sitting beside it.

"You'll find you get along best, Pearce, if you pull your weight, but not so much that you show the rest of us up. There's plenty of work to do, but most of it is easy enough."

Walker turned on his heels and ducked into another of the cells without another word. Apparently the brief tour was over. Charlie went back down, via the men's stairs, hoping that the evening meal was early here, after missing out on his midday dinner. With no instructions from Walker, he headed for Mr Quigley's office.

"That was quick. Walker showed you everything, did he?"

"Enough to be getting on with, Mr Quigley. What should I do now?"

"Take five minutes to have a bite to eat. I asked Cook to put some aside for you. Come back here when you're finished."

"Thank you, sir."

"You did well with Beatrice, Mr Pearce. I like to see a man with initiative."

The plate of stew was warm from the range, if rather dried out around the edges and chewy in the middle. Charlie would have eaten anything by that point, having had an early start and a hectic first day. He made a point of thanking the cook, which both startled and pleased her. She seemed a kind soul, especially as she rewarded his courtesy with a large slice of jam sponge, instead of the congealed tapioca that had been set aside for him.

Life seemed a great deal more bearable as he returned to Quigley's office, licking jam from his lips, ready for his afternoon's work.

The head attendant glanced up briefly and handed him a sheet of paper. "Here's your roster for the next week. We give our new staff a week to settle in before they are put in sole charge on night duty. Head along to the dayroom now, front of the building on your right. Mr Bevan will show you the ropes."

The attendant who had been the victim of the knife attack greeted him. "Pearce, isn't it? I'm Bevan." He pumped Charlie's hand with enthusiasm. "Appreciate your help in the dining room. Bit of a close shave." He pointed to the dressing on his neck with a rueful grin.

"I hope that kind of thing doesn't happen every day. I'd been looking forward to an easier ride after Seacliff."

"I wouldn't say it's easy, but we get very few violent incidents. Mostly they can manage their own hygiene too, which is a blessing you'll no doubt appreciate. We try to wear the men out with work in the gardens in the morning, so it's fairly quiet in the dayroom in the afternoon."

He waved a hand around the room, where the men were quietly going about their activities, playing cards and reading for the most part, although several were staring out the window with blank expressions.

"Good to hear, Mr Bevan. What type of men do you get here? They look calm enough, or is that the medication?"

"We only take the mild cases. None of the criminally insane or severely manic you get at Seacliff Asylum. Melancholics for the most part. They are fairly easy to manage, as long as you keep a close eye on their moods. Nip any tension in the bud, confiscate any sharp objects immediately, and never forget that even a spoon can be made sharp with a bit of effort."

Bevan pointed to a young man with a moon-shaped face, who was rocking back and forth, mumbling to himself, and two men who were pacing back and forth along the length of the room, passing each other without exchanging so much as a glance.

"Those three are feeble-minded. Harmless enough, but prone to wandering and hurting themselves by accident. Especially John, the one rocking. Jacob, in the far corner, is prone to fits. Ring the emergency bell when it happens, then clear the furniture around him."

"Sounds as if they are more likely to hurt themselves than anyone else. That will make a pleasant change."

"There is one group you need to keep an eye on." Bevan coughed slightly, turning his face away in an attempt to conceal his discomfort. "Stillwaters admits men who are accused of unnatural behaviour, on the condition that they control their tendencies. Men who refuse to marry, I mean."

"I understand," Charlie assured him. As if it wasn't hard enough to find love in this world, without putting barriers in the way.

"You will need to watch them around other men, especially the delicate ones." He slapped Charlie on the back. "But you'll have no trouble yourself, not with your build. The men appear to be in awe of you already, which is a grand start."

Bevan took him around the room, introducing the patients and briefing him on their specific eccentricities. After that, the afternoon passed pleasantly enough, with no more than minor disagreements and an episode of inconsolable weeping to deal with.

By mid-afternoon, the dayroom was so peaceful that he was struggling to stay awake. His thoughts drifted to the narrow bunk, with its hard pillow and regulation blanket. Not that he would get much use from it, as his real work would begin under the cover of darkness.

Just as his eyelids closed, the emergency bell rang. Within seconds, Quigley raced in, directing Charlie to the women's dayroom. He was through the dividing door, running towards the sound of the fracas as fast as he could, praying that Grace hadn't stirred up a hornet's nest already.

154

Assorted Inmates

As Grace hurried back to the dayroom after her health check, she was struck with the realisation that the woman in the medical room was the first woman she had seen who was nearing term. And her attendant, Miss Thomas, had not been in the dayroom or the dining hall. Perhaps they believed, as many still did, that ladies in their third trimester should not be seen or heard. In extreme cases, ladies were encouraged to rest the entire time within their boudoir. Quite ridiculous, when working class women slaved over stove and laundry until their waters broke.

Lizzie Trelawney was waiting for her in the dayroom. "How are you coping with your first day, Miss Bennet? It can be rather overwhelming, even for the most seasoned of patients."

"I feel as if I am in the middle of an unsettling dream, but the feeling will pass soon enough, I imagine. Lizzie, can you tell me why there are no women around who are near term. The biggest belly I have seen looks to be no more than six months gone."

"Oh, they are kept in a separate dormitory and have food sent up." Lizzie sighed. "I fail to see why child-bearing must be hidden, as if it is a revolting abomination."

Grace would have no excuse to go there. Not that she needed to, as there was no chance of Amelia being there, but she would have liked to see inside anyway. How many other secret corners did Stillwaters have, to hide away the diverse range of patients they served?

"Are they never let out?"

"They have time in the gardens after we come inside. There aren't many of them, because nature takes its course fairly often, as you would expect. They say that Superintendent Gresham's sermons are so powerful, God forgives our sins. I have never been inclined towards religion, but I have to admit that several girls have been cured even in

155

the short time I have been here. My own view is that fear of Dalloway is the cause, rather than the sermons, awful as they are."

Lizzie was right to the extent that many developing babies were lost early in pregnancy due to miscarriages, but it would be surprising if a high proportion were lost amongst the women here, who would most likely have been committed to Stillwaters only after their pregnancy began to show. Beyond that, Grace was sufficiently trained in medicine to be sure that their condition was not "cured" by divine intervention, whatever everyone else here had been deluded into believing.

She would have to find a way to broach this difficult subject, but first, Grace needed to become acquainted with the cast of players in this theatre of the mad.

Fortunately, Lizzie anticipated her thoughts. "Do come and meet the other women from our dormitory, Miss Bennet."

"That would be lovely. And please call me Jane."

"Jane? Jane Bennet? Like the character in *Pride and Prejudice*? How marvellous."

"I'm afraid my mother was inordinately fond of Jane Austen. I suspect her of choosing to marry my father purely on the grounds of his surname. But why do you find it so amusing?"

"We have a group of women here who simply adore romantic novels. Hence the name of their clique – the Romantics. They like to call themselves after writers and characters. Fortunately for you, the name Jane Bennet is not taken, because no one here is as perfect as the fictional Jane. Beautiful, modest, desirable and thoroughly obedient to the rules of society. Everything we are not."

Grace stifled a groan. The foolishness of her name choice was coming back to bite her. "Is it too late to pretend my name is something else?"

"I shouldn't worry. The Romantics do not care to mix with our group. Sadly, the desire to segregate is as fundamental to human nature as the urge to make love or war. Put enough people together for long enough and cliques are inevitable."

Grace felt fortunate that she had been placed in the hands of Lizzie, who showed every sign of being clever and amusing. "Lizzie. Would it be too impertinent to ask how someone as sane as yourself came to be committed to Stillwaters?"

"The excuse they used was female hysteria. The mere fact of my indiscretion would have been enough to label me as an hysteric. The diagnosis was inevitable even before that, due to my support for women's causes and refusal to marry my father's choice of husband. This is my punishment for disobedience. And you?"

"The circumstances I find myself in have brought my spirits to a low ebb. The doctor diagnosed melancholia."

"You are in good company here, especially amongst our group." Lizzie gestured towards a group of women in a loose circle in the corner by the north window. "We are all fallen women, who have committed the cardinal sin of failing to guard our purity."

"Damned for the sake of love?" Grace thought they looked any normal group of young women, chatting away as their fingers expertly worked at embroidery, presumably on the grounds that "idle hands are the devil's workshop".

"Love?" Lizzie let out an unladylike snort. "For some, that may be true. Many of us find ourselves here due to the unwanted attentions of men, forcibly asserted. Stepfathers, uncles, family friends, acquaintances. Best not to inquire – some of their stories would twist your heart in knots. Suffice to say that more than a few of the women you see before you truly view this place as a sanctuary, after the outside world has robbed them of their innocence in the most brutal of ways. I have heard rumours that several of the long-term patients here are women who refused to return home after the birth of their child."

Grace looked around at the congenial surroundings and silently agreed that there were worse places to be, if one had to be locked away from the world. But how cruel their world must be to view any locked door as a blessing, not a curse. She was not ignorant of life's evils, but to see so many wronged women in one place was heart breaking. How many others were subjected to such violence, who could not afford to hide their shame at places such as Stillwaters?

157

"No need to look so grim, Jane. Despite all that has befallen them, they are welcoming to new friends. You will have to learn to cope with their weeping and moaning under cover of darkness, but we do our best to keep up our spirits during the day."

Heads turned as they approached. "Ladies, this is Miss Jane Bennet. Allow me to introduce Addie, Josephine, Fluff, Cleopatra, Becky, Pinkie, Sarah, Boadicea, Marigold and Phoenix."

Their gazes went first to her belly, then to her face. Several said hello cheerily, others had to make the effort to drag their drooping shoulders up and force a smile onto their lips. As for Grace, her heart sank at their use of such obviously fake names. How would she ever find Amelia or Charlotte if everyone hid behind a pseudonym?

"Delighted to meet you. I look forward to making your acquaintance over the coming weeks." Grace desperately wanted to interrogate them, but equally, she did not wish to frighten them off with too many questions.

Fluff jumped to her feet and embraced her. "You must be taking Isabelle's bed. Lovely, you'll be between me and Lizzie. We shall be friends." Fluff beamed at her, exercising every muscle in her face, making her appear as whimsical and joyful as a fluffy white cloud drifting through a blue sky.

"I hope you do not believe in ghosts, Jane, for this place if full of them," Phoenix added. "That girl Isabelle was only here for two weeks before she ran screaming back to her parents."

A tiny voice piped up, barely audible, from a girl with butter-blonde hair. "She didn't leave, she vanished." Marigold flicked her delicate fingers wide. "Vanished into The Ether without a trace left in the earthly world. I fear her troubled spirit will return to haunt us."

Fluff patted the shoulder of the trembling girl. "Calm yourself, Marigold."

"If it is Isabelle Forsyth you are speaking of, I can assure you she left Stillwaters by earthly means. I met her a few days before I arrived here."

"There now, Marigold, I told you she was alive and well."

Grace opted not to contradict Fluff. "Did she talk to any of you about her reason for leaving?"

Lizzie shrugged at the row of shaking heads. "Isabelle kept to herself. She was a restless one, always wandering amongst the trees, as if she did not care to be with the rest of us. She even dared to go out of bounds."

"That got her two days in the hole," Becky sneered. "Patients who break the rules make it worse for the rest of us. I do hope you will not be like Isabelle, Miss Jane Bennet?"

"Not at all." Grace could hardly admit she fully intended to break every possible rule in her efforts to find out what was happening here. "I rather got the impression that Isabelle was unhappy at Stillwaters. Even a little frightened. Did anything happen that might have upset her?"

"Why all these questions about Isabelle, Jane?" Lizzie asked.

"I am anxious about being committed to Stillwaters, given Isabelle's dislike of the place. I would feel more confident about my stay if none of you had any concerns." She paused, but nobody responded, so Grace added, "I think she was scared of the doctor here."

"Doctor Wilson is no worse than any other doctor," Becky replied. "Cold hands, cold heart, cold instruments shoved in places they ought not go. We know we are with child. There's no point prodding around down there to make sure."

"Don't listen to her, Jane," Fluff said. "Doctor Wilson is not here very often and only sees us when we are unwell. He cared enough to admit many of us here, when others refused to see us. Stillwaters really is a sanctuary, compared to the shame we would have faced outside."

"Well, he is not touching me again," Becky declared. "Clara might still be alive if he hadn't done for her."

"Clara was very sick. You saw her having that fit. We all did. I've never seen Sister Jones so close to panic, like she was that night. She had no choice but to take Clara to the medical room and call the doctor. If he had been able to get here sooner, perhaps she would have lived."

"I could ask her spirit what the doctor did to her," Marigold said. "We could hold a séance!"

"I really don't think that would be on Matron's list of acceptable activities," Fluff replied gently.

"Besides, I overheard Matron telling Miss Dalloway that we are to have a new doctor," Lizzie added.

"A shame that new attendant isn't a doctor," Becky said. "I wouldn't mind his warm hands on my body."

A buzz of enthusiastic agreement rose from the group at this distracting declaration.

Lizzie took Grace's arm and drew her away. "Don't let their idle chatter concern you, Jane. Stillwaters may be a cage, but it is a gilded one, which keeps us safe."

"I'm intrigued by all their nicknames. Do they wish to remain anonymous, do you think?"

"The harsh reality is, we have all been locked away by men who spurn us for not meeting their expectations of what a women should be, in their narrow view. At best, they cannot comprehend us. At worst, they blame us for crimes of which we are the victims. Therefore, many of us choose to be known by a different name from that which was bestowed upon us by our families. Others get given a nickname whether they want it or not. And some end up with a new name for the sheer rightness of it. What else could our dear Fluff be, with that marvellous cloud of wool she calls hair?"

"And you?"

"I have kept my first name, as my beloved gran called me Lizzie. I prefer to use 'de Gouges' as a surname, in place of my father's name, to assert my independence. Or as my father would put it, my repulsive radical leanings that offend the very concept of femininity."

"After the French woman who published the Declaration of the Rights of Woman?"

"Olympe de Gouges. I declare myself impressed, Miss Jane Bennet. I am sure we shall be firm friends."

"I come from a long line of spirited woman and suffragists." As soon as she said it, Grace realised this was probably an inappropriate response, given the reason she was committed to Stillwaters. "My father, naturally, has very different ideas about the role of women. Perhaps I should discard Bennet for something more suitable. I shall think on it."

"Anything you like, although I would advise against using anything from a novel, like Darcy. Or the name of that new attendant, for that matter. It might cause a riot."

The sound of Lizzie's laugh was a much-needed reminder of normality. "I believe I may safely promise you never to dance with either of them. Nor to take their names."

"You will fit in very well around here, Jane, if you can quote Austen at will. Her books are banned, of course, for the rebellious nature of the characters, but the Romantics pride themselves on reciting their favourite books by heart."

Lizzie pointed to the group taking up most of the central area of the dayroom, seated or standing in a circle. A couple of them were twirling dreamily to a tune only they could hear, but the others were listening with rapt attention to the woman who took pride of place in an armchair. When Grace and Lizzie moved closer, they could hear her telling a story.

The words "Mr Rochester" and "gypsy" caught her attention. "*Jane Eyre*, I perceive. So they draw the net wider than Jane Austen alone?"

"Oh yes. Charlotte Brontë is their leader's favourite author. Indeed, she calls herself Miss Brontë, and refuses to answer to anything else, except to her intimates, who may call her Charlotte. I have no idea what her real name is."

Charlotte? Interesting. Could she be the Charlotte who asked Isabelle to pass on a message to Charlie? Grace added her to the "interview urgently" list.

The Romantics were mostly in their twenties and thirties. Despite the strict rules on clothing, most of them had managed to add splashes of colour to their ensemble – a bright yellow flower, a red kerchief, a scrap of blue silk, a bright green sash – so that the overall effect was of a flock of rainbow lorikeets in disguise.

Miss Brontë's ample body was wrapped in a flamboyant paisley shawl. Without it, she would have been dismissed as a plain woman with an unfortunately lumpy nose and square chin. With it, she achieved the drama of Mr Rochester's gypsy fortune-teller. Goodness knows how she had managed to get permission to wear it.

"They will interrogate you until they decide whether you are worthy enough to join their elite ranks," Lizzie whispered. "They fancy themselves as literary heroines. They also enjoy singing, which ranges from tolerable to headache-inducingly awful." She pointed to the women on the right-hand side of the leader. "Miss Austen, deputy commander. The others are Shelley, Radcliffe, Catherine, Ophelia ... you get the idea. Don't ask me which is which."

Miss Brontë paused mid-sentence, as she caught them looking at their group. She opened her mouth to speak, but Lizzie tugged Grace's arm in another direction.

"Charlotte expects that I will introduce you to her first, but I have a mind to make her wait."

Instead, they strolled towards a loose cluster of women, ranging in age from about mid-twenty to middle-age, sitting quietly by the window, engaged in needlework or knitting, or simply staring out the window at an inexplicable world.

"Women who have been cast out by heartless families due to their failure in the marriage market," Lizzie explained. "Their only sins are their inability to flirt sufficiently to attract a man, due to God's curse upon them by making them plain, worthy and intelligent. Melancholy comes as naturally to them as melodrama does to the Romantics."

Lizzie turned her attention to a smaller group of mixed age, loosely together but apart, in the darkest corner. They did not appear to be doing anything but watching, starting at the slightest sound. "Women of nervous disposition, for whom the trials of life are too much, even within the walls of the sanctuary. Wealthy families sometimes visit terrible traumas upon their most vulnerable. Be kind to them, Jane, for no one else has been."

A few singletons stood apart from the clusters. An older woman recited disconnected lines of poetry in a monotonous drone to no one in particular, while a rotund red-head shuffled around the dayroom, starting at any raised voice. Grace recognised her as the one who had spat out her laudanum at dinner. Given her agitated state, perhaps the medication had been necessary after all.

In the far corner, a skeletally thin blonde woman sat motionless, with her head against the window. Another woman stood by the door, scraping her nails up and down the solid wood, as if protesting against her confinement. Grace wondered how long it would be until she felt the same about this place. With luck, she might make it through a day or two without going truly mad.

"Sybil, Flaming Flo, Mouse and Scratch," Lizzie said. "Overlooked, prone to erratic behaviour and fits of pique. Mostly quiet, but occasional frightening. There are a couple of others, like Beatrice, who must be locked away when their mania descends upon them."

Grace took special note of the medication-spitting red-head, although her hair was closer to coppery-red than the pale golden blonde of Amelia's hair. "No need to ask how Flaming Flo got her name."

"Actually, it is not her hair, but the fact she is reputed to have set her family home alight. Her stepmother maltreated her and stripped her dowry for her own daughters."

"What about the one called Mouse? Please don't tell me that frail wee thing went on a rampage with an axe." The poor girl looked as if she couldn't lift a handkerchief, but Grace was beginning to realise that no one here was what they seemed.

"I've no idea. She hardly says a word to anyone. Harmless, unlike Scratch, who goes absolutely crazy when she comes close to a man. They have to put her at the furthest away seat in the dining hall. Her food is brought to her."

163

Grace made a mental note to talk to Mouse and Flo, and the other women who bore any resemblance to Amelia. "Do you ever see the men here, aside from meals?"

"The superintendent and doctor are usually the only men we get to see. The male patients have separate quarters on the other side of the house, with the male attendants. If you go thrashing mad, the male attendants will come and take you away, as you have witnessed. Not recommended, although I must say the new male attendant has a way about him. I hope we do not have an outbreak of hysteria due to his presence."

"Perhaps we ought to invite him in here to take part in a book reading."

Lizzie rolled her eyes to heaven. "Bedlam. Don't even think about it. The very best thing you can do here is endure your time with good grace and pray they let you out as soon as possible. The rules might be draconian, but breaking them will condemn you to a far worse situation."

"Such as?"

"Cold baths and rationed food for minor infringements. Solitary confinement and restraints for extreme misbehaviour."

A stentorian voice brought this unpleasant train of thought to an abrupt end. "Miss Trelawney! Miss Trelawney!"

Lizzie continued to gaze out the window, as if rendered mute by the beauty of the garden. Her lips scarcely moved as she whispered to Grace. "She knows I don't like to use that name."

"Lizzie!"

"It's like training a puppy. Ignore it until it does as you wish, then reward it," Lizzie turned to Miss Brontë with a sweet smile. "My dear Miss Brontë. Would you care to meet my new acquaintance?"

Miss Brontë silenced the chatter within her group with a raised hand. "I can see you wish to do so, and I have no objection to making the acquaintance."

"Then allow me to introduce Miss Jane Bennet," Lizzie said, with a wicked grin.

164

"Do you mock me, Lizzie?"

"It is in fact my real name," Grace replied.

The woman named Shelley narrowed her eyes, making her pinched face look even more shrewish. "But you are not beautiful enough to be given such a name. And anyone can see that you do not match the purity of the real Miss Jane Bennet."

Grace was about to say that the "real" Jane Bennet was only a character in a book, when she realised that might inflame the outrage. "Perhaps you could just call me Jane."

"I know, I shall christen you Plain Jane. That would suit you very well."

The women around Shelley applauded, until Miss Brontë held up her hand for silence. "Shelley, ladies, please remember your manners. We must treat others as we would wish to be treated ourselves."

A woman wearing a gold cloth twisted around her head like a turban pushed to the front of the group, clutching at Grace's arm, her eyes shining. "Did you come up from the station with the new male attendant? We are all most eager to hear about him. Did you note his black hair and green eyes? Perhaps we can persuade him to take the part of Mr Darcy in our rendition of *Pride and Prejudice*?"

Grace suppressed a grin at the chaos this would cause. "I believe his name is Mr Pearce. He was polite and attentive to me, but his display in the dining room suggests to me that he may be a superficial charmer. I rather suspect he may be better in the role of the devious Mr Wickham. Perhaps you could audition him and form your own view as to his character?"

Miss Brontë let out a throaty chuckle of approval. She clapped her hands, drawing attention back to herself. "Capital idea, Miss Jane Bennet. If you can arrange it, I promise to reward you with a part in the play."

All of them were looking at her expectantly. What else could she say but, "You honour me."

"If Mr Pearce is to play Darcy, then I must be allowed to play Miss Elizabeth Bennet," Gold Turban said.

"That's not fair, Ophelia," Shelley cried. "It is my turn. Besides, you look nothing like her."

Gold Turbaned Ophelia turned on her with a lip-pouting glare. "He was destined for me. I knew it in my heart from the moment I saw him."

Shelley lunged forward and pinched the other woman's arm. "The part is mine."

Gold Turban's shriek could have shattered a glass. She slapped at Shelley, landing a skin-tingling blow.

"Ladies! Please, a little decorum," Miss Brontë snapped at the shrieking women.

"Stop it! Stop it!" Flaming Flo appeared from nowhere, with her hair flying and eyes blazing. "Stop your horrid screeching, it hurts my ears."

Flo ripped the gold turban off, allowing a tumble of golden hair to cascade down Ophelia's back. When Ophelia grabbed for the turban, pelting Flo with more shrieks, Flo slapped the gold cloth over her mouth and pulled until the cloth bit deep into her cheeks.

Grace leaped forward and grabbed Flo's arm, twisting it down and around until the cloth dropped away. In the distance, Grace heard a bell ringing and the pounding of running feet, over the uproar of the crowd around her. The two female attendants were struggling to get through the wailing masses.

Flo struggled against Grace with all the ferocity of a wild cat. "Make that hellish harpy stop screaming or I swear I will silence her forever."

Grace was losing her grip as the door burst open. Matron blew her whistle, at which the entire room froze.

166

Ophelia

The shock of seeing the woman's mass of gold hair took Charlie's breath away. Ahead of him, Matron blew a sharp blast on her whistle, wrenching him back to reality.

"Mr Pearce, Miss Dalloway, break up this foolishness. Take both patients to the secure ward to calm them down."

"Yes, Matron." Miss Dalloway strode forward, scattering all before her. "Stop your theatrics right now, Ursula. You know how your screaming upsets Florence."

"My name is Ophelia, not Ursula." Ophelia wrenched her gold cloth from Flo's fingers. She switched her gaze to Charlie, her whole face breaking into a radiant smile. With a flutter of her eyelashes, she swooned, falling in his direction, forcing him to catch her in his arms.

Miss Dalloway pursed her lips at this display of feminine weakness, while jerking the struggling red-head from Grace's grasp. "Florence, you mustn't let a little noise upset you."

"She was screaming like a banshee, Miss Dalloway," Flo mumbled. "I didn't start it, honestly. Please don't punish me."

Florence went along meekly in front of Miss Dalloway, with Charlie bringing up the rear, carrying Ophelia's body, which was limp, but not entirely unresponsive. He had the strong impression that she was faking the faint.

Now that he saw her close-up, he was certain that she was not Amelia. The face shape was all wrong. After the heart-stopping first glimpse of her hair, the realisation was almost too much to bear. He followed the female attendant, as she opened the door next to Beatrice's cell and directed Charlie in.

"Lay her on the bunk, Mr Pearce. I will put Florence in another cell and come back to check on her."

As soon as Miss Dalloway left them alone, Ophelia's eyelids opened, revealing grey-blue eyes, unlike his old friend's bright blue. She leaned towards him, taking him by surprise. "I knew you would come to rescue me, my very own Darcy."

Charlie backed away to the door. "Sit down please, Miss Ophelia. You have me mistaken for another."

The words came out more harshly than he intended. She sank back onto the bunk and burst into tears. Charlie had no idea what to do. He dared not comfort her, in case his attentions were misconstrued. Fortunately, Miss Dalloway returned to rescue him.

"Ursula, you will remain here until tomorrow morning, contemplating your foolish behaviour. If you ever repeat this nonsense, I can assure you that you will be on your hands and knees scrubbing the bathroom floor for a week. Do you understand?"

"Yes, Miss Dalloway."

The attendant ushered him out of the cell and locked the door.

"I did nothing to upset her, Miss Dalloway, I assure you. She appears to have me confused with a man named Darcy."

Miss Dalloway sighed. "It is not your fault, Mr Pearce. The girl is addled-pated. This is precisely why we do not allow the girls to read romantic novels, not that it stops them believing they are tragic heroines. They are all as bad as each other, I'm afraid, but it does not usually result in such drama."

"It has been rather a busy first day for me."

"It is normally much quieter, I assure you. Unfortunately, once one girl becomes hysterical, others tend to follow, as if their madness is contagious. I really must get back to the dayroom to help calm them down. Will you see to the logbook?" She pointed to a ledger by the door. "Every patient in the secure cells must be logged in."

"I'd be happy to, Miss Dalloway. I trust the rest of the afternoon will be more peaceful."

"I wouldn't lay a wager upon it, Mr Pearce, but one can always hope for a miracle."

Ophelia-Ursula had done Charlie a favour by giving him this opportunity to be alone in the secure area. He filled in the logbook, adding Beatrice's name as well, as Walker had omitted to do so. Flipping back through the pages, he could see what Dalloway meant. Days passed with no entries, followed by a flurry of activity. The contagion of madness did not surprise him in the least. He had seen it a dozen times, when an apparently peaceful crowd turned into a riot, sparked by the incitement of a few rascals.

He spent as long as he dared leafing through the logbook, but found no records for any Amelia or Charlotte. Not that he would necessarily know, given the patients' annoying propensity to use false names.

Before he returned to the men's dayroom, he took the time to lift each of the observation flaps of the secure cells. Ophelia blew him a kiss, Florence turned her head away, Beatrice was snoring, and a girl with black hair was facing the wall.

At least they were all calm. He was relieved to see that Stillwaters adhered to the policy of not physically restraining their patients, although he did find a cupboard containing locking gloves and strait jackets at the end of the row. For emergencies only, he hoped.

Spiritual Redemption

Matron's steely gaze moved around the chastened faces in the dayroom. "If I have one more ounce of trouble today, I will have the lot of you locked up for a week on short rations."

The furious hiss of her voice achieved what the shouts of the attendants had not – a cringing obedience. Grace cringed along with the rest of the women. Matron's kindly disposition concealed the iron hand in her velvet glove.

As she retreated to a chair by the window, it was the look on Charlie's face that lingered in Grace's memory. Was she fooling herself to think the expression was only one of hope, when he entered the room and saw that swirl of golden hair? Or was it yearning? Either way, it seemed as if their time at Stillwaters might be shorter than she had dared hope.

Lizzie plopped down beside her. "Poor Jane, what a first day to endure. I promise you this is highly unusual. Stillwaters is a peaceful, dull place most days. Unfortunately, disruptions tend to come in waves, as one drama sets off another."

Grace was beginning to see why they had a full medicine cabinet. "I can see that Flaming Flo's group suffer from disorders of the mind, but what of the Romantics? Why are they here?"

"Hysteria, melancholia, unnatural tendencies – the usual things. One or two are simple minded, others simply delusional."

"Unnatural tendencies?"

"What else can be concluded, when a young lady prefers reading novels and inciting melodrama over their proper roles of subservience and household management? Some even dare to have ideas of their own. Worse still, a few prefer the company of like-minded women over male companions."

"They appear to take their roles very seriously, to the extent that they view the fictional Jane Bennet as a real person."

"As I said, some are delusional, if not completely insane."

"What about the one with the gold turban?"

"Ophelia? I don't know much about her. She is usually the quiet one, hovering on the edge as if uncertain of her welcome. The sight of the dashing Mr Pearce seems to have brought her out of her shell. Hysteria, I presume, with an alarming side-serving of delusional behaviour."

"Has Ophelia been here long?"

"I wouldn't know. I've only been here a few weeks myself. We fallen women come and go, naturally, but many of the other patients are long-term residents. I doubt anyone could tell you, to be honest. Time ceases to have meaning here, for everyone except the women who are with child. They despise us for many reasons, but most of all, I believe, because our time here is limited to no more than six or seven months, while their term is beyond their control. Perhaps also because we have experienced that pinnacle of womanly achievement – being coveted by a man."

The ironic twist to Lizzie's lips fell away as she saw Matron standing in the doorway. "Oh lord, are we not to be spared today, after all this drama? I fear you are about to experience the worst punishment of all – Gresham's ritual thrashing of our souls."

Although Matron gave no signal that Grace could detect, the fallen women rose as one and moved towards the door. Lizzie tugged on her arm. There was nothing for it but to follow her on the rocky road to redemption.

Twelve women, in six pairs, filed into a room off the dining hall. A chapel, Grace realised, once she had taken her seat on the second of five wooden pews, facing the cross that dominated the front wall. As Matron exited the chapel through the door they had come in, Superintendent Gresham appeared from behind a velvet curtain and stepped onto the raised platform at the front of the room.

171

The chapel was lit only by muted sunlight filtering through stained-glass windows and a single candle on the lectern. Gresham clasped his hands in prayer, bowing his head so low his fingers touched his goatee. When each woman was rendered mute by the depth of the silence, he spread his hands wide and lifted his head, his features etched by the eery glow of the candlelight.

Into the silence, his rich baritone burst like the flash of burning sulphur. "Sodom and Gomorrah gave themselves up to immorality and perversion. Would you wish, like them, to suffer the punishment of eternal fire?" He allowed the startled women a moment to reflect. "Do you wish to suffer the eternal fire, girls?"

"No, Superintendent Gresham," they chanted.

"But John gives us hope, does he not?" he continued, with a beguiling sweetness. "If we claim to be without sin, we deceive ourselves and the truth is not in us. If we confess our sins, he is faithful and just and will forgive us our sins and purify us from all unrighteousness. But only if we confess our sins and truly repent."

Grace caught Lizzie's eye. She gave the tiniest of shrugs and rolled her eyes behind her steepled hands.

And this was just the beginning. A torrent of words surged down upon them, a surge of pitiless pity that women were made so selfish, proud and weak, followed by a swell of accusations of wanton lust and depravity, before ebbing into an undertow of dire consequences.

Grace sat like a rock, allowing the words to flow around her, fighting the pull of the current into the gentle eddy of promised redemption.

As the sermon raged on and on, Grace felt her anger surge as she, and all women from time immemorial back to Eve, were chastised for tempting men into sin. By the time the superintendent's voice rose to a crescendo for the final admonition to "open your soul to spiritual awakening and repent", Grace felt as if the burdens of the world had been laid upon her shoulders, in the shape of a lead-weighted apple from the garden of Eden.

By the end, all the women were slumped in their seats, their heads hanging, even the feisty Lizzie.

As if by heavenly command, or perhaps summoned by a hidden bell-cord, Matron reappeared, carrying a silver salver bearing a dozen slim goblets. One by one, the women were summoned to kneel in front of the cross, as Gresham laid his hands on each head and muttered a string of words. As each woman rose, she was handed a goblet.

Grace contemplated the options for escape. There were none. She came forth when called, but was none the wiser once she had heard the muttered words, which appeared to be an incantation in a language unknown to her. Reluctantly, she allowed the goblet to be placed into her hands. She sniffed, but could detect no odour.

"Drink the holy water to purge your sins," Matron whispered.

Left with no choice, she drank. No ray of divine light descended upon her with a triumphant blare of trumpets, but nor did she fall back in writhing agony into a pit of serpents.

When all had received the blessing, the twelve of them were disgorged from the gloom of the chapel into a brilliant sunlit afternoon. Another group rose up from their spot under a shady tree and filed dutifully inside in a line of pairs. Apparently, the enormous fees charged by Stillwaters allowed the Superintendent to spiritually cleanse his patients in smaller groups, each according to their sins. Fallen women, followed by tormented souls, with cursed minds for the finale.

Grace wandered alone for a time amongst the summer blooms, allowing the serenity of the gardens to restore her equilibrium, after the intensity of the chapel. The garden was dotted with small marble statues – a kneeling woman in prayer, a Madonna and child, an angel. With a sudden clarity, Grace realised that it was all part of a grand manipulation – a highly effective carrot and stick scheme to transform wayward women into their proper role of angelic subservience. Darkness and light. Good and evil. Reward and punishment.

She shivered, despite the warmth of the summer sun. The other patients appeared unaffected. No doubt they were used to it. Some tended the flower gardens, wearing gloves and straw hats, others strolled in the shade. Around the front of the house, several Romantics were playing a desultory game of croquet, adding a soothing tok-tok of mallets on balls to the hum of bees and restrained chatter. The attendants were supposed to make sure everyone got their quota of fresh air and exercise, but the only two she could see were dozing in the shade. Nobody moved in haste, or showed undue emotion, as was appropriate for young ladies.

Which made the suddenness of the outburst all the more shocking. Grace ducked as a croquet ball flew past her head and on into the pansies that Mouse was tending.

"You hit my ball," yelled one of the players.

"It's my ball. I always have the red one," the other screamed back.

"You are pink! My red was winning until you hit it, you fly-bitten jolthead."

"It never was, you dizzy-eyed pilchard!"

An attendant hurried towards them, but Mouse was quicker. She raced over, waving a bunch of smashed flower stems in front of her like an avenging fury. When she reached the nearest croquet combatant, she thrust the flowers into her face, startling the player so much that she fell over backwards, twisting her ankle.

The commotion didn't subside until the attendant blew her whistle, bringing instant silence. "Girls, that is quite enough. Alice, please put the flowers down. Need I remind you of our guiding rule?"

"Quiet obedience at all times," the women mumbled.

The trivial dispute was the last straw for Grace. She ran for the sanctuary of the trees. She sank down under a sturdy oak, turning her back to the chaos, with her hands over her ears. After little more than six hours in this so-called sanctuary, she was struggling to hold on to her sanity.

For heaven's sake, she prided herself on her ability to cope in the cauldron of medical school and the bedlam of hospital wards. She had years of experience tending to the appalling medical and social problems of the impoverished women who came through the doors of Lavender House. Why was this place affecting her so badly?

With deep breathing, clarity was slowly restored and Grace realised why this experience was so fundamentally different. Here, she had no control over events. No control over anything at all, even her own actions, let alone those of the women around her, whose emotions were as stable as a rowboat in a storm. It was as if the forced repression of normal behaviour resulted in a compensatory eruption of temper at any minor incident.

The distinctive call of a morepork drifted down to her from within a dense shroud of leaves in a tree on the other side of the wall. Strange that an owl would be out at this time of day.

It called again, adding an odd extra note to the end of its "more pork" hoot. Grace wandered over to the wall, stooping to pick a few daisies as she went.

"Pretty grim in there, I take it."

"Detective Inspector Stewart, you have no idea what a joy it is to hear your voice."

"Grace, my dear, I think it's about time you started calling me Alistair."

Inappropriate as it was to call an older man by his first name, this gesture of friendship brought her close to tears. "It's crazy in here, Alistair."

"Do you need to get out, Grace?"

Tempting, but knowing he was nearby was enough to restore her courage. "Not yet. I think we may have found Amelia. A woman with golden hair got into a fight over the dashing Mr Pearce and has been hauled off into solitary confinement. She seemed to feel she had some claim on him, but then she is delusional, so it is hard to tell. I need to talk to Charlie, to find out for sure if she is Amelia."

"Do you have a sense yet if all is well at Stillwaters, aside from the usual insanity one might expect at a lunatic asylum?"

Grace supressed a shudder and focussed on what she had observed. "Superintendent Gresham appears to believe that women are a curse on mankind and the source of all sin in the world. Any who were sane on entering this place will surely not remain so for long, under the burden of his sermons."

"Gresham doesn't sound like a man who should be put in charge of vulnerable young women. Anything else?"

"The women have mixed feelings about Doctor Wilson. A woman called Clara died under his care recently. Matron is outwardly kind, but rules Stillwaters with an iron hand, with the aid of a shrill whistle and a medicine cabinet that would be the envy of any hospital."

"I really do think you should leave, Grace."

"It's not all bad. Most of the young women here have learned to cope by supporting each other, Their fortitude and companionship is rather inspiring."

"Grace, you need to know what Matron Roberts asked of me, when I completed your admission. I had to indicate which programme of care I wished for you and your child. The basic fee was for you to go through to term and birth the baby. If I wished the child to be cared for and adopted into an approved Christian home, there would be an additional fee for the baby's care until such time as an adoptive family was found for it."

"And if you did not want either of those options?"

"Nothing was said directly, you understand. But I did make a point of saying that our family was mortified by the shame you had caused us and what a pity the clock could not be turned back, so that you might continue your life unblemished by your sin. Matron replied that Stillwaters had had a great deal of success with their spiritual purification programme. I was given to understand that, if you were sufficiently pure of soul, your unfortunate mistake might be purged and your old life resumed within a few weeks."

"For a sufficiently large fee, I presume."

"She did not mention any fee, instead implying that a generous donation would help to secure the benevolent gaze of the divine eye, as it were."

"Thus avoiding any potential accusation of undertaking pregnancy terminations for money. Although she might well be simply referring to spiritual healing and nothing more."

"Exactly so. I was quick to assure her that we wanted the child for a family member who was childless. Of course, the word 'termination' was never mentioned. Hardly surprising, as it is illegal. Indeed, the whole discussion used so many euphemisms that one was left wondering what the exact nature of the treatment would be. The definite implication was that the product of your sin would vanish by divine intervention alone if you were pure of soul."

"I have heard that the number of women carrying their child to term here might be lower than expected, which would suggest their 'treatment' is a success. I have also been subjected to the compulsory ingestion of a tonic, a purgative, and holy water in the short time I have been here, which does rather raise the possibility that the divine powers might be assisted by earthly substances."

"You do not seem surprised, Grace."

"I admit that it has been on my mind ever since seeing Isabelle's reaction to Doctor Wilson on the train. Her exact words to me were: 'He'll kill me and my baby if they take me back to that place.' If it was the doctor, then he may have been requesting an additional fee, entirely separate from those charged by the sanctuary. You'll recall that Doctor Wilson was the one who arranged most of the admissions of pregnant girls."

"Or he might have been in league with others at Stillwaters, taking a cut of the donations and fees. Hopefully, if it was him alone, the terminations will cease. Is there anyone else who could be behind it?"

"Superintendent Gresham and Matron Roberts the wield the most power, but Sister Jones, the nurse, would be well placed to carry on the doctor's work, as she is the one who prepares the medications and examines patients. The head attendant, Mr Quigley, and the ward sister, Miss Dalloway, also have considerable power and keys to most of the doors. I have to admit, I find Dalloway rather terrifying."

"They stand to make an enormous amount of money, whether the child is born or not," Stewart said. "The quicker the women can be 'cured' and returned to their families, the more such cases they can take."

"Stillwaters would be costly to run, I suppose, although the grandeur is only skin deep. We are fed the kind of slop one might expect at any other institution and crammed into dormitories with no luxuries. Only one bath a week and cold water if we misbehave or become overexcited. So yes, I imagine that someone is becoming wealthy from this place, and I suspect it is not the religious organisation that purports to run it."

"I am concerned for your welfare, Grace. Not only through the misery you are suffering here, but due to the consequences if your investigation is discovered. Greed is a powerful motive."

"I believe my cover story has been accepted, which resolves our doubts around Doctor McLeod's loyalties." The silence stretched out uncomfortably long period of time. "Is there something else worrying you, Alistair?"

The tree branch swayed, suggesting restless movement from within. "There are too many unknowns for my liking. I cannot help worrying about the message Isabelle relayed to you on the train – that both Amelia and Josiah are still alive. I'm sure you don't need reminding that Josiah Cowper murdered Amelia's father. I dread to think what risks you may face if he is still be in the vicinity or even on the staff. He must have some link to Stillwaters if he brought Amelia here."

"Even if Josiah was here, he would not know who I am. I really don't think you need be unduly concerned about me, Alistair." Grace tried to make the assurance sound cheerful, but it rang hollow. "Besides, we need more than a single day to get to the bottom of what is happening here, although I would agree to leave if Charlie thinks it necessary to ensure Amelia's safety. The problem is that it is almost impossible to talk to him. You may have to be the conduit for information."

"Of course, although it would be better if we could devise a more rapid means of exchanging messages. Are you sure you are willing to continue?"

"Absolutely."

"Anne said to give you this if you needed reminding of reality."

A silver object sailed over the wall, dropping to the ground at her feet. A locket – one of Anne's most cherished possessions. She didn't need to open it to know that it contained pictures of her grandparents, who had spent four horrendous months on a sailing ship travelling to New Zealand in conditions that would make Stillwaters seem like a walk in the park. A tear dropped to the ground beside it as she hastened to pick it up.

"Thank you, Alistair. This means the world to me. As does your presence." She tucked it deep into her corset. "I should go."

Walking away from him was difficult, but if she had stayed by that wall any longer, so close to freedom, it would have been worse. Grace was determined to focus on the job at hand, like a professional. She swiped a tear from her eye and strode forth into the light beyond the trees.

At least she had learned one thing. The attendants who had dragged Flaming Flo and Ophelia apart earlier in the day had used their real names – Florence and Ursula. And Mouse, who had been part of the croquet fracas, had been called Alice.

There was something about Mouse that drew Grace's attention. In the sunshine, her blonde hair had gleamed with faint golden highlights and she showed every sign of having barely survived a traumatic past. Inside, she had kept her head against the window, while outdoors, she sat amongst the flowers, keeping her head tucked, her eyes scanning the trees through a veil of lank hair. If Mouse was Amelia, Charlie was going to be very distressed by her condition.

Grace spent the rest of the afternoon kneeling in a flower bed, trying to get Mouse to engage with her, with no success whatsoever. Eventually, Mouse got up and walked away.

Another woman was watching her with interest. "Don't bother following. You won't get a word out of her."

"Does Mouse never speak to anyone?" Grace asked.

"When she first arrived, she yelled and screamed and fought the attendants for days, then she tried to take her own life. After that, they drugged her so much she couldn't speak. Poor dear would rock back and forth, mumbling about wanting her rabbit back, for hours on end. Now, she has good days, when you might get a few words out of her or even get her to help with the flower arranging, followed by bad days, when she doesn't say a word."

"Do you know how long she has been here?"

"Years." The woman stared off into the distance. "Maybe five or six years? It's hard to remember." She turned back to Grace. "You're Jane aren't you? I'm Nits."

Grace wasn't sure she had heard right. Calling a person 'nits' seemed too cruel even by the odd standards of Stillwaters.

"That's Knits with a k. I knit a lot you see. Would you like me to make you a scarf? Winter is freezing here." Her gaze dropped to Grace's waist. "Oh, I suppose you won't be here that long, or are you a lunatic as well as a slut?"

She said it in such a pleasant tone that Grace thought she had misheard. "The scarf is a kind thought, Knits, but I won't be here. What rabbit do you think Mouse meant?"

"I expect it was a cloth rabbit she had confiscated when she arrived. There must be a whole cupboard full of seized items somewhere, if they aren't thrown in the incinerator. They're supposed to keep our personal possessions, you see, in case we ever get cured and released."

At that moment, the gong sounded. Knits headed for the door without saying another word, with Grace at her heels, wondering what new challenge she was about to face.

As it turned out, the gong signalled the evening meal, even though the angle of the sun suggested it couldn't be much later than five o'clock in the afternoon. The routine was the same as at midday. Wash their hands, take their allotted seats, queue for food when their table was called, say grace, eat, wash their plates.

With the attendants so close by, Grace didn't dare ask too many questions or risk a glance at Charlie, so she contented herself with listening to the conversations, which mainly consisted of minor chatter about the dramas of the day and requests to pass the salt.

After supper, the head attendant mumbled his way through an uninspiring Bible reading and they sang a couple of hymns, before setting about their allotted chores for the evening. Grace was handed a mop and ordered to help wash the floor of the dining hall, once the tables were cleared away by the men.

At one point, she glanced up to find Charlie looking her way. His expression gave no sign of having seen her, but his hand came up and rested over his heart for a moment, before moving up to touch his lips. Grace rested the mop against her chest, with her hand on the handle at heart level, before wiping a non-existent crumb from her mouth. A ghost of a smile flitted across his lips as he turned away.

The extraordinary warmth of that tiny sliver of connection stayed with her long after the moment had passed.

To her astonishment, once the chores were done, they were directed upstairs to wash and prepare for bed. Even with the delays caused by the extended ritual of washing, undressing and brushing out long hair, they were in bed before the sun had dipped below the level of the trees.

The women opened their permitted books eagerly, with several of them peering over at Grace to see what new literary treasures she had brought into their cloistered existence. She felt bad that she hadn't been brave enough to risk a decent novel. Still, they were probably desperate to read anything new after being in here for weeks on end.

Anne's silver locket felt warm in her hand, hidden under the covers. A beautifully crafted piece of metal, yet so much more. A connection to love and compassion, like Charlie's fleeting gesture after dinner. Grace looked around at the other women, lying in identical beds in their plain nightdresses, with little to remind them of those who loved them. Calming as the décor was at Stillwaters, she was certain that every woman here would have swapped the pretty flower arrangements for a favourite shawl or a personal keepsake in a heartbeat.

Half an hour later, the night attendant came around to pull thick curtains across the windows, shutting out the soft glow of sundown. Grace lay back on her pillow, determined to stay awake, despite the fog of sleep trying to claim her.

She awoke with a start, to find the dormitory dark and still. In the bed beside her, Fluff was whimpering. Grace decided to leave her in peace tonight, but to make an attempt to get to know her and help her tomorrow. The whimpering escalated to groaning for a time, before dying away into a restless sleep.

Grace slipped out of bed, wrapped her robe around her, and padded over to the window in bare feet. Judging by the height of the moon, she must have slept for a couple of hours. A night lamp flickered by the door, throwing a soft glow onto the sleeping figure of the night attendant. The drops of sedative Grace had added to her cocoa would keep her slumbering peacefully for a while yet.

Grace felt a twinge of guilt for having stolen a bottle of sedative from the medical room and used it upon the unsuspecting night attendant and ward sister. But, needs must. Grace tiptoed up to the attendant and gently eased the ring of keys off her belt. Impossible to achieve without a jingle or two, but the attendant slept on.

One of the patients stirred as the door squeaked open, but she turned over and resumed her slumber. Grace slipped out and eased the door closed behind her. If she was caught now, she would be in solitary confinement for the next week, eating stale bread and water.

She wanted to take a closer look at the medical room and chapel, as well as the offices, but she also wanted some leverage to get Charlotte Brontë and Mouse to talk to her. She opted for the medical room first, on the grounds that it was closest.

Frustratingly, none of the night attendant's keys fitted the lock. By the time she had tried them all, it felt as if unseen eyes were watching her. Grace decided to move on, rather than risk being found fumbling around in the dark with her lock picks. Learning to pick locks had been a lark at the time, but now she wished she had practiced more.

She crept along the upstairs corridor, bumping into low chairs and potted palms in the dark patches and rushing through the moonlit patches with her heart in her mouth. As she passed the large arch of the central window, a dark shape loomed up beside her. How foolish she felt when she realised it was only her own shadow on the wall.

Her pulse hadn't recovered when a shape appeared at the end of the corridor and descended the stairs. A moment later, a door opened and closed downstairs. Who else would be about at this time of night?

The sensible part of her told her to go back to her dormitory – the part that whispered "curiosity killed the cat" in her mother's voice – but when had that ever stopped her before?

A Dark Place

After a busy day, the hands on the clock crawled through the last hours of Charlie's shift. Finally, he and Bevan signed off as the night attendant took over, all the patients having been sent to bed well before dark. Charlie wasn't far behind them.

He awoke to the sound of footsteps outside his room. A few minutes later, the footsteps returned in the other direction. A routine patrol by the night attendant no doubt, although there was little chance of the patients sneaking out from the locked dormitory, especially as they had to pass by the attendants' rooms to get to the stairs.

When Charlie heard the squeak of the dormitory door closing, he eased his own door open. The plan was simple – break into the cloakroom to see if he could steal a master key from the key cabinet, to save him the inconvenience of picking locks in the dark. His own set of keys would get him around the patients' areas, but not into any of the offices, where he hoped to find the patient register and financial files.

A pity he couldn't find an excuse to enter the female dormitories and check every face for Amelia's likeness. He'd have to leave that to Grace. A male attendant in the women's dormitory would be the quickest way to find himself ejected into the night with a boot in the rear end. He'd had quite enough of boots on his body for the foreseeable future. Although he wasn't about to admit it to anyone else, dragging his aching body out of the bed tonight had been a darn sight harder than he'd have liked.

Now, as he crept down the stairs to the cloakroom in the lobby, the rush of excitement at being where he shouldn't be damped down any lingering aches. To his relief, there was no guard posted at the main door. Hardly surprising, as the patients were locked upstairs and any escapees wouldn't get past the high walls and gates. Grace would be going crazy, being locked within her dormitory with no way out to snoop about. At least she couldn't come to any harm there.

He paused in the alcove behind the cloakroom, hard against the wall, as someone with a light tread came down the stairs on the women's side. A door opened and closed.

Charlie took the opportunity to slip into the cloakroom, in case the person came back again. Silence descended. He was just about to open the key cabinet, when the scape of metal on metal alerted him to a person at the cloakroom door. With his heart pounding fit to burst, he slipped behind a rack of long winter coats and tried not to breathe.

Across the dining hall, another door slammed and footsteps began to cross the expanse of parquet. The scrape of metal became more frantic, then the cloakroom door opened and closed.

The thin filter of light through the glass panel was just enough for Charlie to make out a slim figure, with a deliciously familiar scent. He reached out and grabbed her, pulling her hard against him behind the coats, with his hand clamped over her mouth.

To his surprise, Grace didn't scream or thrash, but instead sank back into him with a soft expiration of breath through his fingers. Apparently she had recognised him in the dark as easily as he had recognised her, even while under stress. He smiled at the thought and felt her smiling back, even though there was no way she could see his expression.

The clip-clop of footsteps stopped outside the cloakroom. After an agonising few seconds, they resumed, heading for the women's stairs. At a guess, Matron had finished in her office for the night.

When silence returned, Grace loosened his fingers from her mouth. "I'm not sure that the *Ladies' Book of Etiquette* would consider our current position entirely proper, DC Pyke."

Charlie considered the point. His arm was clutched firmly around her chest, where it had no right to be. Furthermore, she appeared to be clad only in delightfully soft garments that left him in no doubt as to her contours. A nightdress and robe, he guessed. Reluctantly, he

185

dropped his arm to a more decorous position around her waist, where the end of her long plait of hair tickled his hand.

"My apologies, Miss Penrose. I don't believe the police training manual addressed the correct way to restrain a unwed pregnant woman in the cloakroom of a lunatic asylum."

"Charlie Pyke, I do believe that consorting with criminals as an undercover detective has turned you into a rogue."

"Not at all, Grace. It's just that if I didn't hold you tightly, you might have blundered into the umbrella stand right beside me, which would have caused an awful clatter. May I inquire why are you wandering the corridors so late in your night attire?"

"I thought if I was caught, I could claim to be a sleepwalker."

"But how did you get past the attendant and out of a locked dormitory?"

"You are not the only one who can do magic tricks, Charlie. I palmed a bottle of sedative from the medical station and added a few drops to the attendant's cocoa. Her key got me out of the dormitory, but I had to use my lock picks to get into the cloakroom."

Charlie was momentarily taken aback by the way she talked of sedatives and lock picks, as casually as most women would say tea and crochet hooks. But then Grace hadn't acted like most women from the instant he had first clapped eyes on her. "Am I going to regret asking where you learned to pick locks?"

"Do you remember Johnny Todd and Tiny Tim?"

"Your pair of devilishly clever street urchins. How could I forget?"

"It turns out they have many useful skills, one of which is opening locked doors."

"I dread to think what else they have taught you."

Grace swivelled in his arms so that she was facing him. He felt her arms go around him, but he didn't have more than a moment to enjoy the sensation. She pulled away again and pressed a hard round object into his palm. He held it up in the faint light. His "magic" shilling.

"Your coin, I believe. You ought to be more careful around pickpockets. Tiny Tim also showed me how to disable a bigger and stronger attacker, which was jolly useful on Flaming Flo earlier today."

"I shall bear that in mind. I see that my absence hasn't turned you into a simpering little miss goody two shoes. What a surprise. Grace, are you shivering?"

"My sleepwalking plan does have a flaw. They certainly don't waste money on heating the corridors here, despite the hefty fees they charge."

Charlie took a thick woollen cloak off the rack and draped it around her shoulders. Tempting as it was having her so close, they were here for a reason and any moment might bring discovery. He leaned towards her ear. "Are you all right? Not gone stark raving loony yet?"

"I'm teetering on the brink of madness, but I haven't fallen into the abyss yet. I'm dying to know if the golden-haired Ophelia is Amelia."

"Unfortunately not. Gave me quite a shock when I first saw her hair though. I've had a look at all the women in the secure cells and everyone in the dining hall. I'm sure none of them are Amelia, with a couple of possible exceptions whose faces I couldn't see. None of the maids or the cook are her either, at least the ones I met today. I had a good look at the logbook for the secure cells and nothing there either. What have you found out?"

"There is a woman called Charlotte, but I haven't interrogated her yet. And a timid woman with gold highlights in pale hair, known as Mouse, whose real name is Alice. She keeps her head down and rarely speaks. I'll try to talk to them both tomorrow. It would be a whole lot easier if they didn't call each other by nicknames."

"Remember that Amelia might look completely different. Drug addiction and fear do have a habit of changing a person for the worse. I have seen that any number of times in police work. But I still think the most likely possibility is that Isabelle was told a story from the past. If there was ever an Amelia here, she may be long gone."

"I agree, but we have to look. Anyway, we still need to find out more about what happened to Isabelle and why she was so desperate to escape Stillwaters."

Charlie was still leaning towards the view that Isabelle's distress was the result of her own mental condition. "If Doctor Wilson did throw her from the train, he must have had an extremely compelling motive."

"I might have a lead on that. I have grave concerns over the treatments here, both religious and medical. I believe they are conducting illegal terminations, under the cover of their spiritual healing programme. Doctor Wilson was not much liked, but I haven't any hard evidence against him yet. That's why I came here to find a key to the medical room."

"I was looking for a master key to the offices, to have a look at the patient admission files and financial statements."

"Excellent. Alistair and I agree that the fees here are high for the service they provide. But we suspect that it is the optional extra fees where they make their real money, for treatments and care of newborns. I find it hard to believe that a religious charity would be so greedy." She shrugged off the cloak, placing it in his arms. "Would you like me to open the key cabinet, or would you care to do the honours?"

"By all means, Grace. Far be it for me to obstruct your latent criminal tendencies."

"That's what I adore about you, Charlie. You're always so supportive of my career choices."

"Wait a moment." Charlie covered the glass panel in the door with the cloak. His fingers searched for the candle and matches in his pocket, finding instead that his lucky silver shilling had been replaced in that pocket.

Grace held up the candle and matches. "Looking for these?"

He leaned forward to whisper sternly in her ear. "Did you know that theft of police equipment is an offence punishable by imprisonment, Miss Penrose?"

"I expect I could get off the charge by pleading insanity, as I'm already imprisoned in a lunatic asylum. Kindly hold the candle, so I can get on with the larceny. I don't know about you, but I would like to get some sleep tonight."

Grace made quick work of picking the lock with the help of the candlelight. Inside the cabinet was a rack of labelled keys. She helped herself to a key for the women's dormitories and one to the medical room. Charlie reached over her shoulder for the spare office keys.

"Take care, Grace. I'd be happier if you left the medical room until tomorrow night. If I get all I need from the offices, you might not need to risk it."

"I'd prefer to do it tonight in case I don't get the chance tomorrow. The sooner we can get out of this place, the happier I will be. Shall we meet again tomorrow night? Or earlier, if there is something urgent to discuss."

"If we can. There is a room off the lobby upstairs, opposite the stairs, where visitors can meet with patients. It would be a safer place to meet as no one will go there at night. Let's try for around midnight, if we haven't found a way to talk before then."

Grace touched her hand to his chest, over his heart, then to his lips, before vanishing like a wraith into the dark. He touched his lips, sure that he would feel a scorch mark, but the heat he felt wasn't on the outside.

Medical Notes

Grace raced up the stairs with light feet and tingling fingers. She hesitated at the top, drawn to the left by the urgency of what needed to be done, but wanting to turn right to the safety of the dormitory (or, better yet, back downstairs into Charlie's arms).

After she had checked the location of the visitors' room, making sure that she had a key that fit the lock, she turned her attention to the medical room. With the stolen key, she was inside in a trice. The doctor's office was more of a challenge, until she found a spare key locked in the cupboard adjacent to the door.

The medical register was in the top right-hand drawer of the desk, a classic location for important documents. Grace crouched down behind the desk and lit the stub of candle she had pocketed earlier.

The register listed all the patients seen in the medical room each day, recorded by whoever had seen them. Her own health check was listed under Sister Jones' name in beautiful copperplate writing. Her entry was incomplete, due to the arrival of the emergency delivery. Grace was relieved to see that was listed as a routine birth of a healthy baby girl weighing seven pounds nine ounces. The midwife had made the entry in childish printed letters, noting that Sister Jones and Miss Thomas had assisted at the delivery.

Flipping back through the pages, it was clear that the medical room was Sister Jones' domain. The midwife was there occasionally for the birth of a baby, as well as covering general medical care on Sister Jones' days off. Miss Thomas appeared irregularly, apparently when needed as a stand-in for the regular nurse aide. Grace remembered overhearing that the usual nurse aide was on leave to look after her sick mother.

Doctor Wilson's last entry was the day of Isabelle's escape. Nothing out of the ordinary was listed that day. Going back through previous days and weeks, it seemed that Doctor Wilson came to Stillwaters on Monday and Thursday, with additional rare visits as needed for urgent cases. Two other doctors were mentioned as attending emergencies. One of them was a doctor at Seacliff, further up the coast, while the other was a local man who signed himself as "Doctor White (retired)".

By far the majority of entries were for everyday ailments that did not require specialist care. Minor injuries, upset stomachs, routine checks, respiratory infections and all the usual minor complications of pregnancy. Cramping and convulsions were rather more common than Grace would have expected, but perhaps patients with mental disorders were more likely to suffer such complications.

Clara's death had occurred a week ago, four days before Isabelle's escape. Her convulsions had begun the night before. Clara was reported to be screaming in agony by the time Sister Jones was called. The nurse had attempted to treat her with potassium bromide, but it was too late. By the time Doctor Wilson arrived the next day, Clara was comatose. Her death was listed as a grand mal seizure. She had been four months' pregnant.

It was hardly surprising that Isabelle had been frightened by the dreadful death of Clara and her baby. She might even have blamed Doctor Wilson for it, especially if she did not trust him. But, unless Sister Jones was covering for the doctor, he was an innocent party. He had not been at Stillwaters the two days leading up to her death and arrived too late on the Thursday to be able to change the outcome. If anyone was at fault – and Grace was loathe to lay blame in any emergency – it was Sister Jones, for waiting for Doctor Wilson to arrive, instead of sending for the local doctor immediately.

Grace continued flipping back through the pages. When she came to the start of the medical register, she searched the shelves for older volumes. Eventually, she worked out that the regular nurse aide had been here less than a year and Miss Thomas had been here about four years, while the midwife, Sister Jones and Doctor Wilson had all been here about seven years. In fact, the daily register had been instigated back then. Prior to that, there were only haphazard folders of loose notes.

Perhaps Stillwaters had moved to a more professional footing then, by employing medical professionals with higher standards. She would have to ask if that was also when Matron Roberts had started here. Any efficiency programme would surely be down to her capable administration.

It would have taken Grace days to go through all the entries, so she restricted her search to the days after Amelia's disappearance from Clyde. The only unusual occurrence was an attempted suicide by a women named Alice Smith. Could that be Mouse?

The files of patient records were even more unhelpful, as they were listed by surname. Isabelle had only mentioned the names Charlotte and Amelia, so Grace had no idea what surname they would be under. Not surprisingly, there was no file for Amelia Lawrence, who would certainly have been admitted under a false name. Isabelle Forsyth's file was there, but her departure had been listed as a routine discharge, rather than as an escape, with no note of her subsequent death.

Grace decided to talk to the other patients again tomorrow, rather than attempting to go through all the documents. Instead, she scanned the shelves, seizing on a file labelled "Reports to Coroner".

For a group of young women from wealthy backgrounds, the number of deaths struck Grace as fairly high, although childbirth was certainly a dangerous time in any woman's life, especially for women with hysterical or melancholic tendencies. Amongst all the patients, self-inflicted injuries – a euphemism for taking one's own life – were dispiritingly common compared to the general populace.

For the pregnant patients, the cause of death was often reported as complications of childbirth or seizures, or more general causes such as heart failure, fever and septicaemia. She was interested to see that the dates of the deaths did not match the dates of the doctor's visits. Indeed, few of the deaths occurred while Wilson was present. Perhaps that was what had been worrying the doctor, when he had expressed misgivings to Doctor McLeod.

Grace was running out of time and candlewax. She decided to do a quick search of the desk drawers, to see if any of Doctor Wilson's personal correspondence had survived his death. However, the drawers held only a row of empty files, with labels such as "correspondence" and "trustee reports".

As she withdrew her hand, it brushed against a piece of paper caught – or hidden – under the top lip of the desk. When she wiggled it loose, it proved to be a copy of correspondence Doctor Wilson had sent to the trustees of the Magdalene Trust, who oversaw the sanctuary, dated the day of his own death on the train. He was probably intending to post it in Dunedin, which meant the original of the letter would have been in the doctor's missing bag.

The letter outlined his concerns at the superintendent's religious cleansing practices, alleging that they went against best medical practice, and, in his opinion, were highly likely to be detrimental the fragile mental state of Stillwaters' patients. Doctor Wilson went as far as threatening to lay a charge of misconduct against Gresham, if no action was taken by the trustees. Furthermore, he alluded to the frequency of deaths at Stillwaters, suggesting that further investigation was warranted.

Hear, hear, Doctor Wilson, she thought. Doctor McLeod had been right about tensions between Wilson and Superintendent Gresham. But, now that she had seen the medical records, Grace was beginning to understand that the doctor was not to blame. One thing was certain – Doctor Wilson would never have written to the trustees unless he was an innocent party. He may not have had much of a bedside manner, but he hadn't been afraid to put his job on the line to force an inquiry into Stillwaters Sanctuary.

Had he also, unknowingly, put his life on the line? Grace thought back to her impression that he had been mildly intoxicated on the train, wondering if he had in fact been drugged. She tucked the letter away in the pocket of her robe with a shiver, feeling as if she was on the edge of a precipice herself, but not knowing who might be behind her, ready to push.

Grace was sure that the religious cleansing ceremony was not the cause of the high rate of miscarriages at Stillwaters, whatever effect it was having on mental wellbeing. Whichever way she looked at it, she couldn't get away from the conclusion that someone here was terminating pregnancies for money, so that grateful parents could have their daughters back unblemished by childbirth.

If not Doctor Wilson, then who? Sister Jones was an obvious candidate, given her control over the medications dispensed. Each patient had been given a specific glass, which would allow the nurse to control who got what treatment. As Sister Jones would not benefit directly from the donations paid for the service, either Superintendent Gresham or Matron Roberts, or both, was likely to be the ringleader.

Time was marching on, bringing with it an ever-increasing chance of the night attendant awakening or one of the patients noting her absence. On the other hand, the opportunity to snoop might come only once. Grace calmed her nerves and set to work opening all the cupboards in the medical room. Aside from the large volume of purgatives, sedatives and tonics she had seen earlier, she found only the normal range of medical supplies one might expect. The abortifacient drug, if it existed, must have been hidden away somewhere else.

As Grace locked the door to the medical room, she weighed up her next move. Common sense urged her to go back to the dormitory, before she was discovered. But the silver locket around her neck emboldened her to look for the storage room, where she might find the means to help her tomorrow.

She had already passed two rooms labelled "Storage". The first contained only supplies of linen, bedpans, soap and cleaning equipment. The second held a treasure trove. No secret cache of drugs, but shelf after shelf of personal effects, bagged and tagged with the patient name from whom they had been confiscated on arrival.

Grace scanned the collection for a tag with the name Alice Smith, finding it on the top row. The bag contained a single item – a stuffed rabbit with white fur, a checked waistcoat and a little embroidered watch. She had to suppress a chuckle. Mouse, whose real name was

194

Alice, had lost her rabbit, which looked just like the one from a popular children's story, *Alice in Wonderland*. She tucked White Rabbit under her robe, hoping she now had the means to get Alice to talk about who she really was.

Many of the other bags bulged with the rectangular shape of books. One of the bags was labelled with the name Charlotte Brown. She left the storage room with a stack of illicit novels, which would have Miss Charlotte Brontë eating out of her hand.

Records Broken

Charlie began his search in Superintendent Gresham's office, on the assumption that he must be in charge of the administration of the asylum. From what Charlie had seen so far, Gresham kept a low profile and left the real work to Matron and Quigley.

Gresham's desk bore only an ornate letter opener, sundry stationery and a basket with three letters, ready to post but not yet sealed. The first letter was to a ladies' philanthropic society, inviting them to tea next Monday. The second letter was to the local floral society, regretfully declining their invitation to give a lecture due to pressure of work commitments.

The third letter was to the trustees of Stillwaters, recommending the immediate appointment of a new doctor to replace the "unfortunate loss" of Doctor Wilson. The letter suggested that suitable candidates be approached in light of the specialised nature of the position, rather than relying on general applications. Doctor McLeod headed the list of preferred candidates. It was signed by Gresham, but appeared to be written by another hand, judging by the bold feminine strokes.

Charlie made short work of riffling through Gresham's files. It seemed as if the man did little beyond acting as a commanding figurehead for Stillwaters, liaising with the trustees, meeting with asylum inspectors, and filing mandatory reports to the Lunatic Asylums Department.

He looked around the office, trying to get a sense of the superintendent's personality. A framed certificate on the wall purported to be from the University of Turin. Charlie wondered if anyone had queried the legitimacy of the qualification, which did not seem to have any connection to medicine, based on his minimal knowledge of Latin.

There were no other pictures or decorations – not even a photo of Gresham with a wife or family. Quite the contrast to Doctor McLeod's office, which had been covered wall to wall with framed certificates listing medical qualifications, as well as and photographs of McLeod with other professional men. A portrait of McLeod arm-in-arm with an elegant lady, surrounded by a gaggle of children, had taken centre stage on his paper-strewn desk.

Charlie was left with the impression that Gresham had no life beyond Stillwaters. Or rather, none that he wished others to know about.

He was about to give up his search, when he spotted a close-fitting door in the far wall, hidden behind a potted palm. Inside, Gresham's character finally made an appearance. It was only a small room, filled with a comfortable armchair, a writing desk, a bookshelf and a cabinet containing bottles of liquor and glasses.

The bookshelf held a collection of works on religion and philosophy, including several books of sermons, along with a few volumes on medical topics. Charlie reached eagerly for the leather-covered box on the lower shelf, sure that he must have found something of significance. He stifled a chuckle when he opened it and saw a stack of paper, probably several hundred pages thick, with the top page bearing the title: "The Miraculous Life and Healing Power of Horace Joseph Gresham, In His Own Words". More pages of his autobiography graced the writing desk, written in tight script with a surfeit of curlicues and exclamation marks. Charlie read one paragraph and put it down again, hoping he would never have to read such arrant puffery again.

He returned to the outer office and blew out his candle, waiting at the door for his eyes to adjust to the dark before he slipped out. Not a sound could be heard as he tiptoed across the great hall under the disapproving gaze of the trustee's portraits.

Within a minute, he was inside Matron's office. The candle wick caught under the flare of the match, revealing a room that perfectly reflected the public persona Matron cultivated. Neat, orderly, efficient, but with compassionate touches – a vase bursting with summer

197

flowers, colourful drapes, a photograph of Matron surrounded by smiling children. Window dressing to reassure wealthy clients? Or a true reflection of her character? Definitely the former, but probably the latter too, although he couldn't be sure from such a short acquaintance.

Her desk was the complete opposite of Gresham's, giving every sign of a busy administrator as well as woman with her finger on the pulse of every aspect of the asylum. The papers he flicked through were all mundane matters pertaining to the everyday running of an institution, so he switched his attention to the inner sanctum.

He made short work of the lock, opening the door to reveal a storage room stacked with row upon row of files and boxes. Financial ledgers, invoices and receipts, staff and patient files – everything Charlie had been searching for and all written in the same bold, feminine hand, confirming that Matron was the financial administrator of Stillwaters, as well as the ruler of the female patients. Gresham must have been so preoccupied with his magnum opus that he left the administration entirely in her hands.

The patient register showed a steady trickle of admissions and discharges, especially to "category three". As Grace was listed, under the name Jane Bennet, he concluded category three referred to pregnant women.

Charlie searched back along the shelf for the register from six years ago. He ran his finger eagerly down the page, but very few women had been admitted around the time of the abduction, none of them named Amelia.

The police had been searching high and low for Amelia after she disappeared, so it would have been safer to admit her secretly and not record her in the ledger at all. But that would only have been possible if Matron Roberts was in on the plan to hide her, which didn't make sense. What benefit could she possibly gain from hiding an abducted woman, especially in a high-class, expensive institution? Unless Josiah Cowper had paid her a hefty bribe to ensure her silence.

Alternatively, Cowper might have admitted her under another name. The most likely suspect was a woman listed as Alice Smith, who was one of the few from around that time who had not yet been discharged. Could she be the same Alice that Grace suspected? He wished he'd thought to get Grace to point her out.

That still left the mystery of why Cowper would have paid for her care. Why would he have bothered, when he could have easily dropped Amelia in the streets of Dunedin before he boarded the ship to Australia? In fact, why bother to take her from Clyde in the first place? Charlie was sure he was missing crucial pieces of the puzzle, but he doubted he would find them within these walls if Amelia was not here.

The financial ledgers appeared relatively straightforward. Income on one side, expenses on the other, with a slim margin of profit. Stillwaters was by no means the lucrative money-maker they had assumed it must be, despite the high fees. The reason was apparent from a quick perusal of the expense column. They hadn't taken account of the huge cost of running an institution.

He ran his finger down the columns of eye-watering sums. The cost of food struck him as high, given the amount of produce they grew in the garden, especially as meat and dairy came from the farm too. Perhaps it was the additional cost of transporting bulkier items, such as flour and oats? Then he saw the wages bill, including his own wage, which was listed as a third higher than the amount Charlie was actually receiving. Some of the incidentals seemed exorbitant too. Did holy water imported from a fancy spa town in France really cost as much as liquid gold?

Now that his detective instincts were tingling, the income side stuck him as off too. Grace had told him there were additional fees and donations for treatments and infant care, but as far as he could see, each admitted patient paid the same fee. If Matron Roberts wasn't squirreling away a plump nest egg on the back of fraudulent accounts, he'd eat his hat.

It took less than two minutes to find the safe hidden within a locked cabinet and another ten minutes to find the Chubb key dangling from the back of a picture frame. A sturdy bag was crammed into the safe, presumably ready for a rapid departure if her fraud was uncovered.

In amongst the bundles of cash and gold coins was another ledger, listing the true amounts charged to patients' families. Not only was the matron pocketing the additional fees for treatments, but she was overcharging for care of the babies born here. The birth mothers' families were being charged for infant care long after the babies were listed as having been adopted, for which a separate, very substantial, fee was charged to the adopting family.

In short, Matron Roberts was making a mint. The amounts escalated over time, presumably as her greed grew alongside the confidence that she would not be discovered. She was about to find out the hard way that crime didn't pay.

Until an official search was made, Charlie did not want to arouse her suspicions. As he packed everything back in the safe the way it had been before, he noticed a wrapped package at the rear, which looked like the parcel Matron had been handed at the train station the day he arrived.

Inside was a pair of medicine bottles in a box labelled "Female Relief", which promised to "cure all ailments of a feminine nature", including "bringing on the monthly waters". He had no idea what that was supposed to mean, but he noted the ingredients listed on the bottles for Grace. Oil of Tansy appeared to be the main ingredient. It sounded like a flower – or was that a pansy?

Charlie shut the safe, returned the key to its hiding place, and extinguished his candle. With the evidence he had found, Detective Inspector Stewart would be champing at the bit to conduct an official raid of Stillwaters.

The corridor was dark and silent as he cracked open the office door. With nobody about, it was worth the risk of going outside to report to Stewart immediately. He made it to the back door with no problem, but, by sheer rotten luck, the night watchman was doing his occasional circuit of the grounds, catching Charlie as he crossed the open ground between the door and the trees.

The night watchman shone a lamp in his face. "Nobody is supposed to be outside after dark."

"My apologies, I didn't know." Charlie jangled his keys in the light, to show he wasn't an absconding patient. "My first day as an attendant. Couldn't sleep with all the strange noises."

"Bunch of fruitcakes, right enough. My sympathies, but I have my orders."

The night watchman made no move, leaving Charlie with no option but to apologise and retreat inside. He would have to get up early to talk to Stewart, although he doubted that his boss would be awake after his long hours on watch, perched in a tree.

The plan was scuppered by his own exhaustion. He didn't wake until Mr Walker hammered on his door, rousing him with a strong dose of ungentlemanly language. By the time he had dragged his body out of bed and squeezed into his uniform, the patients were already congregating in the dining hall, ready to do their allocated chores before breakfast. Not a good start, being late on his first full day.

Charlie was rostered to supervise the laying of the tables. Fortunately, his assigned helpers were already half way through the task without need of his supervision. Grace was on the other side of the dining hall, with a mop in her hand again.

When she saw him, she leaned over to the woman next to her, who had been talking to her at the dining table yesterday. They swapped the mop and broom between them. Grace looked towards him again, raising her hands briefly into the prayer position, before walking to the door of the chapel.

His pulse ticked up, as he realised she must have important information to share with him – something worth the risk of being discovered together. It would be just the opportunity he needed to brief her about the coming raid. Charlie headed for the back door to the chapel, but was waylaid by Mr Bevan.

"Have you seen John? The man with the round face who rocks a lot. He is supposed to be filling water bottles in the laundry."

"I think I saw him near the kitchen, Mr Bevan. My men have done their job here. I'll find John and make sure he gets onto it."

John was in the kitchen being fed bread and jam by the cook, who looked up guiltily at Charlie's appearance.

"Mind if I borrow John for an important task, Cook? Bring your treat with you, John. I won't tell if you don't." He nodded to the cook, who smiled back.

Charlie took John to the laundry, which was between the kitchen and the back of the chapel, and set him to his allotted task of filling bottles from the tap. Bottles labelled "Holy Water". The tap drew its water from a tank collecting rainwater runoff from the roof. So much for the importation of "holy water direct from the blessed springs of France", for which Stillwaters charged an exorbitant price.

"Are you sure these are the bottles you are meant to fill, John?"

"Yes, Mr Pearce. It's my job, every Friday."

"Take your time, John. You can eat your bread and jam, as long as you stay right here. I will be back in a couple of minutes."

Charlie slipped into the chapel via the back entrance, passing through an antechamber and curtain into the main chapel. Grace was on her hands and knees, exploring the various nooks and crannies, with a wet rag beside her to maintain the pretence of cleaning. She started at the sound of his footsteps, leaping to her feet with astonishing speed to resume her sweeping.

"Holy coppers, Mr Pearce, I nearly had a heart attack."

He hurried her into the corner, behind the far end of the curtain that ran around the back of the altar, where they could whisper unseen. Grace leaned so close he could feel her breath against his ear. It was all he could do to resist the urge to gather her up and whisk her to safety straight away, now that he had proof of Matron's wrongdoing.

"We haven't got long. I broke into Matron's office and took a look at the accounts. Matron is perpetrating fraud on a grand scale. Skimming the fees charged for the treatment programme and charging both parties for the care and adoptions of the babies who are born here. In fact, she continues to charge for their care long after they are adopted."

Grace let out a soft puff of breath. "Is that so? I haven't seen or heard any babies. Is there an attic here or another annexe that you know of, where they might keep them before they are adopted?"

"Not that I've seen, but I haven't explored the whole place by any means. I haven't had a chance to go outside at all, but I know there are other farm buildings. There is a separate road to the rear gate, so the adopting parents could arrive unseen to collect their choice of infant, direct from the best bloodlines in Dunedin. I expect that is why they can charge so much."

"Do you think Superintendent Gresham is involved too?"

"I didn't see any evidence of it, but he'd have to be as thick as an stone wall not to realise what was going on here. By the way, I looked at the patient register and the only likely patient listed as arriving within the days after Amelia's abduction was Alice Smith."

Grace's grip on his arm tightened. "I know her. Alice is the real name of the girl called Mouse, who has threads of gold in her pale blonde hair. Her medical records indicate that she tried to take her own life when she first arrived. Charlie, you need to brace for the worst if Mouse is really Amelia, because she is in a very poor state of mental health."

He couldn't face that thought now. Finding Amelia alive would be more than he had hoped for. "Point Mouse out to me at breakfast."

"Charlie, that's not all. I'm sure that the so-called religious purification is a cover for illegal terminations, but I have no hard evidence to support it yet."

"Doctor Wilson, you think?"

"Quite the opposite. Wilson was about to expose the whole scheme, which puts his death in a new light. He wrote a letter to the trustees after Clara's death last week, but I assume he never posted it, as everything is continuing as normal. The letter was probably in the bag taken from the train."

"If not Wilson, then who?"

"It could be the nurse, but I'm sure either the matron or the superintendent must be involved. I would guess the former, based on what you found out about her fraud. She is certainly clever and tough enough. If only I could find the drugs as proof."

"I don't suppose Oil of Tansy means anything to you? Matron had two bottles of it locked in her safe."

"Charlie, you're a marvel. That's exactly it!"

"Doesn't sound that bad."

"Tansy oil can be lethal after ingesting as little as ten drops for intolerant patients. Diluted in water and given gradually over a few days, it can induce uterine contractions, but it can also cause side effects such as vomiting, stomach pains, seizures and an erratic pulse. Exactly the symptoms recorded before Clara's death."

"Didn't you say you were given holy water during the superintendent's religious session yesterday? Holy water that comes straight from the rainwater off the roof, I might add, not an expensive import blessed by a French saint. Could the tansy oil have been added to that?"

"Makes sense. It was Matron who brought us the water, already poured into a separate goblet for each woman, so it would have been possible to give it only to those who had paid for the so-called purification."

"Grace, I think we have found out more than enough to organise an official raid on Stillwaters. I want you out of here today." He tipped her chin up with the tips of his fingers so she could see he was in earnest. "Please, for my peace of mind, get out as soon as you can."

"What about you, Charlie?"

"I'm not the one at risk. I'll stay until Stewart conducts the raid. Always useful to have a man on the inside."

"I admit I'd be happy to be out of here. But I need to stay long enough to talk to Alice Smith and a woman called Charlotte. I have the leverage now to get them to talk."

Charlie weighed up the options, knowing that Grace had a point, but not liking it. Still, a few more hours couldn't hurt, could it? "Stewart will be waiting to help you over the wall this afternoon."

"This evening, after dinner would be better. I am sure to be missed if I disappear before bedtime and we cannot afford to alert Matron before the raid. If I can't escape earlier, we can meet at midnight as planned, and you can help me get out."

"All right, what you say makes sense. Meanwhile, don't take any chances and for heaven's sake, Grace, don't drink the Holy Tap Water."

Charlie was about to give in to an overwhelming urge to embrace her, when he heard a scuffle near the door. He pushed Grace further behind the curtain. Before he could get to the door, Matron appeared at the entrance to the chapel, next to John.

Charlie forced a smile to his lips. "There you are John. I was looking for you everywhere."

"I thought I heard you talking to someone, Mr Pearce," Matron said.

"He was talking to Grace, Matron," John said. His expression was innocent of malice, but the damage was done.

"Who is Grace?" Matron asked, with a look sour enough to make a lemon shrivel.

"John heard me *saying* grace, didn't you John. When I come into a chapel, I like to share a few words with God." He crossed his fingers behind his back, hoping this pathetically weak explanation would pass muster.

"Yes, Matron, Mr Pearce said Grace. I was supposed to stay by the tap. I'm sorry, Mr Pearce."

Matron walked past Charlie and yanked the curtain aside. Charlie struggled to keep his face blank, but the space behind the curtain was now empty. The edge of a toe protruded from behind the raised stage, a gap so narrow, he couldn't believe Grace had squeezed herself into it.

"I have my eye on you, Mr Pearce. If you wish to retain your position here, refrain from leaving your assigned post."

"Yes, Matron." He had to think fast to come up with an excuse to distract Matron and allow Grace to escape. "May I have a quick word with you in the laundry, Matron, while I supervise John? I would like to volunteer for extra duties to demonstrate my commitment to the work."

By the time they were back in the dining hall, preparations for breakfast were almost complete. Grace put her broom away in the closet, then walked in a wide arc to her seat at the table, pausing for a moment to tap a spot on the end of the bench at the far table.

When the rest of the women filed in to the dining hall for breakfast, that spot was taken by a frail blonde woman, who kept her head down. Her hair was nowhere near golden enough for Amelia, but perhaps the drugs and trauma of the past six years had caused her hair to whiten prematurely.

As soon as prayers were over, Mouse was pulled up by the woman beside her and guided to the porridge queue, still with the head held low and her face covered by a veil of straggly hair. Charlie was desperately trying to come up with a plan to make her look up, when John tripped and stumbled into a stack of trays, clattering them to the floor with a fearful crash.

Mouse glanced up, revealing a painfully sunken face, her blue eyes devoid of expression, even as other patients shrieked or giggled at the commotion. She saw him looking, but did not react, other than to avert her eyes. Nor did he feel the least sense of familiarity.

Charlie looked away. He had work to do, calming John, stacking trays, returning the men to a state of order. Even with the trauma of her abduction, he couldn't believe Amelia would have become completely unrecognisable to him.

When he saw Grace looking at him, he shook his head, adding a slight shrug to concede that he couldn't be absolutely sure.

A Novel Approach

Grace couldn't believe her eyes when Charlie indicated that Mouse was not Amelia, although the shrug suggested a trace of doubt. He had been at enough meals now to have seen all the women from a distance. And he had been able to look into all the secure cells and meet all the ancillary staff, such as the cook and laundry maids. It was beginning to look as if they were on a wild goose chase after all.

Disappointing, but not surprising. They had accepted from the start that Isabelle only had second-hand information from the woman called Charlotte. If Amelia had ever been here, she would likely have left by now. In a way, it was a relief. Grace would be delighted to disappear over the wall this evening, safely into the custody of her second favourite policeman, knowing she had done her best to help Charlie.

But first, Grace needed to talk to Charlotte Brontë and Alice Smith. After a night on the prowl, her first priority was to stoke her boiler, even if the only fuel on offer was oversalted porridge, thick slabs of bread with the merest scraping of butter, and tea so weak it scarcely darkened the milk.

She scraped her bowl clean and drank her tea to the dregs, wondering if she would be treated as badly as Oliver Twist if she asked for more.

"Have mine." Fluff pushed an untouched bowl across. "Can't face food this morning."

"You don't look at all well, Fluff." In her distraction, Grace had failed to notice that Fluff's usual rosy pink complexion had faded to the colour of old straw. "You were moaning in your sleep last night."

"My stomach aches. It must be something I ate."

"Shall I get Sister Jones?"

"Miss Dalloway said it's the nurse's day off. She said I was not to fuss, that I'd be as bright as a new penny after a rest. Don't look so worried, Jane, I'll be fine."

Grace shovelled the rest of the food down, then washed both plates. She returned to find Miss Dalloway giving Fluff a small dose of laudanum.

"Will you help Fluff into the dayroom, Jane? Call me if she gets worse."

Grace draped Fluff's arm over her shoulder, while Lizzie took the other side. Together they shuffled her into the most comfortable chair in the dayroom, adding an extra cushion for support. Fluff curled up into a ball, clutching her stomach. Grace took her pulse, which was weak, and wiped her clammy forehead with a handkerchief.

Lizzie took Grace aside. "I wish Sister Jones was here. This is just how Clara looked the day before she died. Superintendent Gresham said she died because the demon had lodged too strongly inside her. She didn't have the strength of spirit to fight it."

"Gresham is a steaming pile of weasel dung. I beg you not to believe a word he says."

"I don't really, I suppose. But he seems to have such power. Sometimes I worry that I will be next, damned for my disbelief."

"Lizzie, this is going to sound like an odd question, but do you know how Fluff's family viewed her condition. Were they willing to raise her baby within the family?"

"Fluff wanted to keep her child, but she told me her father had been ready to cast her out onto the street. It was only by the intervention of her mother and uncle that he agreed to admit her to Stillwaters instead and only if she gave up the child. Appalling behaviour. How could anyone think so ill of a lovely girl like Fluff?"

"And you?"

"My older sister and her husband are desperate for a child. For all my father despises me, he wouldn't hurt her for all the gold in Central Otago."

"Then I think you have nothing to fear. Would you keep an eye on Fluff? I have to talk to Miss Brontë. I'll be back as soon as I can, but please call me immediately if she gets worse."

The Romantics were gathered in a circle, happily arguing over which of their favourite books they would adapt into a play next. Grace hovered at the edge of the circle, directly in front of Charlotte.

Miss Brontë clapped her hands for attention. "Miss Jane Bennet wishes to speak to me. Who am I to refuse such an honour after her heroism yesterday?" She allowed the giggles to subside, then winked at her deputy. "Perhaps we should liven the morning with a little dancing, Miss Austen?"

Her second-in-command soon had the women twirling around their section of the dayroom, conveniently obscuring their leader from the view of the two attendants. Grace was rapidly coming to the view that Miss Brontë was a formidable force.

"I suspect you don't miss much, Miss Jane Bennet. What are you really doing at Stillwaters?"

"I might ask you the same, Miss Brontë. I believe you would be better placed leading a tribe of Amazons into battle. Or perhaps running a school for talented young ladies?"

"Call me Charlotte, my dear. Most people seem to find me rather ridiculous, but you have seen through me." Charlotte smiled – a lovely smile that lit up her eyes. "My parents wouldn't consent to my wish to train as a teacher, thinking it too common a vocation for a well-bred girl. I, in turn, refused outright to marry the obnoxious lard-brain they offered as the alternative. I sank into the world of books and music, until the melancholy became too much for any of us to bear."

"And here, you have found your calling. Lifting the spirits, and probably saving the lives, of young women who might otherwise fall into despair at their circumstances."

"To each, her own small task. Although, in truth, it is me who has been saved from a life of misery. I expect that shocks you, Jane, but I assure you that a life deprived of a meaningful occupation is far worse than the deprivations of Stillwaters. Now, how may I help you?"

"First, I have something for you." Grace checked that the dancers were still shielding them, then reached under the sturdy armchair that was Miss Brontë's throne, withdrawing one of the books she had taken from the storage cupboard and hidden within the springs of the seat.

Charlotte seized the prize from her and clasped it to her bosom. "Oh my sainted days, *Jane Eyre*." A tear slipped from the corner of her eye and dropped to the book in her shaking hands. "My dear Jane, how can I thank you for this treasure?"

"By keeping it safe for the enjoyment of all. There are another dozen or so novels hidden under the armchair, liberated from the confiscated items in the storage cupboard upstairs."

"I shall withdraw them one at a time, never knowing what priceless gem I might pull out next. Oh, the thrill of anticipation will keep me in a state of bliss for months to come! But come now, no need to be coy Jane, I can see you wish to ask me a question."

"Indeed I do. I met a woman called Isabelle Forsyth after she escaped from here last week. She said to tell a friend of mine that Amelia and Josiah were still alive. This woman, Amelia, is very important to us, as she has been missing for six years. Isabelle said a woman called Charlotte asked her to pass the message on, but we were separated before I could ask her anything more."

"How intriguing. I would love to help you solve your mystery, but I'm afraid I am not the Charlotte she was referring to. I never met Isabelle, although she was pointed out to me. She wasn't here long and didn't speak to many of the women, as far as I can recall. She was a restless soul, always prowling the garden, as if seeking a chance to flee. As for Amelia and Josiah, I have never heard of anyone with those names here at Stillwaters. There have been a few patients named Charlotte over the years, but none other than myself at present, I believe."

"Have you been here long?"

"Oh, goodness, I hardly know. Time has no meaning anymore. I was committed in the spring of 1888."

"Over four years ago."

"Has it really been so long? I'm truly sorry I haven't been able to help you, Jane Bennet."

"You have lifted my spirits and eliminated a possibility. I no longer believe Amelia is here, if she ever was. Enjoy your novel, Charlotte."

"Indeed I shall. I see it not as a mere book, but as a gateway into another world, better than any tonic a doctor could concoct."

Charlotte clapped her hands again, bringing the dancing to a halt. Her group was soon flocking to her side, eager to hear what had passed. "Well, ladies, who would like to hear a charming tale about a girl who overcomes great hardship to become a beloved governess?"

The Romantics gathered in a circle, flapping and squawking like a flock of excited parakeets around a particularly juicy slice of fruit. Miss Jane Bennet stood at the edge of the group, basking in their squeals of delight. What pleasure it gave her to see the resilience and companionship of these young women, rallying their spirits with activities they enjoyed, despite the circumstances they found themselves in.

Grace still wanted to talk to Mouse, but that would be best done in the seclusion of the garden. There was still plenty of time for her to finish her task before she escaped over the wall after lights out.

Daisy Chains

After breakfast, Charlie and the other attendant readied the men for their morning session of outdoor work. Bevan directed him to take the men into the walled vegetable garden, while he retrieved the tools from a locked shed. When the tools were distributed, Bevan sat back on a garden seat, beckoning Charlie to join him.

Charlie watched on with concern as the men wielded their spades and hoes with all the finesse of a bunch of children. "Is this safe?"

"As long as we keep a close watch. The tools are blunt compared to what you'd use in your own garden. The real purpose of the work is to tire them out."

"Seacliff was the same. The superintendent there is a great believer in the therapeutic benefits of outdoor work. I must say I agree. Far better than dosing them up with drugs." Charlie allowed his gaze to wander. "Hey, I'll bet there is a great view from the wall."

Charlie climbed on an old milk churn and scrambled up to the top of the wall. The men continued their work like old hands, so he let his gaze drift over the main gate to the sea in the north, across the orchard and fields to the east and around to a tall hedge to the south, with a grove of trees beyond.

"The building behind that hedge over there. Is that the coach house the groundsman told me about?"

"The taller building is the coach house. I believe the stable is behind it, but I've never been there. Quigley told me it is out of bounds, even to attendants. You can walk everywhere else though, in your rare moments of free time. Only you mustn't go into the west garden in the afternoon, as that is the private time for the women patients. Personally speaking, I never hang around here when I have time off. Any chance to get out, I'd advise you to grab with both hands. If you're keen on fishing, I can show you some good spots."

Charlie mumbled his thanks.

"You all right if I sneak out for a smoke?"

"Sure, not a problem." Charlie used the time to study the layout of the sanctuary in more detail. As his gaze swung back across to the building in the trees, he thought he saw a flash of movement in an upper window of the coach house.

Presumably, the lower level of the coach house would be used for the buggy and cart that had collected them on the first day, while the upper storey would be where any stable hands lived. Not that there would be much call for them. Most likely the stable housed no more than four to six horses in all, although they would probably be outside in the field over summer.

Charlie assumed the coach house and stable were strictly out of bounds to stop attendants borrowing a horse for nefarious purposes. After long hours of work at Stillwater, even the meagre delights of Waitati might be tempting. From the number of crates and casks being loaded onto the cart at the station, the local hotel must do a brisk trade. And where there was beer, there were usually other entertainments.

A piercing wail shocked his attention back to his job. One of the men was curled in a ball on the ground, weeping, while another stood by waving a spade and shouting at him. Charlie leaped off the wall, expecting to see gushing blood. He grabbed the spade before anyone else got hurt, then kneeled down to check the victim for signs of injury. There was not a mark on him, despite his wailing.

Bevan sauntered back into the garden, knocking his pipe out behind a stone, making sure to grind the tobacco ash into the ground. "What all the fuss this time, Mr Cuthbertson?"

The patient stopped sobbing and pointed to the ground. Charlie couldn't see anything and, from the look on Bevan's face, he couldn't either.

The other patient bent down and picked up two halves of a still-wiggling earthworm. "He doesn't care for murdering God's creatures, no matter how lowly the victim." He shrugged and popped the earthworm pieces into his mouth, eliciting further howls from Cuthbertson.

Bevan grimaced, but took it in his stride, as if he'd seen it all before, and more. "Mr Pearce, would you take Mr Cuthbertson to tidy up the graveyard. He likes doing that. Take Jenkins and Sunderland with you too." He nodded his head towards two delicate men who were struggling to get their spades into the ground, let alone turn the soil over. "Bring them back inside when the first gong sounds."

Charlie gathered up his charges, delighted to have the perfect excuse to explore the grounds. He was about to ask where the graveyard was, when he realised it would be more useful to roam around until he found it, pleading ignorance if questioned.

He led the men in a sweeping circle around the back of the coach house. Unfortunately the hedge was far too thick to see though, although it did have the advantage of hiding his exploration from anyone in the main house.

Cuthbertson stopped by a patch of daisies in the lawn. He looked at Charlie eagerly. "Can I make a daisy chain, Mr Pearce?"

"Excellent idea. How about you all sit down, so Mr Cuthbertson can show you how to do it." A little to his surprise, they all dropped to the ground and started to pick the tiny white flowers. "I'll be back in a minute."

Charlie pushed through a less dense section of hedge, coming up against an iron rail fence on the other side.

Two women were making their way from the gate to the coach house, chattering companionably. One had a small milk churn in one hand and a wicker basket covered by a checked cloth in the other. The second woman had a single large basket of what appeared to be linen. Oddly, the path they were walking on was not marred by the imprint of carriage wheels or horse hooves. Nor was there the usual smell of horses and hay that permeates the air around all stables.

The women knocked at the door, which was opened by a little boy, who squealed with delight. Arms reached out from behind him and threw him into the air, sending him into gales of laughter. The two visiting women chuckled too. They shooed the boy cheerfully through the doorway, until the whole party disappeared to the sound of happy chatter. Charlie was struck by the incongruity of hearing the pure ring of laughter, a sound he hadn't heard since he arrived, other than in hysterical form.

From the upstairs window, another cry drifted down – this one the distressing cry of a baby, quickly silenced by the soothing voice of a woman. He didn't require a detective's training to surmise that he had found the place the babies were been looked after, prior to being adopted.

When he reversed out of the hedge, brushing twigs off his uniform, he found the men sitting cross-legged in a tight triangle, each with a completed daisy chain on their caps and another in progress. Cuthbertson had created a neat chain which wrapped twice around his head, Jenkins had made a short and ragged version, while Sunderland's cap was adorned by half a dozen loose flowers.

Their happy grins faded at the sight of Charlie returning.

"Do we have to go now, Mr Pearce?"

"You are almost out of daisies, Mr Cuthbertson. Shall we go and find some more?"

The three men got up, their good humour restored. They followed Charlie dutifully as he did a winding circuit around the walls. Trees dotted the parkland they were walking through, but none close enough to the wall to make a convenient exit point. When they reached the corner, they turned north again, finding the graveyard between the edge of the narrow woods and the west wall, hidden from the house.

They removed their caps and entered the graveyard through a mossy lychgate in a low stone wall. Ahead of them, an old wooden cross bore a plaque saying "Peace Be With You In The Arms Of Our Lord".

While the men tended to the weeds in the graveyard, Charlie roamed the rows reading the names of all the young women on the headstones. Along the front was a row of miniature crosses, presumably representing the infants who didn't live long enough to be named.

He was shocked at the number of graves, although Stillwaters Sanctuary had been here for almost a decade, so perhaps he shouldn't have been. He recalled Grace telling him that as many as one in every two hundred women died during childbirth, while up to a third of infants didn't survive. It was a sobering thought. He wished every young rake could be brought here before they lured young women into giving up their chastity, not that it would make much difference to such irresponsible scoundrels.

Beyond the graveyard, tucked away close to the wall, was another set of graves within a simple picket fence. The graves were marked by a row of small plaques, listing only the name and dates of death, for both men and women. Presumably these were the graves of those who took their own lives, buried in shame, apart from the other graves.

A morepork hooted softly in a tree just beyond the wall. He caught a flash of movement amongst the leaves. Detective Inspector Stewart was on the job. Charlie glanced back at his charges, but they were now sitting on the ground again in a patch of daisies. He wandered over to rest his back against the wall.

"Morning, sir. Beautiful day to be a bird."

"And a lovely day to be a lunatic." The voice appeared to be coming from the thick bough of a tree that was close to the wall. "Anything to report?"

"No luck on Amelia and we are almost out of likely suspects. More progress on Stillwaters. There are definitely grounds for concern over what is happening here. A great deal more money is paid in fees than is accounted for in the official ledgers. Matron is skimming a very substantial profit on the side from illegal terminations and fees for adoption and care of the babies, as well as overcharging expenses."

"I saw a buggy arrive at the rear gate yesterday afternoon. A woman took a wrapped bundle out to a well-to-do couple and they drove off, with the bundle in the woman's arms. I should have realised that it had to be a baby."

"This place may be run by a charitable foundation, but I can tell you that they extract a princely sum for supplying desperate couples with a baby born to woman of good breeding, with no questions asked."

"Are you certain enough of the facts for me to arrange a police raid of Stillwaters?"

"Absolutely sure. I found the proceeds of the crime and the real financial ledgers in Matron's safe. I have told Grace to leave as soon as she can. If she doesn't come looking for your help to get over the wall today, she and I will meet around midnight and I will get her to you."

"Can you come back to talk to me again later? Lily has sent a telegram saying she has important information. She's coming up on the afternoon train."

"The patients go to bed ridiculously early here. I expect I can sneak out this evening after nine o'clock. Hopefully, Grace will be with you around that time too. It'll be a weight off my mind to know she is safe."

The gong sounded in the distance. "I've got to go."

"Keep up the good work, Pyke."

Charlie saluted the tree, then hurried back to his charges, who had risen as one at the sound of the gong and were making their way towards the lychgate.

Down The Rabbit Hole

Grace waited in a fever of impatience for the morning to pass, thankfully without further drama. After the midday meal, they were allowed out into the garden.

Much as she ached to melt into the grove of trees for an afternoon of quiet respite from madness, Grace needed to establish for certain that Mouse was not a drug-addled version of Amelia.

She found her tucked into a sunny spot behind a thick screen of Hebe bushes. Grace sat down on the ground an arm's length from her target, angled so she wasn't looking directly at her. To her relief, Mouse stayed where she was.

Grace drew out the White Rabbit from under her skirt and placed it between them. She wasn't sure what to expect – a grab and run, tears of delight, no reaction at all – but she certainly didn't expect the reaction she got.

Mouse seized the rabbit with a low squeal and ripped the side seam apart, shedding stuffing in all directions. Grace flicked her eyes sideways, unsure what to make of this wanton destruction. Mouse extracted an object from within the rabbit's stuffing and began to sob, quietly but fervently.

Grace waited until the tears ran dry. "Miss Smith – Alice – is there anything I can do for you?"

Alice's head twitched in her direction. "Nobody has called me by my real name for ever so long." Her voice was rusty with disuse and emotion. She held out a palm-sized portrait of a young man with kind eyes and a cheeky grin. "My beloved brother. He died."

"Will you tell me about him, Alice?"

Alice considered her question carefully, before answering in jerky sentences. "George was kind. He made me laugh. He … protected me. I couldn't face life without him."

"George would want you to be happy. To laugh a little, as well as cry, don't you think?"

Alice held the portrait to her heart, but didn't reply.

"I could sew the White Rabbit up for you again, if you like. Though I ought to warn you, I am not much of a seamstress."

She looked up at Grace through a veil of lank hair. "Why did you do this for me?"

"I suppose because I don't believe in taking away the things that are important to a person for no good reason. Rules should be to prevent harm, not cause it, don't you think?"

Alice dipped her head, as if uncertain that common sense might prevail over rules.

"May I ask if Alice Smith has always been your name?"

"Of course. Why do you ask?"

"I am looking for a woman who was called Amelia. She had pale golden hair and arrived at Stillwaters around the same time as you."

"I remember her. She was in the medical room when I was there … recovering." Alice unconsciously rubbed at the slash marks across her wrists. "The nurse called her Charlotte, but she said her name was Amelia Lawrence. She was in a terrible state. So very pale, jumping at the least sound, always crying." Alice's voice trailed away. "She told me the dreadful things that had happened to her."

"I know, Alice. No one should suffer as Amelia did. Do you know if she is still here?"

Alice reached out for the White Rabbit, burying her head in its fur. "She was so ill, they took her away. I never saw her again. I fear she must have died."

Poor Charlie, this news was going to hit him hard. "Thank you, Alice. I can't tell you how grateful I am to know what happened to Amelia. The pain of not knowing still haunts her family and friends."

One eye peeked out from behind her hair. "I have seen her ghost in the grove of trees. Her spirit has rosy cheeks and walks with light feet. I believe she comes back to Stillwaters to show me that there is happiness to be found in Heaven. Seeing her helps to keep me alive."

Because she didn't believe in ghosts, Grace wasn't sure what to make of this, except that it kept a spark of hope alight within her. Had Amelia recovered and been discharged? Did she come back to visit occasionally for some reason? It was difficult to imagine why she would ever wish to return here, except out of gratitude for the care that had led to her recovery.

A memory resurfaced from the matron's conversation with the superintendent on her first day. The ladies from Magdalene Charitable Mission visited every month to extend their benevolence to the patients. How wonderful it would be if Amelia was not only alive, but living a good life and coming back here to help other women. She tamped down the hope. It was far more likely that Alice had conjured the ghost from within her fragile mind.

"Alice, I'm sure you would find a lot of good women here who would be willing to help you, when you feel ready to receive it. You have certainly helped me, for which I am truly grateful."

Grace left Alice to her memories of her brother. Now that she knew for certain that Amelia had been here, under the name Charlotte, she was desperate to get into Matron's office to look through the patient files for herself, in case Charlie had missed something. She might even manage another look in the medical records tonight, before she left here forever.

The gardens were quiet today, as most of the women were sheltering from the sun under the trees or in the dayroom. Dare she try to get into Matron's office now?

Grace crept around the side of the house, keeping to the shelter of the larger bushes in the garden. She wasn't sure which of the windows on the south side was the window of Matron's office, but only one was open, allowing the faint breeze to soften the impact of a hot day.

As she got closer to the open window, she could hear Matron's voice, which carried with its usual sharp clarity. She was speaking to a man, whose voice was no more than an infuriating mumble. All Grace could tell was that he was anxious and trying to convince Matron of something, while she remained unmoved. Grace crawled forward as fast as she could, stopping right under the window.

"So what if you saw a Chinese woman on the train. There are plenty around."

He must have moved closer, because his voice became audible, although Grace still couldn't hear the man well enough to identify him. But she did know that Superintendent Gresham went into the city today, so he may well have returned on the afternoon train. Could the Chinese woman have been Lily?

"I tell you she looked like the policeman's wife from Clyde. Why would she be here if the girl hadn't somehow managed to get word out?"

"It's been six years, Josiah. You are worrying needlessly."

"You would worry too, if your neck was threatened by the hangman's noose. We should take the money and get out, while we can. Maybe that damned doctor talked to someone, before his timely death. I told you we should have gotten rid of him earlier."

"As it happens, brother, I think you might be right. Our little scheme has netted enough to keep us in comfort for the rest of our days, along with the windfall from Clyde."

"Then what are we waiting for, Bertha. Let's get out of here right now."

"No Josiah, it will be safer to go tonight, so I am not missed. We will leave at dusk, after the patients are in bed and the place is locked down, but while there is still enough light to get back to the main road. I'll have the cart made ready."

Suddenly, the window was pulled shut with a bang, adding another layer of trauma to Grace's wildly beating heart. Nausea welled up in her throat at the thought of being caught eavesdropping by a murderer and kidnapper. No wonder Amelia had been brought here, if Josiah Cowper was Matron's brother. What's more, he had made it sound as if Amelia was still here.

She had to find a way to alert Charlie and Alistair immediately, especially as Josiah had identified Lily on the train.

Grace was scrambling backwards out of the flower bed under the window when she heard footsteps coming towards her. She stayed on her knees and began pulling weeds from the edge of the path. When she looked up again, Miss Dalloway was standing at the corner of the house with her hands on her hips, regarding Grace with narrowed eyes.

"What are you doing here, Bennet? You are out of bounds."

"Am I, Miss Dalloway? I hadn't realised. I do hate to see a weedy path, so I just followed it around."

'You know the rules. You will be confined to your dormitory and miss supper. Perhaps a little floor scrubbing will help you to remember your place."

Paper Trail

Charlie's afternoon passed with all the speed of a geriatric snail, supervising the men in the dayroom after their morning's work in the gardens. The inaction was frustrating, but there was no way to leave his post without being spotted.

The afternoon ended at last with supper at the ludicrous hour of five o'clock. Charlie kept an eye out for Grace, but her spot at the table remained ominously empty. When the women at her table rose to get their food, he moved towards the serving area, straightening a perfectly aligned stack of plates. He strolled past the woman who sat beside Grace, who was whispering to the woman beside her.

"… Dalloway made her scrub the bathroom floor with a nailbrush. Jane was just doing a bit of weeding … realise it was out of bounds. Oh lord, Welsh rarebit for tea again, is it Friday already?"

Charlie went back to supervising the men. Caught and punished for weeding was not good, but it was by no means as bad as it might have been. He crossed his fingers behind his back, telling himself that Grace would surely find a way out of the dormitory tonight. The sooner he saw her disappearing over that wall, the sooner he could start breathing freely again. He vowed never to let her convince him to put her at risk again.

The patients behaved perfectly that evening, taking their medication without fuss, washing without drama, and tucking up in bed with scarcely a grumble. By quarter past nine, he had left them in the care of the night attendant and returned to his room to change into his own clothes. This close to the summer equinox, it didn't get truly dark for another couple of hours, but he was unlikely to be seen if he kept to the trees as far as possible.

Charlie took the time to ensure the night watchman was at the main gate, before slipping out the back door. He stopped in the bushes under the window to Grace's dormitory. There was no sign of life and no white handkerchief in the window. He contemplated scaling the wall to see if she was still in there, but there were few hand-holds. Besides, the shock of seeing a man's face at the window would set off mayhem in the women's ward. Grace would have to wait until everyone was asleep.

He watched for several minutes, fighting hard against the overwhelming urge to go back inside and storm the place, dragging Grace out of there. When nothing stirred, he hurried to his meeting with Stewart, fervently hoping he had made the right call.

An owl hooted within the shelter of the grove of trees, then a knotted rope arced over the wall. Charlie was up and over in a few seconds, hauling the rope back as soon as he landed. When he turned, he saw a shape disappearing into the trees.

In the clearing beyond, a smaller shape emerged from Stewart's shadow and wrapped him in a welcome embrace. "What's wrong, Charlie?"

"I'm worried about Grace, Aunt Lily. She wasn't at supper. If she doesn't show up by dark, I think we should raid the place tonight instead of waiting for more men."

"Agreed," Stewart replied. "But you need to hear what Lily has found out first."

"We have managed to trace the history of the matron here, Bertha Roberts. We found a marriage certificate between Bertha Cowper and Ernest Roberts, now deceased. With the help of the Reverend Waddell and his band of local ministers, we have established that the Cowper family lived in South Dunedin, with four children, including Bertha and a boy called Josiah."

Charlie let out a low whistle. "Brilliant detecting, Aunt Lily. So the matron here is the sister of Amelia's kidnapper, Josiah Cowper. Finally, a link between Amelia and Stillwaters. I was wondering why she was brought here."

"That's not all, Charlie. Mr Peters used his amazing cross-referencing system to track down further information on Bertha and

Josiah Cowper. Bertha Cowper was previously employed as a nurse attendant at a home for orphaned girls, which was the subject of a fraud investigation. Bertha was released without charge, as the evidence from the financial ledgers implicated the man in charge of the orphanage. He protested his innocence, but was still convicted, though no money was ever found."

"Has DI Stewart told you about Matron's fraudulent activities here too?"

"Yes. It cannot be a coincidence. Mr Peters also found a record of Bertha Cowper being cautioned for the sale of home-made remedies. Presumably as a nurse she must have developed some skills as an apothecary. Apparently she was quite well known locally for the efficacy of her potions, which were sold as 'Doctor Josiah's Miraculous Elixir', the same tonic Amelia was given. It would seem as if brother and sister were in close collaboration even then."

"Matron Roberts is as sharp as a filleting knife. I'd bet she was the one running the show, including the fraud at the orphanage."

Stewart was pacing back and forth, wearing a groove in the soil. "Charlie, how certain are you that Josiah Cowper really did leave for Australia after abducting Amelia and killing her father?"

"Not at all certain. The only evidence was his name on the ship's passenger list and our inability to find him anywhere in New Zealand. Back then, we didn't know he had a sister willing and able to hide him."

"If he was still here," Lily said, "it would explain the message Isabelle gave to Grace, that Amelia and Josiah were both alive. Alistair, you look as if you have a theory to share."

"I'm thinking that such a large-scale fraud would be a lot easier to get away with if the superintendent was in on it. Could Gresham be Doctor Josiah?"

The though turned Charlie's blood to ice, knowing Grace was still in there. "I never met Cowper, so I cannot say. The description we are working to is brown hair, blue eyes, average build and somewhere between about thirty and forty years old, although that is six years out of date. Horace Gresham is the right age and build, and has that evangelical fervour that would work equally well as spiritual healer or quack doctor. I believe Gresham started here several years ago, but I don't have a date. So, yes, it is possible."

"If he is Cowper, you have to give him credit for audacity, to take such a high-profile job."

"I have my doubts he would be daring enough, although I suppose if he had faked his emigration to Australia, he might have been confident nobody would make the connection. If Horace Gresham is Cowper, I'd still guess that it's Matron who is running the fraud. Although he is nominally in charge of Stillwaters, she is the one who keeps the accounts and manages the running of every aspect of the asylum."

"Given the amount of money they are making here, they'd be willing to take a fair amount of risk."

"The evidence on the police file indicates that Bertha was considered the mastermind of the operation to make and sell patent medicines," Lily said, "while Josiah Cowper did what he was told and sold them around the markets of Otago."

"What about the doctor who died on the train?" Stewart asked. "Could he have been Cowper?"

"Again, the right age and type," Charlie replied, "but then so are many other men. Doctor McLeod for one. One of the other attendants here, Mr Bevan, also fits the description, although he seems a decent fellow."

"I went to see Professor Scott, as you suggested, Charlie, to check McLeod's background," Lily said. "Scott was adamant that McLeod was above board. He only arrived in New Zealand four years ago. Doctor Wilson is a different kettle of fish. His qualification is untraceable and his past unknown."

"Grace is convinced Doctor Wilson was innocent. In fact, he was about to expose what was going on here," Charlie said. "Where is Albert Lawrence? He is the only one of us who lived in Clyde at the time, so he is the only one who might be able to identify Josiah Cowper, if indeed the scoundrel is here at all."

226

"I ordered Lawrence to stay at the Saratoga in Waitati and keep a low profile," Stewart replied. "He is keeping an eye on train movements, receiving mail from Lily and Anne and that's it. I didn't want him too close to the investigation as he is an unknown quantity, not like my crack team of trusted investigators." Stewart dropped an arm around Lily's shoulders and received an adoring smile in return.

"I must admit I was pleased to see Albert waiting for me at the station. I was getting some unwelcome attention on the train. You'd think they had never seen a Chinese woman before. It's not like I had the temerity to travel first class."

"My dear Lily, you are worth a thousand times more than those bigoted idiots."

"I know Superintendent Gresham went to the city early this morning," Charlie said. "He could well have taken the afternoon train back. All the more reason to get Grace out as soon as possible. So, what's the plan?"

"I'd prefer to do it by the book, but I'm reluctant to delay much longer, especially if there is any possibility that they are aware of Grace's true identity. Lily might have been recognised too, if Cowper was on the train."

Stewart stopped pacing, a sure sign he had come to a decision. "We need to be ready for any eventuality or to make a quick escape if necessary. Albert Lawrence has hired horses. Lily rode one of them up here from the station, so I can get back quickly to bring Albert and the other two horses. As soon as we return, I'll put Albert on lookout on the front gate and I'll watch the rear gate. Lily can wait here, in case you need to pass on a message."

"And Grace?"

Stewart rubbed his hands over his moustaches, curling the tips tightly, as he did when he was worried. "Unless you have grounds to believe she is in imminent danger, it might best to leave her until we are ready to raid in strength. As soon as we arrest Matron and seize the files, you can use your authority to have Grace released. If she gets out by herself before I arrive, Lily will be here to help her over the wall."

Charlie nodded his agreement. "I'll blow my whistle using the emergency signal if anything goes wrong. Otherwise, shall we set the raid time for ten o'clock tonight? The patients will all be asleep, but there will still be enough light to see if anyone tries to make a run for it."

"Agreed." Stewart handed Charlie his badge, a truncheon and a pair of handcuffs, which made him feel like his old self again. "And Charlie, if you do have grounds to believe Grace is in danger, use whatever force necessary to ensure her safety. That's an order."

Seizures

Grace was still seething at being ordered to miss supper and scrub the bathroom floor as punishment for being a few yards out of bounds. Ridiculous, it was not as if she had been caught trying to set fire to the chapel or drown the miserable Dalloway in fake holy water.

Lizzie slipped her a slice of bread as they got ready for bed. Grace mumbled her thanks as she devoured it. The quiet chatter of the women seemed to last forever, through the brushing of hair, washing, prayers, putting on nightdresses and settling under the row of identical blankets. Now all she had to do was wait until it was dark.

As time crawled by, lying still became almost impossible. She was desperate to get out and pass on the news about Josiah Cowper, Matron and their imminent flight. Finally, the other women settled into slumber, except for Fluff, who was restless and moaning in the bed beside hers. Fluff had slept all afternoon, after being given laudanum, but now its effect was wearing off.

Grace listened with growing concern, as her moaning escalated to groaning, then writhing agony. This was no ordinary stomach upset. Grace should have acted hours ago, when Lizzie had mentioned that Clara had had the same symptoms. She had no doubt now – Fluff had been dosed with tansy oil. From the sound of her, she was in a bad way. Grace couldn't leave her like this.

The night attendant must have heard her too, as she came over with a lamp, turned low, throwing a sickly yellow light onto Fluff. Grace took one look at her sweating, pallid face and knew Fluff was in deep trouble. As they watched, she went into convulsions, which died away again, leaving her semi-conscious.

The attendant was staring with round eyes, not doing a thing.

"Get Sister Jones," Grace ordered.

"It's her day off."

Grace could hear the panic in the attendant's voice. With as much calm as she could muster, she took the attendant by the shoulders. "Get the nurse aide, Miss Thomas, if she is here, or the midwife. If neither of them are here, send a male attendant for the local doctor." The woman just stared at her. "Do it now. I will look after Fluff until you get back. Please go, or she might die."

The night attendant fled, taking the lamp with her.

When the door had banged closed behind her, one of the patients by the window drew the curtain back, allowing the twilight in to reveal a row of terrified faces looking at Grace.

"I have medical training," she said, with more confidence than she felt. "I will take Fluff to the medical room and make sure she is all right. The rest of you should stay in bed."

"I'll help you," Lizzie said.

She had picked up Fluff's limp body before Grace could argue, leaving Grace to open the doors with the spare key she had liberated from the key cabinet. As soon as Fluff was on the bed in the medical room, Grace sent Lizzie back. The last thing she wanted was to get her friend in trouble, especially as Grace planned to be gone from Stillwaters before retribution descended.

Grace had never dealt with anything like this before, but she knew she would have to act fast or Fluff might not make it through the night. As she dithered by the medicine cupboard, her patient went into convulsions again. Grace rushed back to the bed and fastened the straps to keep her from falling and hurting herself, while waiting for the fit to die away. Fluff opened her eyes again as her breathing steadied, but Grace was sure that the convulsions would start again, sooner rather than later.

There was only one medicine to hand that might help – bromide – a common sedative for calming nervous disorders, but also an anti-convulsant. She had seen it administered during her two days at Seacliff, but had never administered it herself. Calm down, read the label, follow the instructions, she told herself.

For a while, the bromide didn't appear to be doing anything, but gradually, the convulsions died down as Fluff's body relaxed and her pulse edged towards normal. There was no sign of blood under her nightdress, so perhaps she and the baby would both make it after all.

Grace covered her friend with a blanket and sat back to wait for help. Every now and then, Fluff let out a low moan or hunched her body in a spasm of pain, but these moments of distress passed quickly and became less frequent, as Grace held her hand and murmured encouragement.

Outside, the sun had gone down, although it was still light enough to see. Where on earth had the attendant got too? Grace needed to get over the wall as soon as she could, before the Cowper siblings made their escape. But how could she leave Fluff in this condition, especially when her medical training compelled her to always put the patient first?

She was staring out the window, plotting an escape route, when the night attendant returned with the jolly, plump nurse aide, Miss Thomas.

The attendant stumbled back against the door at the sight of Fluff's pallid face and motionless body. "Oh no, not another death."

"She is not dead, just lightly sedated." Grace realised she was about to blow her cover, but she had no choice, with Fluff's life at stake. The nurse aide had to know what was happening. "I've given her some bromide to calm her and stop the convulsions. She's responding well."

"And the baby?" Miss Thomas asked.

"Too early to tell, but there is no sign of bleeding."

Miss Thomas eyed her speculatively. "There is never a doctor around here when you need one. I don't know where you gained such skills, but you may have saved two lives tonight."

The attendant was still staring at Grace as if she was a witch. "You can't–"

Miss Thomas steered the attendant to the door. "She'll be fine, thanks to this woman's quick thinking. You may go now."

"I'm getting Matron. Miss Bennet should never be in here, let alone giving medicines to a patient." She fled before they could stop her.

Grace headed for the door too. "If Matron is coming, I need to get back to my dormitory before I get into any more trouble." That wall to the outside world was looking better every minute.

"Please, can you stay, to make sure this poor lass is all right? I will explain to Matron that you saved her life."

Grace hesitated, desperate to leave, but knowing Fluff's wellbeing had to come first, even with her own safely at risk. "Are you not a trained nurse, Miss Thomas? I really need to go."

"I have picked up a few skills since I started helping out here, but I have no proper training. I started out like Fluff, only worse. Terrified, pregnant, delirious. Matron and the nurse saved my life, dragging me back from near-death over two long distressing years."

"You were a patient here? What made you stay on?"

"I felt I owed them a debt, which I was glad to repay by staying on to look after the unwanted children who are born here. For the first time in my life, I feel as if I have a purpose. As if God sent me a terrible trial to show me a new path."

Grace stared at her, mentally stripping back the chubby, self-assured exterior and the prematurely white hair, to see the possibility of a thin, fragile, pale girl with blue eyes, who looked older than her years due to addiction and trauma. "I'm glad you have found your calling. May I ask your name?"

"They call me Charlotte Thomas."

"Oh, Charlotte, I have been looking everywhere for you. Is your real name Amelia?"

The women didn't reply, but her shocked expression left Grace in no doubt. "Charlotte Thomas. Did you choose that name so your friend, Charles Thomas Pyke, would recognise it?"

Charlotte – or Amelia – gaped at her with a combination of hope and disbelief. "You know Charlie?"

"He is here too, looking for you, posing as the new attendant. He is a police detective now. He never gave up hope you were alive, Amelia, but so many lies were told that the truth never came out, until now, by sheer chance."

"My Charlie? He's really here?"

Amelia's eyes flicked to the door. Joy turned to alarm. Her reaction was more of a shrill squeal than a full-blooded scream, but it was all the more potent for the impression it gave of abject terror. Her body went limp and fell forward in a faint.

Grace desperately wanted to know who had entered the room behind her – for surely Matron alone could not have been the cause of such an extreme reaction – but her arms were filled with Amelia's limp body.

Matron stepped forward and relieved her of Amelia's deadweight. "Jane Bennet. What are you doing out of bed?"

Grace got a brief glimpse of a man, before a bag descended over her head and a strong hand clamped over her mouth. He swept her feet from under her and forced her to the floor, holding her down with his larger body weight.

"Give her something to knock her out, Bertha. This is the woman who was with the girl who died on the train. Her name is Grace Penrose, not Jane Bennet."

The voice belonged to the man in Matron's office. Her brother Josiah, who was responsible for Amelia's abduction and her father's murder. Grace tried to struggle, but he held her too tightly. She heard banging and clinking in the background, as Matron searched the cupboards.

A mask slipped over her mouth and nose, forcing a cold swab against her face. The sweet smell of ether trickled into her lungs, slowly robbing her of the will to fight. Her last lucid thought, as the ether overwhelmed her, was one of combined fear and frustration, that at last she knew who the killer was, but it was too late to …

Gone Girl

Charlie walked back through the trees as if he was walking on hot coals. He had no evidence that Grace was in danger, but logic couldn't stop the clawing certainty in his gut that danger was closing in on her. Every instinct was yelling at him to act now, regardless of orders.

He shoved instinct down in favour of scouting the grounds again. There was a lamp burning in the medical room, but that was to be expected. The dormitories showed no hint of light or sound behind the heavy curtains. He circled the front of Stillwaters, but there was no evidence of activity and no light in the superintendent's office, or in his room on the upper floor, above the front door.

Matron's bedchamber was between Gresham's and the women's dormitory. Lamplight glowed softly through a crack in the curtains, but that was comforting, not worrying, as Matron would surely be out of her bedroom if there was the least hint of trouble.

Should he risk trying to reach Grace in her dormitory, before Stewart had returned with the horses? Male attendants were absolutely forbidden on the female wards, so that would have to be a last resort. He tried to calm his agitation. Ten o'clock was not long to wait. Two of them would stand a better chance of success anyway – four including Lily and Albert. As policemen, they could enter places an attendant would be barred from.

Charlie slowed his pace to a stroll as he approached the front gate, trying to look like a man taking a constitutional before bed. The night watchman poked his head out of the guard house at the sound of his feet on the gravel driveway.

"You're the new attendant, aren't you? I thought I told you not to go out at night."

234

"You did. That's why I've come down to ask permission to walk the grounds. I feel like I'll go crazy if I don't get a moment of peace before bed."

"I suppose that makes sense. I'll turn a blind eye, as long as you are discreet about it. To be honest, it'd be nice to have someone to chat to."

"I know how you feel. I'm not used to such a quiet place. We don't get many visitors here, do we?"

"I feel sorry for the patients. Their parents are all very charming when they drop their daughters off, but that's the last we see of most of them. Rotten way to treat your own flesh and blood if you ask me."

Charlie leaned casually against a post. "Nobody visited today?"

The night watchman checked the register of visitors. "Just a man to see Matron. Been here before. Her brother, I believe. Came up on the afternoon train, so he must be intending to stay."

Matron's brother, here. Charlie forced himself to ask one more question, just to be sure. "He must have arrived on the same train as Superintendent Gresham."

"I expect so."

"Ah well, I'd best be getting back. Have a peaceful night."

"Never anything but, around here."

The night watchman had no sooner retreated into his shelter, when Charlie ran for the house, keeping to the grass to muffle his pounding footsteps. Unless Matron had another brother, Amelia's abductor was already in the house. No wonder Lily had had the unsettling feeling of being watched on the train.

Charlie rushed inside, not caring if he disturbed the peace in his desperation to find Grace. Matron's office was empty, but there were signs of a hurried attempt to burn documents in the fireplace. The safe door was open, the safe empty. A thousand eternal damnations – he was too late.

He ran upstairs. Matron's bedroom door was open. The drawers were pulled out, leaving clothes scattered on the floor. Charlie hesitated for a fraction of second only, before bursting into Grace's

235

dormitory. The night attendant gaped at his door-crashing entry. The patients sat up in their beds, drawing their blankets around themselves, adding a shrill chorus of squeals to the attendant's piercing shriek.

The attendant thrust her lamp in his direction, blinding him. "Get out of here, you imbecile."

"I'm Detective Constable Pyke," he yelled over the uproar. "Where is Grace Penrose?"

"Grace? We have no Grace."

Satan's horns, what was the name she was using? "Bennet? Jane Bennet."

"She was in the medical room with a sick patient, but you cannot go in there."

Charlie had already pushed her aside and was sprinting along the corridor, leaving bedlam behind him.

The medical room was empty, aside from a woman with fluffy hair, who was too woozy to answer his questions. What now? He rushed along the corridor, checking all the secure cells, but he saw only startled, unfamiliar faces.

Panic rose up inside him, threatening to swamp his brain. He shook it off and checked his watch. With any luck, Stewart would be back by now. He raced down to the rear door of the house, blowing three short blasts, three long blasts, and three more short blasts on his whistle as soon as he was outside.

Hooves galloped towards the rear gate and pulled to a halt before he finished the final blast. An outline of a man stood up in the horse's saddle in the soft light of dusk. He leaped onto the wall, before dropping to the other side and running towards Charlie, his gait slightly stiff on one side. DI Stewart was back in the nick of time.

"Damn it, I'm getting too old for these shenanigans. What's happened, Pyke?"

"I can't find Grace, but Josiah Cowper is here and Matron has cleared out the safe. They must have left while I was looking for Grace. They're going to make a run for it with the money."

A shout rang out from the front gate, as the drumbeat of another horse approached the rear gate, topped by a slight figure who was struggling to stay in the saddle, with her skirts around her knees.

"Lily, take my horse and met us on the other side," Stewart called out.

Charlie was already running for the front gate, where the night watchman was refusing to admit Albert Lawrence.

"Charlie, two people have left on a cart," Albert shouted. "A woman and a man. It's hard to tell in this light, but I think the man was Doctor Josiah."

Josiah Cowper, you're about to get what you have deserved for a very long time. Charlie stopped at the gate, catching his breath. "Was Grace with them, Albert?"

"I only saw two people, but there was quite a lot of luggage in the back – sacks and trunks and the like. I wouldn't have seen her if she was lying amongst them."

"We can't risk her being taken away. If we lose track of them, they might hide anywhere."

Stewart limped up behind him and showed his badge to the night watchman, who rushed to open the gate, at the same moment as two horses cantered around the outside perimeter. Lily bounced to a halt and slid from the horse into Stewart's arms, while Charlie secured the reins.

Stewart took time out from the crisis to plant an enthusiastic kiss on Lily's lips. "Lily, my darling, you are magnificent. Marry me."

"Yes, of course I will, Alistair." She allowed herself a moment to enjoy his embrace, then pushed him away. "Now, go get that murdering fiend."

Stewart turned to the night watchman. "Take my fiancée to the matron's office. Then come back to the gate and don't let anyone but us in or out. Lily, secure any documents they have left behind. Lock yourself in the office until I get back." He wrapped an arm around her and kissed her again.

"Unhand my aunt, Uncle Alistair. We have work to do." Charlie put the second pair of reins into Stewart's hand. Without a backward glance, Charlie leaped onto his horse and kicked it into a gallop, with Albert hard on his heels.

Stewart shook his head ruefully, but couldn't hide his grin. "That lad is becoming jolly full of himself lately. I hope he doesn't think I will go easy on him if I am his uncle."

"You know he'll just try all the harder, Alistair, my love," Lily replied. "Now go, before that horse tugs your arm out of its socket."

A cart was never going to be a match for three determined riders, however fast Cowper whipped the terrified horse into a lather.

As they drew level, Stewart shouted, "Stop, police."

Josiah Cowper hauled on the horse's mouth, pulling it to a halt. He threw the reins to Matron and scrabbled in the box at his side, drawing out two pistols. He stood above them, with his legs apart, the black hole at the end of each pistol uncomfortably close to the tops of their heads.

"Turn around and skedaddle, or I'll blow your heads off."

Charlie knew he had seen that bushy moustache before, but he couldn't place him until he heard his voice. Josiah Cowper was the guard on the train from Dunedin. Charlie dug into his memory of the day he had arrived in Dunedin. His mind had been on Grace at the time, but he was fairly sure he recalled that the same man was the guard being questioned at the station over the two deaths.

The same train guard who had told Grace that he had tried to stop Doctor Wilson from jumping. If Wilson had discovered what was going on at Stillwaters, then Cowper had a strong motive to kill him, and now he knew he had also had the perfect opportunity.

"I am Detective Inspector Stewart. Give yourself up, Cowper, we have you outnumbered." He gestured for Charlie and Albert to back off and circle the cart.

Cowper didn't budge. "It ain't over until the man with the firepower says it's over."

"You're under arrest for the murder of Edward Lawrence, six years ago in Clyde. And for the abduction of his daughter, Amelia Lawrence."

"I didn't kill him. She did. Then she forced me to take her to Dunedin. It's her you should be arresting, not me."

"We are also arresting you for the murder of Doctor Wilson," Charlie said.

The tips of the pistols wavered as Cowper turned from Stewart to Charlie, who was now behind him.

Charlie stared into the barrel of the gun without flinching. "How very convenient being the train guard, going past Stillwaters every day, seeing who was arriving, and who was trying to escape. Passing information and drugs to your sister, the matron, at the station. Did you throw Isabelle Forsyth off the train too, before you killed the doctor?"

"I never killed that girl. I never even saw her out there." Cowper's denial was fervent, but also contained a telling gap. He rushed to fill it. "I didn't kill the doctor either."

Albert joined in from the other side of the cart, causing Cowper to twist around again. "What about my sister Amelia, Cowper? Did you murder her too?"

The tips of the pistols jerked at this new threat, but steadied again all too quickly. "You'll never find out if you try to arrest me. That interfering hussy you sent to spy on Stillwaters will die too, if you don't let me go."

Charlie lunged from his horse onto the back of the cart, but even in his fury, he was too slow. Stewart, a notable fast bowler in his heyday, had already hurled his truncheon, catching Cowper on the back of the head. Albert had the presence of mind to duck, as one of the pistols went off, cracking a branch of the tree overhead.

Cowper crumpled, crashing into Charlie's bulk. Charlie let him fall onto the pile of luggage before clipping the handcuffs on him. He dragged the scoundrel upright by the chin, putting just enough pressure on the man's windpipe to let him know who was in control. "Where is

Grace Penrose? I swear I will squeeze the life out of you if you do not tell me this instant."

Matron shot a pleading look at Stewart, but he busied himself with fastening her wrists. She looked back at Charlie, who did nothing to disguise his wrath.

"You'd better tell me, Matron, or your brother is dead meat."

Matron crumpled. "Please don't hurt him. She's in the old stables, behind the coach house. I begged him not to kill her."

Charlie flung himself back on his horse, waiting only for Stewart's sharp nod, before taking off at a full gallop.

Dire Straits

Grace awoke to the odd sensation of her head being pulled to and fro across a hard surface, as rough sacking rubbed across her face. She tried to put her hands out to stop it, but they were clasped against her chest. For some reason, she couldn't seem to move them. In fact, her whole body seemed to be tightly constrained, making it difficult to breathe.

Slowly, it came back to her. If her memory wasn't playing tricks on her, she rather wished she had stayed knocked out. Although, considering she had been disabled by a murderer, she ought to be grateful to be alive … so far.

Suddenly, the bag slid off her head, leaving her gasping dank, stale air instead of dank, stale hessian. Just enough light filtered into the brick-lined chamber to make out another person. Amelia. She was in a strait jacket too, but she had managed to drag the sack off Grace's head with her feet. Thanks heavens for a dextrous fellow prisoner.

Amelia put her face close to Grace's, showing her the cloth gagging her mouth. Grace struggled to sit up, her head whirling with the effort. She dragged Amelia's gag down with her teeth, grimacing at smell of liniment.

"Yeesh. They might have used a fresh bandage to gag me. Disgusting. Are you all right, Miss Bennet?"

"My real name is Grace Penrose. I'm still a little woozy from the ether, but I'll be fine in a minute or two. Do you know where we are?"

"The old stables, behind the coach house. Nobody comes here anymore, except to throw another pile of junk on top of the heap. We are in one of the old horse stalls."

Grace examined her surroundings. The outside wall and floor were solid brick, the side walls were thick oak up to horse-head height, then

241

barred. A single small window was set high on the wall. The only exit was the stall door. "Locked?"

"Bolted on the outside. No way out I'm afraid, even if we could extract ourselves from these strait jackets."

"Do you think the Cowpers are planning to come back?"

"I doubt it. I overhead enough of their discussion to get the impression they were leaving forever with a large sum of money. How that evil man talked his sweet sister into this is beyond me. He wanted to kill us, but Matron stopped him."

"I know Matron has helped you, Amelia, but I think you should know that she was also defrauding the charity that oversees Stillwaters. With the huge fees they were charging, plus the money from selling babies to adoptive parents, they were making a fortune here. They were even charging for raising children who were long gone."

"Selling babies? Oh no, Grace, that cannot be right. The babies went to good Christian homes with the consent of the girl's families. A gift from God, for women who could not conceive."

Grace didn't enlighten her any further as to the true situation at Stillwaters. She was relieved to know that Amelia was not part of the scheme to extract money from both the birth family and the adoptive family.

"You think I am being naïve, don't you Grace? Matron isn't perfect, I know that much. But she sat by my side for hours, calming me when my craving for that dreadful tonic drove me to the edge of insanity. My mother cannot have known what evil she was pouring down my throat, but even when she saw its effects, she refused to stop, until I couldn't live without it. If it hadn't been for Matron I would have lost my life and my baby."

"You were pregnant before you left Clyde?" Grace had suspected as much from the way Mrs Lawrence had kept Amelia hidden away, saying she was ill.

"Being pregnant was the reason I had to leave Clyde and never go back. Josiah Cowper didn't kidnap me – I begged him to take me away. Oh Grace, it was such a mess. I was so desperate for the tonic, I offered

242

him all the money I had, so I would have enough to keep me going while he went away to sell in other towns. Cowper came to our house and made me open the safe. I swear I didn't care by then what he took from my family, just as long as he gave me what I craved."

"But then your father came home unexpectedly."

Amelia dropped her head and shivered. "I don't think Cowper intended to kill my father, only frighten him. I tried to knock the pistol away, but it went off instead. It was me who caused my own father's death. That is why Cowper agreed to take me away with him, so I could testify for him if he was caught. That's why he kept me here."

"Amelia, I am so very sorry for all you went through. You cannot blame yourself for what others forced upon you. He was the one holding the gun on your father."

"It's all in the past, Grace. I've come to be happy here, despite everything. Matron has been good to me. I found my purpose in life, looking after the babies, and my own little Frankie brings joy to my life."

Grace stared at her with sudden comprehension. "Your baby lived?"

"Yes, of course. He is almost six years old now, the light of my life. I know he cannot stay here forever. He needs to go to school, make friends, have the freedom to live a proper life. I'll take you to meet him as soon as we get out of here. I think Matron put so much effort into helping me because she believed her brother Josiah was Frankie's father. I didn't tell her otherwise, because I was so desperate for her help. She loved my son as if he was her nephew and, goodness knows, Frankie needed all the love he could get."

"Oh." Grace couldn't think what else to say. She dreaded the thought of seeing the child. The vehemence of Mrs Lawrence's hatred for Charlie had left her in no doubt who she thought was to blame. What if the boy had black hair and green eyes flecked with gold? Even if he didn't, Charlie might feel honour-bound to marry Amelia out of a misplaced guilt for her disappearance. Either way, Grace was going to lose him forever.

"Grace, how did you know I was here? And why did Cowper recognise you?"

"I meet your friend, Isabelle Forsyth, on the train after you helped her escape. Cowper was the guard on the train."

The guard's face had been etched in her memory from the moment he had shut the rear door of the carriage and reported the disappearance of both the doctor and Isabelle. If only she had known then that the guard from that fatal train journey was Josiah Cowper, the pieces of the puzzle would have fallen into place a lot sooner.

Grace recalled his calculated look at Isabelle, as if he knew exactly where she had come from. Cowper had even overheard their conversation about Amelia and Charlotte and Constable Pyke. He would have had a powerful motive to silence the escaping girl, so she couldn't tell tales about what was happening at Stillwaters.

And the doctor too, who was suspicious of what was happening here and threatening to expose their fraud and medical malpractice. Knowing that Cowper had a strong motive to silence Doctor Wilson completely changed her perspective of what had happened on the train. They had all relied on the train guard's version of events, assuming he was an entirely independent witness.

The image of the doctor's body, lying face up on the boulder, suddenly made her realise what she had been an idiot to miss before. How likely was it that a man who had jumped from a train would land on the back of his head? But a man who was pushed or thrown over backwards – that was a different story. Cowper had nothing to lose by getting rid of the interfering doctor, as he already faced the hangman's noose for the death of Amelia's father, whatever she might say in his defence.

"Enough of the past," Grace said. "Any ideas for getting out of here?"

"Grace, I admire your spirit, but our hands are bound and we are in a bolted stable. Slim as you are, I doubt you could squeeze through that tiny window, even if you were free. Charlie will rescue us."

Her faith in him was touching, but Charlie he had no idea where they were. What if Cowper came back to finish them off before Charlie was even aware they were missing? Besides, escape was far preferable to the ignominy of being rescued.

"I'm feeling better now that the effect of the ether is wearing off. Perhaps I could open your buckles with my teeth?"

"Worth a try, I suppose."

Optimism was no match for the tight straps that bound the ends of the sleeves behind Amelia's back.

"I have a knife." Grace had taken to heart the joke about Charlie giving her a knife. This one wasn't a throwing knife, but a small folding blade that fitted into her fake baby bump, alongside the lock picks and Anne's locket. "Amelia, can you reach the padded pouch under my skirt?"

She hoped no one was watching them, as Amelia tugged at her skirt with her teeth, until the pouch dropped onto the floor.

"Put your foot on it so I can pull on the end of the bow."

Using a combination of teeth, nose, feet, and desperation, Grace extracted the contents of the pouch and opened the knife, grateful for the extra money she had spent to get a spring-loaded, locking blade that opened at her touch. Now for the tricky part.

"I think it will be easiest if I try to cut through the sleeves at the front, to get your hands free. Let me know if I hurt you, Amelia. Tell me as soon as the knife pierces the fabric."

Grace took the knife in her teeth, working the end of the sharp blade carefully through the fabric, then ripping outwards to avoid cutting Amelia's arm. It took a long, long time, and many, many unladylike curses after dropping the knife, but eventually the fabric came away and Amelia had one hand free. Thank heavens Stillwaters used strait jackets of thick cotton, rather than the heavy canvas ones used for the criminally insane.

"Great work, Grace." Amelia wiped blood off her wrist with her sleeve. "Hardly a nick." Within a short time, she had ripped through the other sleeve, then cut Grace free too.

Grace jiggled her arms to get the blood flowing, then went to work on the bolt, using the knife to tease it from its slot. But the bolt was old and stiff with rust. It didn't budge an inch. The bars were even more impossible – old but designed to withstand the strength of a stallion.

That just left the window, too high above the brick floor for Grace's liking, but not too high that she would be badly hurt if she fell, with luck.

Amelia followed her line of sight. "There is no way you will get through there."

"It's amazing how flexible the body can be. I once saw a contortionist squeeze himself into a box that wasn't much larger than a small valise." Grace took off her robe to reduce her bulk, figuring that her soft nightdress would help her slide through the gap.

She took a deep breath and hoisted herself up to the bars, using the feed box as a step. When she sidled around to the window, it was at chest height. If it had ever been glazed, the glass was long gone. An evening breeze wafted delicious, fresh air through the hole, bringing goosebumps to her body.

Only two things now stood between Grace and success – the narrowness of the hole and the fact she might drop head-first to the ground if she could not find a way to climb down on the other side. Perhaps people react to a fall like cats, tumbling in the air and landing on their feet. She hoped rather than believed it to be true. The recent experience of Doctor Wilson was not encouraging.

Truth

Charlie slid from the sweating horse in front of the coach house. As he made his way around the back to the stables, an odd grunting sound caught his attention. It seemed to be coming from above.

Dusk was rapidly turning to night, but there was still enough light to see … what in the name of Zeus was that object wriggling in the narrow window of the stable? As the object twisted on the sill, he realised it was a person. A hand reached out to grasp the shutter, which was hanging by one hinge against the wall.

As he watched the body emerge, the hinge gave way and the body plunged towards the ground. With a sense of inevitability, he rushed forward and plucked her out of the air, cradling her in his arms like a child.

"Charlie. Excellent timing, as always. It turns out that humans are not cats."

"Grace. Nice of you to drop by." He could feel her body through thin fabric. "Are you in your night attire again? You really must stop doing that if you wish me to behave like a gentleman. It is extremely distracting."

"You could put me down, if my body offends you."

Offends was the direct opposite of the word he would use, but now was not the time to discuss such matters. "I could, but I don't want you running away until I find out what happened and why you are attempting to leap from a height like a fledgling bird."

"Matron and her brother, Josiah Cowper, locked us in the stable. Did they get away?"

"I handcuffed the villain myself. What a perfect cover, a train guard who sees everything, but is noticed by no one. Pity you weren't there to see the look on his face when I accused him of the murders of Doctor Wilson and Isabelle Forsyth, as well as Amelia's father."

The delight on her face was reward enough. "Grace, did you say he locked *us* in the stable?"

"Did I forget to mention I found Amelia?"

"You did? Where?" He dropped her onto her feet so fast she fell backwards. He grabbed her again and hauled her upright. "Sorry, Grace. You're shivering, take my coat."

She put it on with a sigh. "That's better. Lying on a cold brick floor in a strait jacket isn't nearly as pleasant as a warm bed. Follow me."

Grace led him around the corner to the stable door, which he forced open with the help on an old length of iron bar from the junk pile.

"Amelia?"

"Charlie, is that you?"

He ran to the stall and threw the bolt. Amelia was in his arms before he had the door half open. He embraced her with all the emotion of a man whose worst fears have proven unfounded.

"Amelia, I'm so happy you're alive."

She wrapped her arms around his neck, laughing and crying at the same time. "I knew you would come for me, Charlie."

He couldn't see her very well through the dark and tears, but he could feel her vitality and curvaceous body. "I feared you would be a broken woman, even if I found you, but you seem miraculously well."

"And you too. Whatever happened to the skinny little boy I used to know? Grace told me that you are a detective now. I'm so pleased you achieved your dream." She planted a joyful kiss on his cheek. "It's wonderful to see you again, my dearest friend."

Charlie turned to look for Grace, but she was disappearing through the door, letting it bang shut behind her.

"She's perfect for you, Charlie. Kind and brave and clever."

"Grace and I are … I'm not sure what we are to each other, to be honest. Or rather, I'm not sure whether she sees me as anything more than an amusing distraction. Besides, she has half the medical professionals of Dunedin at her beck and call."

"I may not be a detective, but I am in no doubt about where her affections lie." She held his face between her hands and kissed his cheek. "Come and meet my little boy."

"Amelia, you're married? How wonderful. I didn't dare hope to find you in such good spirits. Albert is going to be excited to meet his nephew. He should be here soon."

"Albert? He is here too? I long to see my brother again. But I am not married, Charlie. The shame of it was what made me leave Clyde. I'll explain later. I'm desperate to make sure Frankie hasn't been harmed."

They found Grace sitting on the steps of the coach house, staring at the ground. Amelia took them inside and lit a lamp, illuminating a small sitting room with a few toys, a kitchen and several closed doors. She gestured for them to take a seat, while she crept upstairs.

Grace stood up again as soon as she was out of sight. "I shouldn't be here. This is a moment for the two of you to share."

"What do you mean, Grace? Of course you should be here." He reached for her hand and pulled her onto the sofa beside him. "I would never have found my old school friend without you. Seeing her not only alive, but thriving, is an enormous weight off my shoulders. I know I had no reason to feel guilty, but I still wish I had done more."

Amelia reappeared carrying a squirming child.

"Put me down, Mama. I'm a big boy now." He wriggled out of her arms and dashed across the room to a rocking horse. Suddenly, he saw them and came over shy.

Charlie smiled at the typical childish behaviour. "Hello, Frankie. My name is Charlie. I'm an old friend of your mother."

Amelia took her son by the hand and led him over. When the boy raised his head, Grace gasped. Charlie managed to restrain his reaction, but only just. He plastered a fake smile on his face as he held his hand out for the boy to shake.

He looked at Amelia and saw the confirmation in her eyes. Now wonder she had fled Clyde. Those bulging eyes and that thin, sharp nose were the very image of the devil, in the form of the meddlesome vicar, Randall Barclay.

The sound of horses clattering up the driveway broke their silence.

"I'll bring Albert in to meet his nephew," Grace said. "Should I warn him?"

Amelia hung her head and whispered, "Perhaps that might be best."

Charlie had the lad on his knee, telling him a funny story about his mother, when Albert came in. He rushed to Amelia and crushed her against his chest, the tears running freely down both their cheeks.

Charlie bent his head down to the boy's. "Would you like to meet your Uncle Albert, Frankie. I'll bet he knows loads of funny stories about your lovely mama."

Albert picked up Frankie and hugged him until the boy squirmed. Charlie was glad to see Albert's delight, no matter what other emotions he harboured inside.

Amelia gestured him over. "Albert says he's going to demand that Randall Barclay meet him in a duel. Please don't let him do anything so stupid."

"Amelia, as a policeman, I have to ask. Did Barclay force himself on you? If he did, I will make sure the full force of the law slams down on his loathsome, sanctimonious head."

"I'm so ashamed. I trusted him, as a man of God. I went to ask his advice one day, when I was feeling wretched after taking too much tonic. My memory is hazy, but he pretended to help me, encouraging me drink more to calm my nerves. Afterwards, he blamed me for enticing him into sin by taunting him with my body, but I don't remember anything apart from the pain and pleading with him to stop. I had no choice but to leave Clyde. My mother would have forced me to marry him. I hated him."

Charlie felt his fists forming into tight bunches, but he forced himself to calm down for her sake. "Amelia, it was not your fault. None of it was your fault – not in the slightest. Barclay is a vile swine who took advantage of your weakened state."

"I know that now, but I was so muddle-headed at the time."

"Whatever happens, I vow he will never come near you again."

She took both of his hands in hers. "Dearest Charlie, you don't need to protect me anymore. I have to see him one more time, with my head held high, to expose his despicable behaviour. My mother needs to understand that her loyalties were woefully misplaced, for my sake and for yours. After that, I do not know what will happen. From what Grace said, Stillwaters may not survive the scandal and Frankie and I cannot stay here forever, regardless."

"Brava, Amelia," Albert said. "I would be overjoyed if you and Frankie came to live with my family. I'm sure Violet would say the same. We have so many years to make up for." He jiggled his giggling nephew on his knee. "You're such a big chap already, Frankie. Would you like to go to school with your cousins?"

The boy's beaming smile spoke a thousand words.

"Will you come home with me tomorrow, Amelia?"

"Yes, Albert, nothing would give me greater pleasure. Edith, who works in the laundry and helps out here, can look after the babies." Amelia lifted her son from his uncle's knee. "I'd better get Frankie back to bed now."

Charlie and Grace found DI Stewart finishing up his interview with Superintendent Gresham, who had transformed from imperious oracle to gibbering wreck.

"Mr Gresham, I will have to ask you to remain in your room until the Dunedin police arrive tomorrow to take a formal statement. Please hand over your keys." Stewart locked Gresham's door behind him and gestured for them to follow him to the visitors' room. "Not surprisingly, he denied all knowledge of Matron's schemes. I have to say I am inclined to believe him. A sorry state of affairs."

"His ignorance doesn't speak well of his leadership," Charlie agreed, "but we have found no evidence implicating him."

Stewart sank into a chair, stretching his gammy leg out with a sigh. "Gresham seemed most shocked by the revelation that the 'success' of treatment was not due to the power of his oratory."

251

"He had everyone here convinced of his extraordinary powers." Grace sat down, then immediately stood up again, pacing the room like a caged animal. "What have you done with the Cowper siblings?"

"They are locked in the secure cells, where they belong. I have arranged for all of us to be taken to the first train back to Dunedin tomorrow morning."

"What will happen to Stillwaters?" Grace asked. "The patients will need reassurance that their care will continue."

"What do you suggest, Grace?"

"Miss Dalloway and Mr Quigley should be able to manage until the trustees decide what to do. Sister Jones appears competent, but she might value some assistance from a specialist, such as Doctor McLeod."

Stewart rubbed a hand over his red eyes. "Right. Charlie, can you bring Dalloway and Quigley to me, then help Lily secure the documents in Matron's office. Grace, can you secure any medical files we will need as evidence. Get some sleep if you can. It's going to be another busy day tomorrow."

By the early hours of the morning, Charlie had finished his tasks. He found Grace dozing in the medical room, next to a patient with fluffy hair, who was snoring quietly. As he eased the door closed again, her head came up.

"Charlie?"

The tremor in her voice caught him off guard. "Are you all right, Grace? You must be exhausted."

Grace tiptoed over to where he was standing by the door, shutting it gently behind her as she exited. She slumped back against the door frame. Moonlight flooded through the arched window, illuminating the misery etched in every line of her face.

"It's over now, Grace. Try to get some rest."

"I'm worried about what will happen to the patients, especially the ones in a fragile mental state."

"No need for you to worry about that. Dalloway and Quigley have talked to Stewart and agreed to take over the running of the sanctuary. They will tell the patients that Matron is on leave to attend to an urgent matter. As far as the patients are concerned, everything will continue as normal. There is no reason why Stillwaters cannot continue, with a more enlightened approach to care."

"I suppose so."

"Grace, would you like me to stay with you?"

"That's kind of you, Charlie, but you must see to Amelia and Frankie. I will be fine after a few hours of sleep."

Before he could reply, she had retreated to the medical room, shutting the door between them with a firmness that reverberated straight through his heart.

The Final Piece

On the morning train back to Dunedin, Grace tried to shut out the noise around her. After the intense emotions of the previous few days, she ought to be looking forward to resuming normal life. Instead, her brain was swirling with half-formed images, from meeting Isabelle on the train to finding Amelia.

They had a lot to celebrate. The mystery of Amelia's disappearance was finally solved, not to mention busting Matron's money-spinning schemes at the expense of her patients' welfare. But there was one piece of the puzzle that refused to slot into place.

As the train rattled along beside the precipice once again, the connections between Isabelle and Amelia struck her for the first time. Both young women had shown extraordinary resilience and determination despite overwhelming challenges. Both had one supportive parent and one who had thrown them to the lions. Both had the support of worthy young men who loved them, despite a gap in their social positions.

Grace glanced down the carriage to where Amelia and Charlie sat close to each other, her white hair next to his black, as they shared their lives again for the first time in six years. Albert and his newly-found nephew were sitting opposite them, giggling as Charlie casually flipped his shilling, making it vanish, only to reappear behind Amelia's ear.

Sleight of hand, misdirection – call it what you will, but the magic was always about failing to see what was right in front of your eyes. As the train drew level with the platform at Port Chalmers, the puzzle pieces rearranged themselves in her mind, causing her to laugh out loud with the sheer boldness of it. Time would tell if she was right.

Detective Inspector Stewart had telegraphed ahead for the local police to meet them at Dunedin station. Mrs Lawrence and her vicar had also been notified.

Grace was first off the train. For once, her preference was to stand back and watch. Stewart and Lily had charge of Matron and her brother. With his usual brisk efficiency, Stewart briefed DI Wallace, who handed over the prisoners to a pair of constables, while Lily supervised the unloading of the boxes of evidence.

Amelia's mother paced up and down, scanning the windows for signs of her long-lost daughter. The vicar, for once, was not hovering by her side, but watching from the far side of the platform, pacing nervously. Grace noticed that another local constable had taken up position nearby.

Mrs Lawrence let out a shriek when Amelia appeared, clinging to Charlie's arm. She rushed forward, pushing her way through the crowd, stopping dead when Albert descended to the platform with a child in his arms.

Grace recalled the scene later as a series of images. The mother's expression shifting between weeping joy, jaw dropping realisation, a murderous glare at Charlie, a closer examination of the child, and, finally, pirouetting to face her devoted vicar with a glare of such ferocity, Satan himself would have fallen to his knees.

Randall Barclay confined himself to a single expression – abject terror – before taking to his heels, right into the clutches of the constable. Mrs Lawrence turned her back on him and threw herself into Amelia's arms, begging forgiveness. Albert and Francis joined the reunion, while Charlie walked away with a sad smile to see to the luggage.

The rest of the morning was absorbed into a flurry of explanations and witness statements. Grace signed the final document at last and emerged into the sunlight. Only one more task and she could go home to a long, hot bath and long, undisturbed sleep.

Charlie was waiting for her outside.

"Charlie, what are you doing here? I thought you had gone with Amelia."

"She needs time with her family." He linked his arm through hers. "I told her what you did to help her. She was astounded that you would risk your life for a stranger."

"Not a stranger. A dear friend of yours."

"Her whole family is in your debt, as am I. A terrible burden has been lifted from my soul, seeing Amelia not only alive and safe, but looking so capable and well."

"I did it for Isabelle too. She would be glad that we uncovered enough evidence of fraud and medical malpractice to put Matron behind bars for a long time. I just hope there is enough to convict Cowper of the murders of Mr Lawrence and Doctor Wilson."

"We'll get him all right. When I left the police station, Matron was making a full confession of her brother's wrongdoings and her own saintly innocence." Charlie swept his free hand in a vague arc. "Such a beautiful day. The sun is shining, not a cloud in the sky, and we have a whole day and a half to do as we please before I have to go back to Wellington. Starting with taking you to the Christmas Ball tonight."

"Is it Saturday? I have quite lost track of time. It would seem absurd to go dancing tonight, after all we have been through over the last few days."

"All the more reason to wrench ourselves back to normal life. Unless you do not wish to go. I'm sure I could find someone else to dance with."

"Don't you dare, Charlie Pyke. If you have to go back so soon, I intend to extract every last ounce of enjoyment out of your remaining time. I wish you could stay for a few days, at the very least."

"So do I, Grace. Hopefully, I won't be in Wellington for much longer. Stewart is trying to arrange a transfer to Dunedin for both of us. He asked Lily to marry him."

"He did? How wonderful. I've no doubt she agreed, they are such a perfect match."

"He is threatening to leave the police force if that is what it takes to be with his fiancée. And I could always take up another occupation. Something quiet, with regular hours, and no risk of bodily harm to me or my friends and family. A bookkeeper, perhaps."

"Do you miss Dunedin so much you would accept a life behind a desk, risking only paper cuts and boredom?"

He tucked her arm a little more firmly under his. "Dunedin certainly has its attractions, for the next three years at least."

"I would hate for you to have to give up police work, Charlie. You were born for it."

"Unfortunately, the local force has a full complement of detectives at present, with no vacancies on the horizon."

"Maybe I could offer my professional services as an assassin to create a couple of positions on the local detective team. Which detective constable would you prefer I get rid of? Or I could remove a detective sergeant, if you wish to apply for a promotion."

"How very thoughtful of you, Grace, but I would rather not return here, only to have you arrested for murdering a police officer."

"Charlie Pyke, I'm deeply offended that you think I would be clumsy enough to get caught. As a matter of fact, I have been reading up on rare poisons. I fancy using venom from a snake known only from the equatorial highlands of New Guinea."

"Too clever, Grace. Far better to go for something simple and direct, like throwing the victim off a train over a precipitous drop."

Grace let the seconds pass, as she decided whether to confide in him. "It is Isabelle's fate that still troubles me."

"What's done is done. On the available evidence, I doubt we would have enough evidence to convict either Doctor Wilson or Cowper for her murder."

"As a matter of fact, I am sure you couldn't, for the very good reason that neither of them killed her."

"I know that expression of yours, Grace Penrose. What clever deduction are you bursting to share with me?"

"If I tell you, it must be as a friend, rather than as a policeman. I know it is a lot to ask that you take it no further, but I don't think you will regret it."

"Very well, but only because I cannot bear the suspense. What is it?"

"We need to make a slight detour. Meanwhile, consider the remarkable coincidence that Isabelle disappeared at the only place on the journey where her body might not be found."

Grace refused to say anything more until they arrived at the Forsyth house. By good fortune, they found Isabelle's mother having a glass of sherry on her own.

When the butler showed them in, alarm streaked across her face. She laid the photograph she had been looking at face down and resumed her usual bland countenance. In front of her, the window framed a view across the city, with the sun sparkling on a harbour dotted with masts.

"I'm very sorry to intrude upon you so unexpectedly, Mrs Forsyth," Grace said. "May we talk with you?"

Mrs Forsyth waved vaguely at a sofa.

Grace took a moment to settle and smooth her skirt, giving her time to gather her thoughts into a coherent order. She picked up the photograph that Mrs Forsyth had laid face down and smiled.

"I can't believe it took me so long to put the pieces of the puzzle together. No matter which way I placed them, they just didn't seem to fit properly. I never believed that Isabelle intended to commit suicide. When I found out the doctor was also innocent of ill intent, the whole incident opened up to new possibilities. In fact, I began to wonder if the guard had told the truth when he said he had seen her fall, after struggling with the doctor."

Mrs Forsyth continued to sip her sherry. "I'm sure I don't know what you mean, dear."

"I never understood why Isabelle would have rushed out of the carriage, when she was far safer inside. After all, there was nowhere to go, or so it seemed. It was the guard's van being locked that stopped

258

me from seeing the truth, even after I knew the guard had reason to lie about what happened."

Grace turned the photograph towards her hostess, showing dark-haired Isabelle on the arm of her lover. Even in a photograph, his slight figure and white-blond hair was unmistakable. "Otto Jensen, I presume. The very image of the slim, blond porter who I bumped into while he was loading a large trunk at Oamaru, who also bore an uncanny resemblance to the porter who offloaded it again at Port Chalmers. How else could the same porter be in both stations, if he wasn't on the train, in the guard's van with the baggage?"

Mrs Forsyth opened her big blue eyes wide, pretending innocence, but the tiny smile that tugged at the corners of her mouth said otherwise.

"Otto was waiting in the guard's van, having unlocked the door," Grace continued. "A simple matter for Isabelle to run across the gangway and into the van, locking the door behind her again. No wonder the doctor lingered on the rear platform in a panic, wondering how she had vanished so suddenly. How fortunate for the guard, that the man he needed to get rid of put himself into such a vulnerable position."

"But surely she would have been found, when the guard's van was opened?"

"I rather suspect nobody thought to look inside all those trunks stacked up in the baggage section. Port Chalmers was only a short distance away, after all, so the chance of discovery was minimal, especially as she had made her state of mental agitation crystal clear. Outwardly, she acted the distressed woman on the verge of panic, but her conversation with me was entirely rational. She was excited to see the man she loved, not in suicidal despair over being abandoned."

Mrs Forsyth shook her head. "Goodness me, what a vivid imagination you have, Miss Penrose."

"I wasn't half so clever as your daughter. I suspect you were in on their plan all along, Mrs Forsyth. For a moment there, you must have been worried that the plan had gone terribly wrong. I recall your shock when Detective Constable Pyke told you that both the doctor and your daughter were dead, when you were expecting her death to be announced as a tragic suicide. Smart of her to throw her hat and shoes off the train to make us believe in her fate."

Mrs Forsyth swapped her fake innocence for a wry smile. "You must understand, my dear, that my husband would have moved heaven and earth to stop Isabelle marrying her beloved Otto. It wasn't only that he was in trade, it was that he wasn't English. But they were so in love, so very right for each other, and with a baby on the way."

Charlie leaned forward. "So you arranged for Isabelle to leave this house for Stillwaters Sanctuary, thinking she would be safe there, until she could escape and fake her own death."

"I told Otto where she was going. They arranged to communicate by throwing messages over the wall, so Isabelle knew when to escape and board the train."

"While Otto got on the train dressed as a porter at a distant point to waylay suspicion."

"I am very grateful to you, Miss Penrose, for helping her."

"I tried to, but I nearly ruined everything by not stopping the guard from getting the doctor. I must admit, it is a huge relief to know that Isabelle is still alive."

"Isabelle would have been discovered on the train earlier if not for you."

"May I ask where Otto and Isabelle are now?"

Mrs Forsyth hesitated.

"As far as the police are concerned, the case is closed," Charlie said. "A tragic accident. I promise to let sleeping dogs lie."

"Isabelle sent me a message from the port to say the plan had succeeded, although only just. I thought my heart would burst with the relief of it after your visit. They boarded a ship to Melbourne the next day."

Mrs Forsyth was positively glowing now. Very likely she was happy to have another person with whom she might safely share her joyful secret. "Mrs Jensen went with them. My only regret is that I was not able to go too, as I was needed here to act the role of grieving mother. I am proud to say I did everything I could to assist, including giving Otto Jensen the funds to buy the tickets and start a new life."

"The missing jewellery, I presume," Grace said.

Her hand unconsciously sought the gaps on her ringless fingers and the unadorned skin of her neck. "It was the only decent thing my husband ever did for me, giving me that jewellery. I was sorry to lose my beautiful necklace and rings, but I never did like those garish gold cufflinks of his."

"Fortune certainly does favour the bold, and the clever."

Mrs Forsyth sipped her sherry, but her eyes shone with delight. "I admit, it gave me a terrible shock to think how close their plan came to going wrong. The doctor's attempt to rescue her was nearly her undoing. She said she only just managed to close the door to the guard's van before he burst onto the gangway."

"Thank goodness, or she might have been killed as well."

Mrs Forsyth let out a long puff of breath. "May I ask what you will do, now that you know her secret?"

Charlie took the photograph from Grace and set it face down on the table again. "Not a thing, Mrs Forsyth, other than to wish the young lovers well. Isabelle did my family a great service, by letting us know that a missing friend of ours was still alive. She has also been instrumental in putting a double murderer and fraudster behind bars. Perhaps you might pass on my heartfelt thanks when you write to her."

"Or when you sail over to join her," Grace added.

"Please do not tell my husband, but my passage is already booked. I leave the day after tomorrow."

They left Mrs Forsyth sitting in her armchair, smiling adoringly at the picture of her daughter and future son-in-law, ignoring the gorgeous view from the window.

Grace couldn't help but smile too as they walked home, arm in arm. "Was it Shakespeare who said, 'The course of true love never did run smooth'?"

"There's also an old proverb that says 'where there is a will, there is a way'. Those two young lovers certainly proved the truth of that."

They took a shortcut through a stand of trees, enjoying the cool breeze, scented with fresh leaves and glorious freedom.

Grace stopped in a glade, where a fallen tree allowed the sunlight to filter through the green. Flecks of gold on green, like the eyes looking at her now, only a few inches away. "It gives me great satisfaction that the murder which started this whole affair was not a murder at all, but a love story with a happy ending."

Charlie brushed a stand of hair off her cheek, letting his fingers linger. "Isabelle's plan was ingenious, but there was one thing she couldn't take into account – a chance meeting with one of the sharpest minds in the country."

"I rather admire Isabelle. Knowing what she wanted was not possible, yet finding a way despite the obstacles." Grace brought her hand up to touch his. "Charlie, I want you to know that I will always be here for you, even though I can see that you and Amelia are overjoyed to be reunited."

"Amelia and I were never more than friends and never will be, Grace." His fingers twined with hers, touching her hand to his heart and then his lips. "I seem to have an unfortunate weakness for an altogether more exciting and unconventional type of woman. Perhaps someone so daring, she might take her shoes off and paddle in the shallows at the seaside with me tomorrow, after we have danced the night away at the ball? Do you think we could manage a whole day together without stumbling over a dead body?"

"I'm willing to risk it, if you are." She paused, trying to find the right words. "Charlie, I hope I don't have to wait another two years before I see you again."

"I don't know how long it will be, Grace, but I can promise it won't be anything like two years. I'd prefer not to leave you alone for two minutes, not with all the murderers and doctors on the loose in this city."

"Charlie, you can't think–"

Grace never got to finish her sentence. But she did get an answer to a medical question that had been occupying her mind for some time, on the nature of the body's response when two pairs of lips meet for the first time.

Naturally, being of a scientific bent, she felt the need to test the response more than once, just to be sure, with entirely satisfactory results.

Read on

In Book 3, *Murder By Vote*, Penrose & Pyke are flung into an explosive new mystery.

With the women's suffrage campaign and temperance movements gaining momentum in 1892, opponents are desperate to keep their liquor flowing and their womenfolk tending home and hearth. How far will they go to stop women from getting the vote? Grace Penrose and Charlie Pyke are about to find out.

Thank You
Thank you for reading this story. If you enjoyed it, I would be very grateful if you would leave a rating or review to help other readers discover it.

Find out about other books and sign up for notifications of new releases at https://RosePascoe.com

Historical Notes

Although this story is entirely fictional, the broader themes were inspired by the real social constraints under which women lived in 1891 and the mental health practices of the time.

I hope readers will forgive me for using the vocabulary of the day. Words like "lunatic" and "hysteric" are appalling in retrospect, but they were in common usage at the time. Institutions for people with disorders of the mind were officially known as lunatic asylums and were administered under the 1882 Lunatics Act by the Department of Lunatic Asylums.

When I began researching lunatic asylums of the era, I was surprised by the benign philosophy of care. The prevailing "moral management" approach was established well before Dr (Sir) Truby King became its champion. Fresh air and outdoor exercise, meaningful work, uplifting entertainments, and a nutritious diet were the cornerstone of treatment, while physical restraints and punishments were discouraged. Asylums were built in the countryside on a massive scale – and none grander than the gothic Seacliff Asylum, north of Dunedin.

Which is not to say that abuses were uncommon, as one might expect when minimally trained staff worked extremely long hours in overcrowded conditions with challenging patients. Even the massive asylums of the day filled quickly, used as a dumping ground for every manner of person from the criminally insane, to chronic alcoholics, epileptics, elderly people with dementia, and everything in between. My fictional Stillwaters Sanctuary is very much a toned-down version of reality, as I had no wish to write a horror story.

Fifty years earlier, asylums were very much worse – little better than brutal, overloaded prisons. Fifty years later, patients might well have faced horrific medical interventions such as electroconvulsive therapy, brain surgery and "unsexing" operations, as famously recorded by one of New Zealand's best-known writers, Janet Frame. She was held at Seacliff Asylum during the 1940s, narrowly escaping a lobotomy after being wrongly diagnosed as a schizophrenic.

As Frame notes in her autobiography (*An Angel At My Table*): "*There was a personal, geographical, even linguistic exclusiveness in this community of the insane who yet had no legal or personal external identity – no clothes of their own to wear, no handbags, no purses, no possessions but a temporary bed to sleep in with a locker beside it, and a room to sit in and stare, called the dayroom. Many patients confined in other wards of Seacliff had no name, only a nickname, no past, no future, only an imprisoned Now…*".

For anyone interested, I have posted additional information and photographs on my website (https://RosePascoe.com), including photographs of Seacliff Asylum. For more detailed accounts of the asylums of the era, I would highly recommend: *Unfortunate folk: essays on mental health treatment, 1863–1992* (Barbara Brookes and Jane Thomson, University of Otago Press, Dunedin, 2001) and *A choice of difficulties: national mental health policy in New Zealand, 1840-1947* (Warwick Brunton, PhD thesis, University of Otago, Dunedin, 2001).

The combining of a private asylum with a home for fallen women is of my own devising, because Grace Penrose was unable to resist the opportunity to raise the issue of a woman's right to control all aspects of her medical care. The baby farming aspect of the story is a nod to the most famous criminal case of the era. In 1895, Minnie Dean became the first – and only – woman to be hanged in New Zealand, for murdering children in her care. Baby farming was the notorious practice of taking in babies and children for money, often keeping them in squalid conditions, because their mothers had no other childcare options.

The train north of Dunedin still runs as The Seasider (https://dunedinrailways.co.nz), although an extra tunnel has reduced the terror value of the original route. I am grateful, once again, to The Lothians blog for a marvellous description of the first journey from

Christchurch to Dunedin in 1878 (https://the-lothians.blogspot.com/2016/05/washington-and-josephine-open.html), which includes the following description of the cliffs:

"The dizzy depths of the sea below which washes the foot of the rocks are enough to appal [sic] weak nerves, and I would suggest to all tremulous people who may happen to travel on this line to keep well inside the carriage doors. Having rounded the cliff, which is quite a quarter of a mile in extent, the dangers are not yet over, as the track has been hewn for some yards out of an almost perpendicular mountain side. To effect this, men had to be slung down from the top in ropes to hew the rock with pick and chisel; blasting could not be resorted to on account of its unreliable character."

The vast volume of online research material on every conceivable subject never ceases to amaze and delight. My gratitude to all the enthusiasts of the world who share their passions so freely. Special thanks to the Hocken Library, National Library and Papers Past for preserving an incredible range of images and news clippings, and to Heritage New Zealand and places like Ferrymead Heritage Park for preserving the physical reminders of our history. My only complaint is that they offer too enticing a rabbit hole to disappear down, when there is so much writing to do.

About the author

Rose Pascoe writes historical mysteries with a dash of romance, when she isn't plotting real-life adventures. She lives in beautiful New Zealand, land of beaches and mountains, where long walks provide the perfect conditions for dreaming up plots and fickle weather provides the incentive to sit down and actually write the darn things.

After a career in health, justice and social research, her passion is for stories set against a backdrop of social revolution. Her heroines are ordinary women, who meet the challenges thrown at them with determination, ingenuity, courage, and humour.

Visit her at: https://RosePascoe.com

www.ingramcontent.com/pod-product-compliance
Lightning Source LLC
Chambersburg PA
CBHW011509170626
46810CB00009B/3296